PLANET HERO

Civilian

M.A. Carlson

Cover designed by B Rose Designz

This book is a work of fiction. Names, characters, places, and incidents either are products of the author's imagination or are used fictitiously. Any resemblance to actual persons, living or dead, events, or locales is entirely coincidental.

M.A. Carlson
Visit my website at https://macarlsonauthor.wordpress.com/

Printed in the United States of America

First Printing: Apr 2020

ISBN- 978-1-7348021-1-5

CONTENTS

PROLOGUE

"You won't escape us, Dr. Portal," Private Eye Light shouted, beams of light firing from the tip of his index fingers toward the purple clad villain. Private Eye Light was a hero, only a 38th Milestone hero but still a hero. His superpower wasn't the most powerful by far. Finger guns of light were effective and there weren't many powers that could negate it, except, Dr. Portal's ability to create portals was able to do just that. Each shot fired was completely negated by transporting the light bullets away.

"I've already won, Dick Light," Dr. Portal snapped back. "With the power source I now possess, I can go wherever I want, and you can't follow. No one will ever be able to follow." Dr. Portal was not a hero. Dr. Portal was a villain, a 31st Milestone villain, a footnote in the annals of villainy. He seemed to be able to spawn dozens of short-range portals, it meant every shot Light took was transported behind the villain. A few more Milestones and Dr. Portal might learn to transport those shots so that they came out shooting back at him. It meant it was extremely important that the villain was caught before he could increase his Milestone even further.

"And where do you think you can go that can escape the long arm of the law," Light countered, his hands twitching in pain, a sign that his energy was starting to run low. If he didn't capture Dr. Portal soon, then Light knew he'd be forced to bow out of the fight. At least, until he was able to recover some of his energy. He just hoped that Dr. Portal ran out of energy before then.

"By going to another world," Dr. Portal boasted. "With this new power source, I will tear a hole between dimensions. To a world untouched by you heroes. A world ripe and just waiting to be conquered," Dr. Portal answered, cackling madly as dozens of little portals opened around him, creating a shield preventing anyone or anything from getting to him.

Light's eyes widened at the implication of all the damage Dr. Portal could do if he were to succeed. Not only would the villain do untold damage to a world without heroes, but the madman would be able to return to this world to commit crimes and escape back to the other world. He looked around for his temporary partner, the man known as Wind Mage, another hero, though of the 36th Milestone and one that Light had worked with in the past. He caught sight of the green clad hero flying in from his left and shouted, "Wind, we can't allow him to escape!"

"I know, Light, but his portals, there are just too many of them," Wind said, sounding tired, as if his own energy levels were getting low as well. "How can he keep creating so many portals?"

"It must be that power source he stole," Light answered, targeting the long metallic tube Dr. Portal was now fiddling with.

"You're too late," Dr. Portal cackled, as blue arcs of electricity sparked off the tube and a green portal opened behind him. "But don't worry, I will return." And just like that, Dr. Portal stepped backward into the green portal.

"We must stop him," Light said, running as fast as his feet would carry him. Trying to reach the portal before it closed, the effort making him wish that he had upgraded his body with his last Milestone increase.

Light was almost there when the portal wobbled as if it had suddenly become unstable. Too late he realized that was exactly what was happening. The portal shrank then enlarged and shrank again before bursting in a wash of energy that sent Light sprawling across the pavement and Wind tumbling from the air.

Light groaned in pain as the light of day returned to his vision. He was slow to climb back to his feet and even slower to move in the direction the portal had previously occupied. The street was completely wrecked, and a crater replaced the intersection that was at the epicenter of the explosion. Thankfully, the civilians had been evacuated as soon as the fighting began or there would be a lot of casualties as well. As for the damage, Hero Repair Company, or HRC, would have that righted within a few days.

For now, Light would need to call in a specialist to try to trace Dr. Portal. He pitied whatever world was forced to deal with that madman now.

When Light reached the edge of the crater, it was about what he expected to see. Exposed sewer lines, sparking electrical lines, and busted water mains quickly filling the hole with water. It wouldn't be long until those services were blocked off or shutdown. Sighing, Light was about to turn away when he spotted white fabric bobbing up to the surface followed by a flash of pink skin and dark hair, a person.

Light quickly slid down the side of the crater and into the water. Somehow, someone had been caught in the explosion. He grabbed the body and pulled it over to the edge of the pit. Light didn't have time to worry about the how or why, a life was in danger and as a hero, it was his job to save lives. "Wind, help me get him out," Light called up, hoping his sometimes partner was conscious.

The swirling of air was all Light needed to know he had the requested help, lightening the load as Light lifted the man onto his shoulders, hopefully he didn't make any injuries worse but he needed to get him out and on to the road above so he could be treated.

"Wind, can you pull the water from his lungs?" Light asked as soon as he laid the young man down.

"Yeah, give me a sec," Wind replied, his voice reedy and light. It took a moment, but a small vortex of water began flowing from the unconscious man's mouth until suddenly the man coughed, expelling the rest of the water and splashing Light's battle worn costume.

The man opened his eyes, blinking several times before letting unconsciousness reclaim him.

"At least he's breathing," Wind commented.

"At least," Light replied, sitting back, breathing tiredly. It was finally his turn to look at who he just rescued. With one look, Light was rolling the man over and pulling his arms behind him putting restraints on him. "And you thought you'd get away Dr. Portal."

"Was Dr. Portal that young?" Wind asked.

Light rolled the man back over and looked again. "His son maybe? Or . . . a brother?" Light questioned.

"We better call this in," Wind said, tapping on his wrist communicator, connecting him to Dispatch.

1

I looked at my watch through bleary eyes. The digital display of my smartwatch read '1:07 PM', in bright blue letters that faded after a moment. It was still early afternoon and I groaned with exhaustion. "How did Becky convince me to work an extra shift?" I just completed a 30-hour shift as part of my residency at Oak Memorial Hospital. Becky was the cute nurse that knew exactly how to push my buttons, which left me pretty much wrapped around her little finger. I could probably be with her right now, but after 30-hours on shift with barely 3-hours of sleep squeezed in, I was ready to go home and really sleep before I was back on shift in 10-hours.

As tired as I was, I chose to walk my bike rather than ride it. Better to not risk the ride through traffic. That would be a lame way to die and probably deserved. Thankfully, it was only a mile between the hospital and home. Home was just a shoddy apartment that I could barely afford on my salary. It was unlikely that the hospital that owned me for the next year would ever give me any kind of a raise that would allow me to even consider upgrading, but that was the way things were. My best hope was for the hospital to eventually offer me a residency.

"Four years of college, four years of medical school, and so many years of residency to go. Focus Davis, Lucy is counting on you," I grumbled to myself. My mother fought cancer for most of my life . . . until she lost. First it was breast cancer, which she beat. Then breast cancer again four years later, thanks dad for leaving her when that happened. Still, she beat it again. When it hit her liver a year after that, it was just too much. I've been looking after my sister Lucy ever since. My

5

sister who was only a few months from graduating college. My sister who was depending on me to keep her afloat. My sister, who would probably still need me to help her keep afloat until she could find a job once she did graduate. Something that would likely take a while due to the current economy.

I yawned again as I stopped at a crosswalk and waited for the signal to turn. When the little sign flipped over, I stepped into the crosswalk only to jerk back when a car horn made itself known. I made a rude gesture as the vehicle cruised past and through the clearly red light. When the brakes slammed and the tires screech, I realized what I had just done. I didn't live in the best neighborhood. The hospital I worked at had more than its fair share of gunshot victims and other gang related violence.

When I heard the click of the car's door opening, I didn't wait to see what would happen. I jumped on my bike and peddled for all I was worth. The sound of an engine revving behind me encouraged me to ride faster. I knew my neighborhood decently well. I knew where to turn and when to turn. I just hoped that whichever gang I just pissed off wouldn't open fire on me or any of the innocent bystanders nearby.

I crashed through from one alley to the next as my feet worked furiously to keep me ahead of the relentless gang member or members, whatever the case may be. Didn't these guys know I would be the one patching them up if they got shot later?

And then my lack of sleep finally caught up with me. I made a wrong turn down a dead-end alleyway. I cursed then cursed louder when the white car that had been chasing me pulled into the end of the alley, blocking any avenue of escape.

"You gave me one hell of a chase," the large and imposing man that stepped out of the vehicle stated, a red bandana on his forehead to match the black hoodie with red highlights. Those gang colors were a bad sign.

"Look, I'm a doctor," I said, desperately trying to reason with him.

6

"You think I care about that," he replied, pulling a gun and stalking forward. "You disrespected me. I can't let that go unpunished."

Still, unwilling to just give up, I tried again, "And if you ever get shot by one of your rivals, you will need someone just like me to keep you alive. I can't do that if I'm dead."

He snapped back angrily, stating, "And you think that makes up for you disrespecting me?"

"You almost hit me with your car. I reacted poorly to almost getting run over," I said. I realized I wasn't doing anything to defuse the situation, but my sleep deprived brain decided this was the best course of action.

"You got a lot of balls, doc," the man replied, lowering his gun slightly, giving me some hope that I might live to see my sister graduate.

Before I could reply, the alley was illuminated in green light. I could see the eyes of the gangster that had been pointing a gun go wide as the hand holding the gun started shaking. Without another word or any kind of warning the man turned and ran. He ran right past the car and kept running.

I, however, was confused, until I turned around to face the green light that made the gangster run. It was like a hole in the world filled with green energy. It was more disturbing when a man stepped backward, out of the miasma.

As soon as he was clear of the swirling energy vortex, he howled triumphantly, "Yes! I did it! I knew it would work!" The man coughed once. "Now, to start conquering this wor-" he was interrupted by another cough. He turned away from the portal and saw me. He looked like he wanted to say something but was stopped by another coughing fit. A coughing fit that included the misty red of hemoptysis, flecks of blood coming up with each cough. "No . . . what . . . what is-" he didn't finish his sentence as he fell backward, his coughing growing stronger, his body suddenly beginning to convulse.

I wanted to pretend I hadn't just seen a man step out of an energy vortex because such things were impossible. I wanted to pretend he wasn't coughing up blood, that he wasn't experiencing respiratory failure. I wanted very much to just walk away. But I couldn't. It wasn't in me to leave someone to die like that. "Damned the Hippocratic Oath," I complained, rushing forward, dropping my medical bag next to the man. Pulling out a mask from my medical supplies and covering my face. The last thing I needed was to breathe in whatever was causing this man's distress.

His pupils were completely blown when I flash my pen light in them, it was about then his eyes began to bleed, I could see the veins in the eyes turn black. He was dying in a hurry to a very virulent pathogen, at least that was my theory with the limited information I had available to me.

I pulled my small medical kit from my bag and pulled the emergency EpiPen and jabbed it into the man's leg, hoping the shot of epinephrine would help him survive just a little longer. I didn't have an actual shot of adrenaline to give him in my pack, or I would have tried that instead. Hopefully it would keep his heart beating just a little longer. I checked his pulse again, but it was getting fainter, not stronger. "Come on," I said, starting chest compressions, trying to save the purple spandex wearing weirdo. But it was no use, he was already gone.

I sighed, closing the now dead man's vacant blue eyes, noting the time as 1:48 PM if my smart watch was to be believed. I sat back, picked up my phone, and dialed 9-1-1. The phone only rang once before I finally took a good look at the dead man. He was probably in his forties or else he had lived a very rough life, one that was not conducive to a healthy appearance. He was pale but that could have been due to the blood loss. He had a five o'clock shadow, a salt and pepper of black and silver hair

8

to match the hair on his head. His nose appeared to have been broken several times and never quite healed correctly, and a myriad of scars that dotted his face and neck. The most disturbing thing I saw . . . his face . . . it was my own, older, but still mine. I knew my father's face well, this was not it, I looked more like my mother and as far as I knew my mother didn't have any siblings.

I vaguely heard the operator on the other end of the phone when I saw a strange blue spark from something on the dead man's belt followed by a beep. Another spark and another beep. Another spark and another beep, though faster this time. The beeps and sparks started coming regularly, picking up speed. This was something I had seen too many times in action movies. This man was about to go boom, and I had a feeling I didn't want to be anywhere near him when he did.

I couldn't be sure I could run far enough with the time I had available, so I unclipped the man's belt and threw it and the beeping device back into the portal they came from. When the portal wobbled, I feared I may have just made a mistake. I turned to run, trying to get as far away as I could. I heard something behind me and looked over my shoulder. The portal was ballooning outward, rapidly closing in on me, finally swallowing me whole. It was about then everything went white and I felt my body suddenly get lighter before darkness took me.

2

I didn't remember drinking so much after my hospital shift, but it must have been one killer of a bender. A bender and . . . shrooms? Maybe? Whatever happened, it gave me very strange dreams.

I moved a hand to my face to try to rub the sleep away only to find my arm firmly secured. Did Becky and I get up to something kinky last night? I wish I could have remembered that.

It was then a distinctly male baritone said, "Ah, good, you're awake."

My eyes peeled wide only to recoil shut at the bright light that was being shined in my eyes. "Ow," I complained, trying to blink away the spots of light. "What the hell, man! Is that really necessary?"

"I'll be asking the questions here son," the same male voice stated.

I blinked a few more times as I tried to figure out where I was and what was going on. My arms and feet were secured to the chair I was sitting in, and very tightly secured at that. I think even my fingers were secured as I couldn't even wiggle them. I couldn't see much of the room as there was a bright yellow light shining directly in my face. It reminded me of an old cop show where they try to sweat a suspect.

I tried to see past the light but between my throbbing head and the direct shine of the light in my eyes, that was unlikely to succeed. When my vision flashed and blurred, I figured I should stop.

"What? What happened? Was I arrested?" I asked. "I swear, I tried to save the guy. He just . . . died."

The man asked, "Who died?"

I took a deep breath, trying to calm myself before I began to speak. I started with the obvious, "I have no idea. Some guy, in some kind of purple outfit, stepped out of a strange green vortex at the end of an alley. Said something about it working then started aspirating blood," I explained, then I went into doctor mode, "His pulse quickly became thready and weak, so I gave him a shot of epinephrine to see if it could give his heart a jolt, but it didn't slow down whatever it was he caught. When his heart stopped, I tried to resuscitate him, but he just . . . it was so quick. I'm not sure what killed him so quickly, but you should call in the CDC and quarantine any remains after that explosion. I should also probably be quarantined as well. It's entirely possible I contracted whatever killed him."

The man probed further, asking, "This man who stepped through the portal, you didn't know him? You'd never seen him before that day?"

"No sir," I answered, then I asked, "Was that really a portal?" Suddenly, I was getting the feeling this wasn't a police station but some kind of secret government facility, one I was likely not going to be leaving alive.

"Yes, it was real," the man answered. "You've never seen a portal before?"

"Only in the movies or video games," I answered with a nervous laugh. I don't know why I laughed. It wasn't funny. Then my vision flashed again, only this time there was a spike of pain through my head and into the back of my eyes. For a brief moment, I thought that was me dying. Thankfully, I wasn't dead, at least, not yet. As the pain subsided, I blinked a few more times and shook my head. My vision was fuzzy and seemed to be developing obstructions. Was this a symptom of what killed that man?

The man asked, "Are you okay, son?"

"I think . . . I think I might be symptomatic. My vision is blurring and has become partially obscured. And there is a pain in my head and behind my eyes," I answered, trying to be direct. "I think I need a doctor, head CT, Chem-panel and standard blood test."

"I'll call you a healer, just hold on," the man said.

I didn't hear a door open or close, just a brief 'wooshing' sound, like in those sci-fi movies, with the sliding pressurized doors. If it was true, it lent some credence to the idea that I was being held in a government facility of some kind. And what did he mean 'a healer'?

I didn't wait long before I heard the 'wooshing' sound again.

"This is him, Ward," my original interrogator stated.

A new male voice, this one much deeper, chuckled, then asked, "You don't say? I'm not sure I could have figured that out if you didn't tell me, Light."

"Just, check him out," the man now identified as Light said.

"Cool, codenames," I joked, blinking again as I was assaulted by more pain. This time it seemed to be everywhere at once. Seepimg into my muscles and bones. I would have convulsed and dropped to the floor if I hadn't been so securely . . . secured.

"What's happening to him, Ward?" Light asked.

Suddenly, I felt a hand on my shoulder.

"He is . . . or was, Nanoless," Ward said, sounding surprised. "How is that even possible?"

"Dr. Portal really did it," Light said. "He actually crossed a dimension."

"Wait, is that real? I heard a rumor . . . but . . . seriously?" Ward asked, sounding more surprised.

"Yes," Light said. "But forget that for now, pay attention to him. Is he going to be okay?"

I had so many questions, but my ability to speak seemed to have been severely impaired. I wanted to ask what 'Nanoless' was. I had never heard of such a disease or disorder. Then again, from what the two men said, it sounded like I was in a different dimension. Was that really a thing? Then again, that might be a hallucination on my part. I really couldn't tell with all the pain I was in.

Ward answered, though his voice didn't carry much hope or optimism, "I don't know yet, there hasn't been a Nanoless since the Advent. And that was thousands of years ago. If you bothered to study your history, you would already know, the Advent wiped out 87% of all life on planet Hero. Not a very high survival rate."

I wanted to cry out '87%!', instead, all that came out was an odd burbling sound that was completely unintelligible.

"Yeah, yeah, yeah, I know," Light said.

"And then there are the untamed wilds outside of the fortress cities, the areas we still haven't been able to reclaim," Ward continued.

"Enough about that. Is he going to make it?" Light asked.

I felt a hand on my shoulder, even through the pain. There was extra warmth in that touch but that might have just been due to my body temperature dropping. I couldn't be sure, and if I didn't survive whatever was happening to me, I would never know.

"It's still too soon to tell," Ward answered. "And if he really is from another dimension, there is no telling if his physiology is different from our own."

None of that sounded good to me. I found myself hoping I really was delirious. Another bout of pain spread through me like wildfire, and much more intense than previous. and I was ever so thankful to be embrace by darkness when I finally succumbed to whatever was attacking my body.

3

I woke with a start, my eyes peeling wide and blinking several times as I tried to take in my surroundings only to be confronted with a large video screen about a foot in front of my face.

Congratulations!

You have survived the Advent! What is the Advent? The Advent was humanity's last hope of survival. Humanity was on the verge of destroying all life on the planet. Our environment was heavily polluted. Species were being hunted to extinction. Birthrates were in freefall. At most, we would have survived a century, if that.

To combat the inevitable extinction of our people, we came to the conclusion that our only hope, was to forcefully evolve the planets population. Hence the Advent. We unleashed a Nano-virus, a biomechanical nanomachine virus, one capable of ushering in a new era. One that would evolve life. Making life more robust, enhancing strength, and granting great power. Though with great change, also comes great sacrifice. We estimated at least 60% of the world's population would be lost during the great change we called the Advent. We mourn for those losses, but again, without those deaths, humanity would not have survived, would not have evolved.

I blinked several more times as I read through the message, then I read it three more times. I couldn't believe what I was reading. Some nut job, or a lot of nut jobs, decided the best way to save humanity was to wipe most of them out. And if that wasn't enough, they also forcefully evolved people.

I tried to lift a hand to turn the screen off, but my hands were once again bound. I struggled for a few more seconds before deciding it was futile. Instead, I just glared at the message and wished it would just go away. It was much to my surprise when it did, only to be replaced with a new message.

As a survivor, you will find your mind and body have been significantly changed. First, somewhere in your peripheral vision, you now have a digital interface that will communicate the status of your body directly to your mind in the form of a Life or Health Bar, results will vary. This will inform you when you are close to dying as it catalogues any injuries to your body.

Second, you now also have access to an energy source previously unavailable to humanity. This energy source will grant you power, though the nature of that power will be very different for each person due to the forced nature of your evolution. You might be able to command fire, ice, lightning, or all three at once. You might be invulnerable to physical damage or be super strong. There is no way to predict exactly what ability you will be granted.

My eyes now widened as I digested that bit of information. If I was reading this correctly, it meant I now had superpowers. I read the message a few more times, feeling slightly excited by the prospect. It also kind of explained why I was constrained the way I was. If I had to hold someone with superpowers, I would not want that person to be able to move in the slightest, especially if I didn't know what that person's powers were. The question now, how do I find out what my superpowers were and how do I use them?

I waited again for the message to change and hopefully give me more information but after a minute it didn't move. I frowned and mental shouted, 'move on' wishing once again that it would get on to the next message or just go away so I could start figuring things out. And it did, which gave me pause. I was curious now. I thought 'Back' and the screen changed back to the previous. I thought 'Next' and it moved to the next message. I grinned a little. This was some rather impressive technology.

> Due to the possibly volatile nature of your new ability, the Nano-virus put a system in place to slowly unlock your potential over time and with experience.
>
> With each Milestone, you will be able to apply two enhancements to either Body or Ability, or one enhancement to each.
>
> Body enhancements fall into three categories, Athleticism, Resistance, and Recovery. Athleticism will increase your strength, agility, accuracy, and speed based on your muscle and body type. Resistance will increase your ability to take a hit, to keep on fighting through injury, and even possibly reduce the amount of damage you receive based on your muscle and body type. Recovery determines how fast you are able to heal from injury and how quickly you regain expended Nano energy.
>
> Ability enhancements fall into two categories, Power and Control. Power will increase the raw power of your ability as well as increasing the amount of energy you can command. Control will increase your manipulation of your ability, allowing you to refine how you use your ability.

My mouth might have dropped a little at that. It felt like something out of a video game. Milestones were like levels. And each level granted two stat points to apply however you want. I was even more eager to find out what I could do. I thought 'Next' again and the message changed once again.

> At the first stage, you have been awarded one enhancement to each category. You will need to absorb more Nanos to advance.

> Once you close this message, you will be able to access your Body and Ability measurements by thinking or saying 'Status'.
>
> Good luck! You and those like you are humanities hope for the future.

I thought 'Next' again, but there were no further messages. What I thought was a video screen placed above me, vanished from view. Suddenly, I was aware that I was now in a room. I could see light peeking through window shades next to my bed. I saw an unoccupied chair. I also saw two doors, one of which I assumed was a bathroom and the other an exit. I might have thought it was a hospital room based on the white linen sheets and the general feel of it, but it lacked the smell of disinfectants I knew only too well from the years I've spent working in a hospital. There was also the fact that I was firmly secured and unable to move at all, something that was not exactly standard practice in a hospital, even for the criminals the police regularly brought in for treatment.

Seeing as I wasn't going anywhere, I decided to try out the only instruction given by the messages. So, I thought 'Status' and a new video screen appeared.

Davis Malory
Aliases: N/A
Occupation: N/A
Alignment: Neutral
Milestone: 1st
Nano: 0/1,000
Body
Athleticism: 1
- Strength: Average
- Agility: Above Average
- Accuracy: Above Average

- Speed: Average	
- Stamina: Average	
Resistance: 1	
- Physical Resistance: Average	
- Energy Resistance: Above Average	
- Mental Resistance: Above Average	
Recovery: 1	
- Physical Injury: Average	
- Nano Energy: Average	
Ability	
Power: 1	
- Time: Weak	
- Space: Weak	
Control: 1	
- Time: Weak	
- Space: Weak	

And that was it? I thought I would have this sudden and impressive boost in power that would make me a god among men. But that was it? According to this video thing, I was physically, mostly average. I had better Accuracy and Agility, but I had no idea how that was supposed to make me a stronger person or into any kind of a super anything. And what was that nonsense with my Power and Control. Weak? What did that mean exactly? Weak? I scoffed aloud but didn't actually say anything.

Apparently, the scoff was enough as I had no sooner made the noise than the door opened. I didn't recognize the man or the blue and gold suit he was wearing, but the giant 'W' emblazoned on his chest made me think this was Ward, the man that showed up during my interrogation. A voice matching the man I heard called Ward by the other guy, asked, "Ah, finally awake, are you?" Ward was tall . . . I think he was tall. I couldn't really tell from laying down as I was. I could see he was

Black from the little bit of his face that wasn't covered by his cowl and mask. He also appeared to be very physically fit. The skintight suit did very little to hide his physique. It honestly made me feel a little uncomfortable.

"So it would seem," I replied carefully. I still wasn't sure what was going on here. The costume the man wore made me think he was some kind of superhero. But then, that man was wearing a purple suit and talked about taking over the world. It was entirely possible this man was also a villain . . . was that even a thing?

"It would indeed," Ward boomed, grinning broadly and confidently. "I, for one, am very glad to see you have recovered. I am the hero, Blue Ward. Might I have your name?"

"Davis," I answered. "Davis Malory."

"Pleased to meet you, Davis Davis Malory," Ward replied.

"No, just Davis Malory," I said, feeling embarrassed for the man. That was such a played-out joke, but the sincerity in the way he said it made me think that was what he thought my name really was.

Ward grinned broadly again, "Ah, even better. Your name will fit well enough in this world. We can discuss that later. For now, how are you feeling?"

"Fine . . . confused. The, uh, the messages, is that real?" I asked. It was entirely possible I was still hallucinating. Or maybe I died, and this is some strange version of heaven . . . or hell, maybe purgatory?

"Very real," Ward answered, walking up next to the bed. I watched in fascination as his hand glowed blue with golden sparks shooting off at random. He set the hand on my shoulder and I felt the warmth from the previous day . . . was that the previous day? How long had I been asleep? "Good, very good. It seems the Nanos have successfully integrated with your system. I wasn't sure how your biology would compare to our own, but it seems that following the Nano infusion, our biologics are now identical."

"What does that mean?" I asked.

"Well, you had an extra organ that I couldn't identify but it seems your body has successfully broken it down. You were also missing an organ that appears to have grown in quite nicely," Ward answered.

"I gained an organ?" I asked.

"Mmm, you did indeed," Ward said with a nod and a friendly smile. "Your bio-energy converter has grown in nicely."

Bio-energy converter? What was that? Did it have something to do with my new ability? "And what organ did I lose?" I asked. There was only one organ I could think of that was dispensable. I shuddered to think what else I might have lost.

"I consulted some very old anatomy books. I believe it was called an appendix," Ward answered.

I sighed in relief. Of everything that I could have lost and kept living, that was the best option.

"Now, I am sure you have a great deal of questions," Ward began. "But before we get to that, we need to finish asking you about the events of two weeks ago."

"Two weeks?" I asked. "How long have I been asleep?"

"About two weeks," Ward answered. "The Nano Infusion did a number on your body. There were a few times I wasn't sure you were going to make it."

"Two weeks," I repeated. I tried to look down at my arm for an IV, but they were covered so I couldn't see anything, not that I could get much of an angle to see by.

"That is correct," Ward said. "Again, I will be happy to answer any questions you have, but first, we need to finish discussing what happened to Dr. Portal."

"Dr. Portal?" I asked, is that what that guy was called. And wait, was that his real name?

"Yes, the villain, Dr. Portal. You said that he appeared near you?" Ward asked.

"Yes, the portal," I said, pausing. That was still so weird to say or think. "It opened a few feet behind me."

Ward nodded, then asked, "And you had never met him before? Maybe an uncle, or a long-lost father or much older brother?"

"No, I take after my mother. My father left when I was young, but he didn't have any brothers and neither did my mother," I answered honestly.

"And teleportation or Portalmancy don't run in your family?" Ward asked.

"What is Portalmancy?" I asked. I had a vague idea.

"Portalmancy is the ability to open a portal that allows for the instantaneous transit from one location to another. I've seen Portalmancers tear through space, open wormholes, summon celestial worms, create an actual door, or use an existing door to create a connection from one place to another. I've even heard of one guy that used an old Police Box. Anyway, many methods, same results," Ward answered. "But you still have not answered my question."

"Sorry," I said with a blink. "No, my . . . I guess, my Earth doesn't have superpowers."

"Earth? We haven't called our planet that since Pre-Advent," Ward said with an amused grin.

"Then what do you call it?" I asked.

Ward grinned, and then with a great amount of pride, he put his hands on his hips and struck a pose, then stated loudly and clearly, "Planet Hero!"

4

The main conference room of the New Haven Fortress City Hero Association was situated deep underneath the association's headquarters, the tallest building in New Haven and positioned in the very center of the fortress city. While the building stood out as a beacon of justice and hope, it was targeted on too regular a basis to place anything of real importance above ground. Within the main conference room were the six members of the council of heroes, three permanent members and three rotational members. Plus, for this meeting, a single guest sat watching and listening to the casual questioning of the young man now identified as Davis Malory, trying to decide what was to be done with him.

Major Miracle, a hero that had reached the 87th Milestone, was a permanent member of the council and current leader of the New Haven Fortress City Hero Association. He leaned slightly forward and pressed a button to mute the speakers, silencing the interrogation. Major Miracle was tall and broad-shouldered. He appeared as if he was about to burst out of the crimson body suit that covered him from his hairline to his feet. And emblazoned on his chest was a bright yellow circle with a crimson 'M' in the middle. He was also currently considered to be the strongest hero in New Haven, his ability to fly and his super strength made him something of a paragon within the community. He looked to the other members of the current council one at a time then asked, "Thoughts?"

Mental Star answered, "I don't sense any falsehoods, only confusion and a little fear. I would need to get closer to do a more thorough scan." She was lithe and wore a silver bodysuit with an 'M' fashioned out of stars. She had achieved the 81st Milestone, so not as powerful as Major Miracle but still exceptionally powerful. This woman was something of a mystery to the city of New Haven. The legends say she simply appeared one day, fully grown, and immediately put an army of villains to sleep with a thought. That wasn't actually what happened, but she never bothered to correct anyone. She also quite enjoyed the air of mystery that surrounded her. And though her ability to read thoughts was well developed, her telekinetic skills were more so, not that anyone knew that, which was just how she liked it.

Para-Hypno added his two unwanted cents to the conversation, "It's too convenient. Dr. Portal dies and is replaced by a doppelganger from another world. Give me an hour and I'll break him. We'll get to the truth then." Para-Hypno was in his 58th Milestone, though unlike the others at the table, he preferred an unkempt look, black bodysuit covered by a brown trench coat and brown fedora on his head. He was what was known as an investigative type. His ability to turn into a nearly invisible apparition made it rather easy for him to enter into places that others could not. His ability to hypnotize others made it even easier for him to gather information and then be forgotten afterwards. He was not a permanent member of the council, his presence, like the two other rotational members, was due to being randomly selected from those of a sufficiently high level.

"For all we know, he's completely innocent," Private Eye Light stated loudly. "Your illusions and hypnotic suggestions might be . . . acceptable on criminals, but this man isn't one." Private Eye Light was also an investigative type of hero, though considerably less well known. He relied on old fashioned detective work, running down leads, following the clues. His powers were not well suited for that kind of work, but he made do.

23

"Not yet," Para-Hypno retorted. "And who said you could speak in here. Last I checked, you weren't part of the council Sparkle Fingers."

"Remind me, is Para short for Paranormal or Paranoid?" Light quipped, feeling annoyed and earning a chuckle from several of the members at the table.

"Calm down you two," Major Miracle ordered, silencing the pair instantly. "Para, we don't yet know if he's a criminal or a trick from Dr. Portal. And Light, we don't yet know that he isn't."

Para-Hypno looked like he was going to retort but held back after a slight glare from the Major.

"I understand that, I just don't want to see him hurt unnecessarily until that can be established," Light said calmly.

"And he won't be," Major Miracle promised. "That said, we do need to do our due diligence and make sure he doesn't pose a threat."

"Do we know his powers yet?" Wet Work asked, the gills on the 85th Milestone's neck struggled with the atmosphere. He spritzed his neck and face with a water from a small bottle he pulled from the belt of his dark navy wet suit. Wet Work was well known for his work in anything to do with water, whether it was the various rivers that ran through the wilds and the city, or the scattered lakes and oceans. When it came to water, he was the man to ask for help, not just in New Haven but across the globe. He was the third and final permanent member of the council.

Mechanic Parts answered, "No, the suppressor is set to maximum. He might be able to see his own status, but we can't get a read on it while he's still being confined so tightly." The 56th Milestone man was the only one at the table that wore street clothes, a pair of overalls and a white t-shirt, both of which were smeared with the occasional grease or oil stain. He was another of the rotational council members. He was also an exception as he was not a hero, not even a retired hero, just a failed sidekick. He was selected to sit on the council due to his Milestone being the highest among his peers, and because no one else within his categorization had a suitable Milestone to be able to sit on the council.

"Says the only non-Hero at the table," Hammer Jack grumbled. The 50th Milestone hero wore a grey bodysuit with the outline of a jackhammer on the front with an 'HJ' inside the outline. Hammer was nearly as large as Major Miracle, but he lacked any finesse or subtlety. He was a blunt instrument, which sometimes you needed to fight villains. His power allowed him to create vibrations, something he used to power his weapons of choice, two jackhammers that he wore like gloves. Anyway, his spot on the council was luck of the draw and in a few months, he would vacate his seat and another hero would replace him, hopefully one with a little more than just brute strength.

"If you want me to fix those stupid jackhammers of yours the next time they break, then you'll keep your trap shut," Mechanic snapped back. He was a Nano-Engineer, which meant he designed and constructed weapons, tools, and other various equipment for the heroes to use. Once upon a time, Mechanic was in line to become a hero. He was a sidekick to the Machine Maker, a hero known for building all kinds of automatons to fight villains. Then a villain killed him. After that, Mechanic just didn't have the heart to go on in the hero program.

"There are other Nano-Engineers, maybe I'll take my business to them next time," Hammer replied.

"Be my guest," Mechanic replied. "See how long your toys last after you try that. Just don't come crying to me afterward."

"Enough," Major Miracle said loudly, scowling at the pair. "Focus on the matter at hand. Para, what are the villains saying?"

"My sources tell me they are looking for Dr. Portal in a bad way. That power supply heist really made someone angry," Para-Hypno answered. "Which is why I think that," he paused to point at the screen, "is just an act. Dr. Portal must have known someone else wanted that power supply. What better way to get them off his back than to fake his death and pretend to be someone from another dimension."

"That seems really convoluted," Light commented, hopefully expressing an appropriate amount of doubt.

"He's a villain, of course it's convoluted," Para snapped back. "It's what they do!"

"I can't believe I'm saying this, but Para might have a point," Mechanic said, rubbing his temples. "I hate villains, bunch of insane people."

Major Miracle sighed, then looking at Para-Hypno, he said, "For now, focus on finding out who wanted that power supply and why."

Para-Hypno scoffed but nodded his agreement.

"What can I do?" Light asked, he was by far the weakest Hero at the table. "I know I was only allowed to sit in this meeting due to my being there during the incident and for the initial questioning, but I want to help if I can."

Major Miracle studied Private Eye Light, then shifted his gaze to look at the rest of the council members gathered at the table before speaking. "Mechanic, go ahead and lower the restrictions just enough so Mental Star can complete a clean scan, I think she should speak to him next. While you're at it, and if you can, lower it just enough to get a power-scan. Any objections?"

Light frowned, feeling like he was being excluded. Even though he was a member of the Hero Association, he was an independent hero and at a much lower Milestone than the others, it was to be expected.

"Assuming everything comes up clean, Private Eye Light, you can help him acclimate to the new world he's in," Major Miracle said. "But keep him in the building, at least until we've concluded our investigation."

Light's frown reversed and he nodded once. This was his chance to really help the council. To get his name known by the higher ups. And if he did a good job, there was a good chance they would involve him more in the future. "Yes sir!" Light all but shouted.

<u>5</u>

My hand flew up to my nose to scratch it the instant the contraption that held me captive was disengaged. "Oh, thank God. I needed that," I said, feeling instant relief. Then came the stretching of my neck, the rolling of my shoulders, and then the twisting and bending every which way to get the rest of my body moving again.

The man that introduced himself as Private Eye Light minutes earlier smiled then said, "Sorry for that, but your situation is rather unique. With shapeshifters, cloners, and the multitude of available powers, one can never be too safe." He was tall, though not quite as tall as me. He wore a gold colored trench coat with an attached hood, though it laid back. He wore a simple mask over his eyes, but it didn't do anything to hide his youthful appearance or the nearly glowing blonde hair on top of his head. Below the trench coat I caught a glimpse of a simple white bodysuit and golden boots. He looked like something out of a comic book, though that wasn't saying much. Ward and Mental Star also both looked like they should have been in the pages of a comic book and not walking the streets.

I wanted to say I understood, but I really didn't. I didn't understand much about this world, even after talking to Ward and then that woman Mental Star over the last couple hours. Well, more talking to Ward. Star didn't really say anything, she just kind of sat down next to me and smiled. It was super awkward. I talked . . . a lot . . . and she didn't even twitch until she just got up, nodded to me, and then left me alone again. Oh, and some guy that looked like a mechanic came right after Ward but before Star. It was just for a minute and he did something to my bed. He didn't say anything, but I assumed that he was just a mechanic or a rather dirty and greasy looking orderly.

It was a little while later Light entered the room. He inserted a key into my bed and a few minutes later I was free.

"Feeling better?" Light asked after I stopped stretching.

"Yeah, I think so," I said. I half expected my knee to ache after being so stationary for so long. In fact, nothing hurt . . . like, nothing. Curious, I may have glanced at my new status bar, specifically my health . . . life bar, it was full still, not even a sliver missing. It made me wonder if the Nano-virus fixed old injuries. If it did, then it made me wonder if I was out of a job.

Light gave me a friendly smile and a nod. "That's good. Now, I'm sure you have more questions, I have been assigned to help you acclimate to your new situation."

I nodded, that was probably a good thing. Who knew what kind of trouble I could cause if I had superpowers when they sent me home and I didn't learn something about them now? Thinking of that, I asked, "How long before you can send me home? I mean, after you give me some basic training, so I don't accidently end the world."

Light grimaced. I really didn't like that grimace. "The thing is, we don't have a way to send you home, or at least, not yet."

"What do you mean? This is a world of superpowered people. You can't tell me you don't have someone else able to create portals," I protested, feeling panic starting to creep in.

"We do have people with the ability to create portals, that's true," Light said quickly. "We just don't know how Dr. Portal got to your world. We are investigating. Our best Nano-Engineers are working on it, even now."

"Nano-Engineers?" I asked. "Is that like a scientist? Preferably one that studies portals specifically?"

"Sure," Light answered, grimacing again, though this time he also looked slightly confused by my question.

"I'm never going home, am I?" I asked.

"We don't know that yet," Light replied. "But I promise, we are working on finding a way to send you home."

I supposed that would suffice for now.

"Look, you've been cooped up for a while, how about we go for a walk? You can ask me questions and I'll see what I can do to answer them?" Light suggested.

I sighed. It wasn't like I had any better options. "Lead the way."

It was actually kind of nice to walk. Light took me out to an atrium. It must have been in the center of the building, or I assumed it was. The rectangular garden and walking paths were surrounded on all sides by tall walls with windows, going up a dozen or more floors. It was nice as hospitals went.

"I don't recommend trying to fly out of here, there is an energy field over the top of the atrium to keep out birds," Light said.

"Killer birds?" I asked jokingly.

"Not often, but better safe than sorry. Birds tend to avoid the fortress cities. They generally live in the wilds. But every now and then one will sneak in," Light replied seriously.

"Wait, you're serious?" I asked.

"Of course," Light replied. "But mostly it's a precaution to keep out any villains that think sneaking into the New Haven Fortress City's Hero Association is a good idea."

What a backwards place. "And why would killer birds exist in the first place?" I questioned.

"Nanos didn't just change people," Light replied.

"Right, Nanos," I said. I had a feeling there were going to be a lot of things explained away as 'Nanos' in the coming days.

"I suppose that is a good place to start," Light said. "How much did Ward tell you about Nanos?"

"Not enough," I said.

"Alright, then I'll start at the beginning," Light said. "So, it all started with the Advent. We don't know all the details, but at some point, in the past, an individual or a group developed a virus capable of fundamentally changing life at a cellular level. This killed most of the population on Hero while trying to force evolution. It also evolved plants, animals, insects, or any other life form you can name. It either perished or evolved. Those who survived found themselves suddenly blessed with new abilities and enhanced bodies. For a few hundred years it was like the wild east out there."

I wanted to ask about the 'wild east' comment, it was jarring. "Sorry to interrupt? Wild East?" I asked, hoping my face expressed the proper confusion.

Light tilted his head slightly as if he too was confused. Then as if a light went off for him, he explained. "The wild east was a time of eastward expansion a few thousand years ago, back before the advent when gun duels were commonplace."

"Oh," I said. I supposed it made sense that this world would have a different history. "Sorry, you were telling me about the advent. Please continue."

"Happy to help." Light said before continuing where he left off. "Eventually, the first Major Miracle appeared. She was amazing. Unbelievably powerful. She was what most consider to be the first real hero. She created the first Hero Association. Helped to build the first Fortress City to protect against the wilds. Without her . . . well, let's just say life on Hero would have been wiped out a long time ago," Light said, looking slightly solemn.

"Anyway, with the Hero Association, things got better. There were still villains and evolved animals, but the heroes were able to keep them at bay. Suddenly, people were able to start living again. It wasn't a battle to survive every day. People didn't need to try to gain as many Nanos as they could in the hope to be strong enough to kill before being killed," Light explained. "Eventually, more fortress cities were built. More people chose to don the cowl and be heroes. The result is the mostly peaceful lives we live today."

It was an interesting history lesson but didn't tell me nearly enough about Nanos.

"Okay, that's the history of how we got to be here. Back to the Nanos," Light said, redirecting. "Wild Nanos are everywhere and in pretty much everything. It's in the air we breathe, the water we drink, and the food we eat. Wild Nanos are just that, wild. It can't be easily absorbed into the body. It must be tamed before it can be added to your Nano Colony."

"So, I can absorb it from water, food, and even the air, but I need to tame it . . . bring it under my control?" I asked.

Light nodded thoughtfully, then answered, "Yes, but as a 1st Milestone, you probably won't be able to cultivate more than one or two Nano per day, at least at first. Once you learn to properly cultivate it will get a lot easier."

"Cultivate?" I asked.

"Wow, this is going to take some time," Light said. "Okay, so, with some time and practice you will eventually be able to feel Nanos. Cultivating Nanos in the body is a matter of learning to feel the wild Nanos and then command those Nanos, essentially taming them and making them your own."

"Okay, and how do I do that?" I asked. While I had no idea what I would do with Nanos, I was intrigued by the concept. Plus, I had superpowers. There was no way I wasn't going to learn to control my ability, no matter how long or short my stay in this world was.

Light smiled. "How about I teach you?"

"Sure," I said.

Light led me over to a grassy area and told me to have a seat before sitting down across from me.

"Close your eyes," Light instructed.

I wasn't sure what closing my eyes was going to do but I humored him.

"Now, send your focus inward," Light said.

"You've got to be kidding me," I groaned, opening my eyes to stare at him incredulously.

"What?" Light asked, meeting my gaze unflinchingly.

"Really? Send my focus inward? Is this a bad kung-fu movie?" I asked, wondering once again if I wasn't hallucinating.

"Hmm, I'm not sure I understand," Light said, looking honestly confused at me.

"You sound . . . silly saying it like that," I said.

"Oh, do your heroes not speak this way?" Light asked.

"No," I said. "And we don't have heroes, not like you do here anyway. We don't have powers, we don't fly without an airplane, we are not able to move faster than a speeding bullet, and we do not shoot lasers out of our eyes."

"I apologize. We have learned over the years, that citizens feel . . . reassured and even hopeful when they hear heroes speak this way. I thought that as you are more like a citizen that this would put you at ease," Light explained.

"Well don't, just . . . be direct. Scientific if you can manage it," I said.

Light frowned. "Scientific, huh? I'll try. Okay, close your eyes again, and before you complain, it should help you block out distractions. I would also have you plug your ears, but seeing as you need to hear me, we can skip that for now."

I nodded, only slightly reluctantly. I closed my eyes again.

"Now, within your body there is already a very small tamed Nano colony. It exists within your Bio-Energy Converter," Light said.

"Which is where?" I asked.

In response, I felt a hand pat my stomach, just above my navel and below my diaphragm. Then Light explained, "It is in the center of your intestines and connects to all your internal organs, lungs, heart, kidney, liver, pancreas, and so on. If you concentrate on it, you should feel something. I've heard some people describe it as a burning feeling, others as a cool feeling, for me it felt like the sun on a bright spring day."

I cocked open an eye to look at him. At least he had the good sense to look slightly embarrassed.

Light shook away his brief embarrassment and with a stern look, he said, "Focus."

I suppressed a smirk and resumed the mental exercise. I tried to feel for that area of my stomach.

Light tried to coach me along, saying, "It can help to think about your ability, what your ability does."

That was great help. Time and Space. What exactly was Time and Space supposed to feel like? Time . . . this was taking too long. Space . . . I wonder what space is really like. Is it all . . . floaty and out of control? Is it really cold? Or is space like that closet at home that you just can't stuff anymore junk into? And then I felt a kind of emptiness. Or was that just hunger. No . . . no, definitely an emptiness. And it had a kind of pulse, fast then slow then fast again. Was that time?

"Do you feel it?" Light asked.

"I think so," I answered. Trying to puzzle out what this was exactly.

"Good, focus on it and feel it. Just keep feeling it. Focus on how yours feels," Light instructed.

"For how long?" I asked.

"Until you can differentiate between it and the wild stuff around it," Light answered.

Wild stuff around it? What was that supposed to mean? I didn't feel anything around it. I asked for clarification, "So, if I keep feeling . . . whatever this is, I will eventually feel something else around it?"

"Correct," Light replied.

I frowned. This felt so strange. That said, I never would have made it through medical school if I didn't learn to focus single-mindedly on a task, like studying anatomy. So I sat there, feeling the pulsing emptiness in my gut. Eventually, I started to wonder if I really was just hungry when I felt something . . . off. It was like something with a different rhythm rubbed against mine for an instant and then it was gone.

I must have perked up because Light seemed to have noticed. "Starting to feel it?"

"Should it feel like something with a different rhythm rubbing against mine?" I asked.

"For you, that might be the case. It's different for everyone," Light replied. "For now, just keep focusing on it. Eventually, you'll be able to feel those . . . odd rhythms more easily."

He wasn't kidding. After that first bump, I felt another, then two at once, then more. It wasn't overwhelming and there didn't seem to be a lot of them, or maybe there was, and I just couldn't feel them yet. Either way, I reached a point where I was feeling them regularly and not with increasing frequency. So, I asked, "I think I've got the feeling, what's next?"

"Okay, so you know your rhythm, next time you feel one of those odd rhythms, try to pull it into your rhythm or try to send your rhythm into it. You might need to try a few different things to find what works for you," Light explained.

The next odd rhythm I felt was gone too fast to try anything as were the next fifteen. Eventually, I started trying to anticipate when the next odd rhythm would strike. When it did, I tried to grab on to it and it stopped. I was so surprised it worked that I let it go. I groaned in frustration but tried again. It took a few minutes to grab another and hold it. This time, I tried to push my rhythm on to it only for my rhythm to do nothing except to push it away, letting it get loose again. The next one I grabbed, I tried to pull into my rhythm only for it to bounce off and flitter away. The next attempt I tried to surround it but that did nothing. Ah, how I love the scientific process, hypothesis and experiment. I wished I had a notepad to take notes on my various experiments. Finally, after exhausting everything I could think of doing to it with my rhythm directly, I tried to just change the rhythm, and it worked. It took time, first to get it to feel like empty space. Then to add in the fast and slow pulsing of time. Eventually, the odd rhythm was gone and only my own existed. It was effortless to then pull that matching rhythm into my body.

"It worked," I said.

"Nicely done. Make sure you check your 'Status' to confirm. Wouldn't want you to think you're cultivating only to find out you really haven't been," Light said.

Davis Malory		
Aliases: N/A		
Occupation: N/A		
Alignment: Neutral		
Milestone: 1st		

Nano: 1/1,000
Body
Athleticism: 1
- Strength: Average
- Agility: Above Average
- Accuracy: Above Average
- Speed: Average
- Stamina: Average
Resistance: 1
- Physical Resistance: Average
- Energy Resistance: Above Average
- Mental Resistance: Above Average
Recovery: 1
- Physical Injury: Average
- Nano Energy: Average
Ability
Power: 1
- Time: Weak
- Space: Weak
Control: 1
- Time: Weak
- Space: Weak

"Hey, it says I have 1/1,000 Nano now," I said excitedly.

"Good, you just need to do that 999 more times to reach your 2nd Milestone," Light said with a laugh. "Then you'll be attributed 2 enhancements to work on improving either your Body or Ability."

"No problem," I said sarcastically.

"But you might want to get something to eat first, we've been out here for almost six hours," Light said.

"Six hours?" I asked in disbelief. Six hours to gain one point of Nano. Did it really take me six hours to convert just one wild Nano? If it really took six hours then it would take me about 250 days if I did nothing but cultivate, not even counting any time for sleep and other necessities.

"Don't worry, that was just the first step," Light said, seeing the look I was now giving him. "Granted, this is something we start teaching children usually, but as an adult, you should be able to pick it up much faster."

"Oh, great," I said. If this was something taught to children, I could see why a year or more to gain a single Milestone would be acceptable.

"Look, let's go eat and then I can give you some tips that will help," Light promised, guiding me back inside the building.

6

I was surprised by how much I ate. I didn't even notice I was hungry until I smelled food and my stomach gave an embarrassingly loud rumble. After eating, Light led me through the building and back out to the atrium for more learning.

"Okay, so you learned how to tame wild Nanos, or at least one Nano," Light started. "The trick is to learn how to tame more than one at a time. It will significantly increase the speed at which you can cultivate Nanos and build up to the 2nd Milestone."

"That's good, I was afraid it was going to take me a year to build up that much," I said, feeling relieved. "So, how do I get started?"

"Just like last time, close your eyes and focus on feeling the wild Nanos," Light instructed.

I fought against my desire to sigh and closed my eyes. It was much faster this time, feeling my Bioenergy Converter and the wild Nanos that ran rampant all around me.

Light continued, "Now, once you feel them and feel like you're ready, begin. As you work on the first, try to stay open to more Nanos coming within your sphere of influence. Once you are comfortable doing both actions at once, start adding the new Nanos to your cultivation process."

Just like last time, I grabbed hold of one of the wild Nanos. Before I even started trying to change its rhythm, another came close and I grabbed it as well. Holding two was as easy as holding one. Then I added a third and a fourth. After I had a hold of forty-four wild Nanos, it seemed like no others were coming closer to me, or I just couldn't sense them.

So, I started coaxing the Nanos I was holding to match the rhythm of my own Nano colony. Having experienced this once before, I felt like I had a better handle on the process, which in turn made it feel like it went a lot faster this time. However, the dark skies above me suggested that was not the case. Still, 45/1,000.

"Better this time?" Light asked, seeing my eyes open.

"I think so, but how long did that take?" I asked.

"Almost 9 hours," Light replied.

"Did I do something wrong?" I asked, concerned by the increased time it took.

Light shook his head, "No, the more Nanos you try to cultivate, the naturally longer it is going to take. How many did you manage to tame, fifteen, twenty?"

"Forty-four," I answered, hoping that was really good. If he only guessed fifteen to twenty, there was a chance I did exceptionally well.

"Hey, that's pretty good for your second cultivation attempt," Light congratulated me. "Tomorrow, you'll want to try to double that number."

"Is that even possible?" I asked. "It felt like after I had the forty-four, I couldn't sense any more Nanos around me."

"Very possible," Light said. "As you increase your Nano cultivation, the more acutely you will sense the wild Nanos. You'll see next time you cultivate. For now, you've done a lot today, you should get some rest. We can start again early tomorrow."

I could only nod.

A few days passed like this. Cultivation after breakfast, cultivation after lunch, and cultivation after dinner. Cultivating was the only thing that was keeping me from going mad with worry over going home . . . of worrying over my sister. So, just like in medical school, I threw myself into the work. And just like Light said, with each successive cultivation, I was able to draw in more and more Nanos until one day, I heard a chime and a new message appeared in front of my face.

Congratulations! You've reached the 2nd Milestone. The Nanos have accumulated within your body to a point in which it is now possible to enhance your Nano Evolved Body or Abilities. Be intelligent with your decisions as all choices are final.

You may now open your Status and apply two points of enhancement.

I couldn't help but grin a little.

"What's with the grin?" Light asked.

"I just reached the 2nd Milestone," I answered proudly. "Did I set a new record?"

"Not even close," Light answered with a laugh. "Still, not bad. Do you know what you want to enhance?"

"My abilities of course," I answered. I had the chance to build up superpowers. Who wouldn't want to make their superpowers stronger? Then again, I had yet to use my powers so there was still the possibility that my superpower was lame. I mean, I hoped it was going to be awesome, but there was always a chance it wouldn't be.

Light smiled and nodded. "That is usually where we have children start, ideally we want them to get their ability scores up to Weak before we start teaching them how to use them."

"Weak? But I started at Weak, I thought that was bad," I said.

"Well, that is a surprise," Light said. "I wasn't given the results of your scan, so I had no idea. Anyway, most children start at Zero or Very Weak. Zero means they have an ability but absolutely no control or power in the ability. Children with a Zero don't usually become heroes. The gap between them and other children is just too large. Not that there aren't the occasional outliers. Anyway, starting at Weak is actually really good."

I nodded. That was interesting to hear. But I didn't completely understand why it was such a hurdle to overcome.

Light grunted, "You know, I don't think I ever asked you what your ability is?"

"Oh, I have Time and Space," I answered.

Light tilted his head. "I don't think I've heard of Time and Space as an ability before. Space yes, Time . . . I'm not sure about Time. Anyway, I've never heard of that combination. I wonder how that is going to work."

"Uh, no, I mean I have Time as an ability and Space as a second ability," I corrected.

"Ooh, dual abilities, those are rare. And the both of them started at Weak?" Light asked excitedly. "And Time? I've never heard of Time. Then again, I don't know everything."

"Yeah," I replied.

"I'm a little jealous, I only have Light as an ability," Light lamented. "Still, my Light will power up quite quickly compared to your dual abilities. That said, you will have a lot more versatility in what you can do. For now, if you intend to improve your abilities, I would choose one ability to enhance first. Get one ability to Below Average before you work on the other. Also, I would split your points between control and power, raise them up equally until you know what you can do with your ability. Then you can decide if power or control benefits you more. You might end up raising both up equally forever."

"What about your Light ability then? How did you raise it up?" I asked, before realizing it might have been rude to ask something like that. "Sorry, is it rude to ask?"

"Culturally, yes. People usually won't discuss how they develop their Body and Ability, especially not heroes. We tend to covet our development plans, especially when villains might use that information to kill us. But I know your situation, so I don't mind helping you out," Light said with a friendly smile. "I raised both control and power to Average by my 20th Milestone. Then I was able to really evaluate how to best progress my ability. As a result, I boosted my power to Good and now, at my 38th Milestone, I'm just starting on my way to Very Good."

"Wait, you're a 38th Milestone? Then you've gained what, 74 enhancement points?" I asked, confused as to why his power was only at Good.

"That's right," Light answered with a friendly nod.

I hoped he'd volunteer an explanation. When none was forthcoming, I asked, "Why are you only Good if you have had that many enhancement points? Or did you put all your enhancements into your Body?"

Light didn't hesitate to answer my question. "My Body is Average across the board. I suppose I should explain how the enhancement points work. From Zero to Very Weak, from Very Weak to Weak, and from Weak to Below Average requires five enhancement points each. From Below Average to Average, from Average to Above Average requires ten enhancement points each. From Above Average to Below Good to Good and from Good to Above Good requires twenty-five enhancement points each. Above Good to Below Excellent requires fifty points. From Below Excellent to Excellent to Above Excellent also requires fifty points each. And from Above Excellent to Master requires five-hundred points. I've never heard of anyone that has reached Master level, but New Haven is a small city."

That actually explained a lot. It also made me sigh. It would need four more Milestones to raise just one of my abilities to Below Average in both Power and Control. Ten Milestones past that to get to Average. And finally, another fifteen Milestones to get my other ability to Average.

"Anyway, once I get my power to Excellent, I'll be investing in my Body, probably start by balancing them at Average. After that, I'll be working on bringing my Recovery of Nano Energy and Stamina up to Good," Light continued, his eyes now focused on the space in front of him. I guessed he was looking at his Status.

"What do resistances usually start at?" I asked. If Light was just now planning on raising his Resistances to Average, then were mine abnormally high?

Again, Light just answered the question. "Most of them are Average or Below Average with one being elevated based on your ability. My Energy Resistance started at Good because of my ability. Unfortunately, my Physical Resistance is Below Average. Same for my Nano Energy Recovery."

"Okay, then why do you want to get Nano Energy Recovery and Stamina up to Good?" I followed up.

Light smiled and happily explained, "Being able to recover Nano Energy allows you to keep using your ability and continue fighting for longer. As for Stamina, if I'm chasing a villain through the city on foot, I risk getting tired. If I get tired, the criminal might get away. Stamina can offset that."

I nodded. I understood, mostly. "Then how do you chase criminals now?" I blurted out the question, not thinking about how it might sound slightly accusatory.

Still, Light answered, looking happy to do so. "I usually don't. I corner them. I'm what's known as an investigative type. Sometimes, I get a tip from a citizen, but usually, the Association gets information on villain activity that they deem to be within my capabilities. Anyway, whoever it is, gives me a little information and then I follow the lead to wherever it takes me. Usually, when I'm confronting a villain, I'm already inside their base or waiting to ambush them wherever they are going to attack," he answered.

Now I actually understood. I suppose it made sense that not every hero was suited to chase people through the streets. Just as not every hero was suited to find the hidden boss of a criminal syndicate. Comic books back on Earth suddenly made a lot more sense now that I was more or less living inside one.

"Now," Light started. "Why don't you apply your points?"

I nodded and accessed my Status. I had been thinking about this for days, ever since I first saw that Weak level on my abilities. With so many days of cultivating and getting a feel for Space and Time, I knew that I didn't fully grasp just what Space was or what it could do. I suppose I could have asked Light, but I have already bombarded him with so many questions as it was, not that I thought he would refuse to answer. But that wasn't the point. I didn't feel comfortable enough with how Space felt to want to put points into enhancing it, at least until I felt I understood it better.

That left me with Time. And Time, I felt keenly how it worked. The fast and slow rhythm my Nanos moved at told me a great deal. I felt comfortable pursuing that ability. And who knew, maybe one day I would have enough control and power over Time that I could move through Time. Maybe I would even be able to go back in time to before I was sucked into this strange world.

With a mental command, I applied the points and a (1/5) appeared on the line with my Time: Weak, first under Power then Control.

Davis Malory	
Aliases: N/A	
Occupation: N/A	

Alignment: Neutral	
Milestone: 2nd	
Nano: 1,006/2,500	
Body	
	Athleticism: 1
-	Strength: Average
-	Agility: Above Average
-	Accuracy: Above Average
-	Speed: Average
-	Stamina: Average
	Resistance: 1
-	Physical Resistance: Average
-	Energy Resistance: Above Average
-	Mental Resistance: Above Average
	Recovery: 1
-	Physical Injury: Average
-	Nano Energy: Average
Ability	
	Power: 2
-	Time: Weak (1/5)
-	Space: Weak
	Control: 2
-	Time: Weak (1/5)
-	Space: Weak

"So, feeling any more powerful?" Light asked with a light laugh.

"No," I said. "Should I?" I asked, slightly worried that I should have felt something.

"No," Light answered. "If you were already using your powers, you might feel a slight increase, but as you have yet to use your abilities, you won't know the difference."

"Which brings up a good point," I said, grasping the fact I had yet to use my abilities. "When do I learn to use my ability?"

"Whenever you're ready," Light answered. "I thought you would have been chomping at the bit to get started on your first day, but you really got into the cultivation training."

"You mean, I could have started training with my ability days ago?" I asked, not wanting to believe what he just said.

"Yes," Light answered.

I could have smacked myself. I'd been looking forward to learning to use my abilities for days and this whole time I could have been practicing. Instead, I was cultivating because that is what I thought I needed to do. I really should have asked more questions. I was almost a doctor for goodness sake. My ability to diagnose problems was one of my best qualifications. And instead of acting like a doctor and getting all the facts before I made a diagnosis, I was jumping on any little bit of information I could get my hands on and running at it like an out of control freight train. If I'd done that as a doctor, I might have gotten someone killed. That would need to change.

"I've been going about things all wrong," I grumbled. "Okay, Light, I need more information. I know you've been really great about telling me things when I ask, but there are things I need to know before I act any further. I also need a note pad or something to take notes on. It's time I started treating myself like a patient and getting to the bottom of exactly what is going on with me. Are you willing to continue helping me?"

"Of course," Light replied without hesitating.

"You really are a good guy," I said.

"I'm a hero, it's what I do," Light replied with a proud smile.

7

As requested, Light provided me with a notepad of actual paper and a pen. I couldn't remember the last time I actually wrote anything with an actual pen and paper. But that is exactly what I did. Starting with all the skill levels and the requirements for each. Then I went through each of the Body categories and got a thorough explanation of what each meant.

Strength was fairly straight forward. It accounted for how much you were able to lift and how hard you could hit something. Agility accounted for your flexibility and how well you moved. Accuracy accounted for your ability to land an attack, both physical and ability based. It also had something to do with your eyesight and seeing incoming attacks, which when combined with Agility and Speed helped you to dodge an attack. Speed wasn't just how fast you could run, but how fast you could react, which again, helped with dodging attacks. Which left Stamina, and that determined how fast you recovered from physical exertion.

Resistances were a mixed bag of straight forward and complex. Physical Resistance was your ability to resist damage from a physical blow. In other words, if I got really high Physical Resistance, I could be shot multiple times and just shrug off the damage. I was tempted to immediately raise this with my next several Milestones, then I learned about the other Resistances. Energy Resistance was ability to resist damage from energy-based attacks, like Light's Light attacks, or laser beams from the freaking eyes. Mental Resistance stopped people from using mind control on you or just from reading your mind without your permission.

Recovery was almost as straight forward as Athletics. Physical Injury was more or less just how fast you healed without assistance from a healer. My doctor brain basically looked at it as a quantifiable way to determine how well my body was able to recover naturally. Nano Energy was a little more complicated in its mechanics. The short and easy explanation was that it determined how quickly your Nanos recovered the energy they expended after using an Ability.

When I got to my Ability descriptions, Light actually needed to bring in some help. Thankfully, the help came from someone I already knew, Ward.

"Space and Time, huh?" Ward wondered aloud. "That's a pretty interesting combination."

"So, what can they do?" I asked.

"Well," Ward started and paused to look at Light. They communicated something silently between them, I almost wondered if one of them had some kind of telepathy, maybe Light hadn't told me all his abilities. "So, your doppelganger, Dr. Portal, had Portal as an ability . . . hold on, I'm jumping ahead here. So, most abilities have their own hierarchy. For example, Private Eye Light here. His ability is Light, which is considered the top tier of Light-based abilities. A subset of Light would be Flash. A person with Flash can emit a bright burst of light to temporarily blind an opponent. At higher power rankings, that flash might be able to burn people or permanently blind someone. Or if they go with a higher control ranking, they might be able to use the light for some manner of hypnosis. Anyway, because Flash is a subset of Light, Private Eye Light is able to use the same kind of ability and many more."

Ward paused to let that sink in. If I understood correctly, and I like to think that I did, it meant that Light could use any ability that fell under the Light hierarchy.

"What other abilities fall under the Light hierarchy?" I asked.

"Hard Light Constructs, Light Beams, Light Armor, Light Wards, Light, Light, Light, I think you get the idea," Ward said.

"And you can do all that?" I asked, looking at Light.

"I can do some of that," Light replied. "Remember when I told you I focused more on Power than Control. Well, a lot of those Light abilities require more Control than I possess. So, for now, I have a level of Control over Flash and Light Beams. Someday I might build my Control higher, but I have other priorities. Currently, my Ability setup fits with my style."

I nodded. "Okay, then just how does the Portal Ability have anything to do with me?"

"Portal is a subset of Space. As is Teleport, Gravity, Anti-Gravity, and more," Ward answered. "If you develop your Space ability, someday you might be able to open Portals between two locations just like Dr. Portal was able to."

"What about Time?" I asked.

"The closest thing I've heard that could fall under Time was Haste and Decay, assuming Time is the primary ability, which I'm pretty sure it is," Ward said. "I suppose some experimentation is in order."

"Okay, so how do we start?" I asked, eager to begin.

"There isn't any one way to start," Ward said. "Everyone is different. The only thing that most agree on, is that in the beginning, the Nanos will show you the way."

"Stop," I said instantly. "Don't do that Hero and mystic speak thing with me. Be direct and be scientific about it."

Ward looked slightly put off by my statement and I swear I heard him grumble about rude children, but before he could reply, Light jumped in, placating Ward and answering me. "So, each person's Nanos have a unique feel to them. That 'feel' is an instruction from the Nanos into how you can wield them. For me, my Nanos originally felt like bright beams bouncing off the walls of my Bioenergy Converter. Eventually, I learned to harness that feeling and direct it to the tips of my index fingers," Light said, then showed me the now glowing index finger on one of his hands. "For you, it will be much the same. In some respects, spending so much time cultivating Nanos in the beginning should make things much easier."

I think I understood. It was about that rhythm. The fast then slow pulsing feeling. It was time speeding up and slowing down. That was what my ability was trying to tell me. "So, do I just, take hold of that feeling and force it out?"

"This is where the 'Everyone is different' part comes in," Ward said. "You'll need to experiment until you figure it out."

"Great," I said sarcastically.

"That's the spirit," Ward said, either completely missing my sarcasm or ignoring it.

"Why don't you give it a try?" Light said, then added, "Close your eyes and feel your energy source."

I should have seen the 'close your eyes' instruction coming. Still, I did it anyway.

I had become rather adept at feeling my Bioenergy Converter and the steady fast and slow rhythm that kept playing in the background. I tried to focus on that rhythm. I tried to coax the rhythm to show me something but felt instantly that it wasn't going to do anything. I tried pushing at it but again nothing. Then I got to wondering if it was like my cultivation. It seemed it wasn't responding because I wasn't taking hold of it like I did the wild Nanos. So that's what I did, I took hold of it and instantly felt like there was something there. I focused on the familiar rhythm. I felt a need to wrap it all around myself. So, I did. But nothing happened, at least not that I could tell.

I frowned and opened my eyes. Ward and Light were still there, looking at me expectantly. And there was something new. Just under the faint red bar that monitored my health, there was now a gold-colored bar that was steadily getting shorter. It was confusing, but with Ward and Light right in front of me, I could just ask them.

I tried to speak but could hardly move my mouth. I tried to breathe, but it felt like I was trying to breathe through molasses. Thankfully, I wasn't suffocating, and I didn't seem to be running out of breath from holding it in too long. Then I focused on Ward and Light. Was it me or were they moving slowly? I tried to move, but again, this time it felt like my whole body was trapped in molasses. Was this my ability? Did it change my perception of time?

As soon as I understood what was happening, I wanted to jump for joy. This was an amazing ability. I could already see so many applications. And then the effect suddenly ended, and I collapsed. My breathing was labored, and I felt as if I had just run a marathon . . . maybe a few marathons . . . back to back to back. I could see in my periphery that the gold-colored bar was gone.

"You okay?" Ward asked, immediately dropping to a knee next to me, his hand on my shoulder again. He breathed a sigh of relief a moment later. "Phew, just Nano-Fatigue," he said.

"Congratulations," Light cheered for me. "I didn't see anything, but if you have Nano-Fatigue then you definitely activated your ability."

I would have said something, but honestly, I just wanted to sleep.

"Let's get him back to his room to rest," Ward said. "Now that he's activated an ability, he's got a lot of training ahead of him if he wants to learn to really use it."

With that, Light and Ward carried me back to my room and deposited me in my bed. I would like to say I could remember the trip or that I laid awake imagining all the things I would be able to do, but I'm pretty sure I was asleep before my head even hit the pillow.

When I woke up the next morning, the gold-colored bar was back, and I also understood what it was there for. It measured how much energy I had left to use my ability. I thought it would be a great tool. With that, I wouldn't need to count the seconds until my Time Compression came to an end. I would know when the bar drained.

I took a quick shower and dressed in the sweatpants and t-shirt that were provided for me. As I left my room, only Light was waiting for me just outside my door. He immediately asked, "Feeling better?"

"Yeah, how long did I sleep?" I asked, worried I slept for several days again like I had after the Nano-virus had its way with me.

"Just the night, maybe a few hours extra but not bad, it's just half past nine. It's not unusual for first time power use to cause Nano-Fatigue," Light said. "Now, I want to know what happened? I assume you activated your ability, what was it? We didn't see anything external so I'm guessing something internal. Ward was also excited to hear about it, but he couldn't be here because he's on duty today."

"I slowed down time," I said, then added, "I think."

"You haven't checked your status yet?" Light asked.

I shook my head, then said, "No, should I have?"

"It should give you a list of activated abilities, and maybe some descriptors," Light answered.

I opened my Status with a thought.

Davis Malory		
Aliases: N/A		
Occupation: N/A		
Alignment: Neutral		
Milestone: 2nd		
Nano: 1,006/2,500		
Body		
	Athleticism: 1	
-	Strength: Average	
-	Agility: Above Average	
-	Accuracy: Above Average	
-	Speed: Average	
-	Stamina: Average	
	Resistance: 1	
-	Physical Resistance: Average	
-	Energy Resistance: Above Average	
-	Mental Resistance: Above Average	
	Recovery: 1	
-	Physical Injury: Average	
-	Nano Energy: Average	
Ability		
	Power: 2	
-	Time: Weak (1/5)	
	o	Time Compression: 51%
-	Space: Weak	
	Control: 2	
-	Time: Weak (1/5)	
	o	Time Compression: 6-Seconds Uncompressed Time
-	Space: Weak	

I was slightly confused by the update to my abilities. Time Compression. Is that what it was called? I suppose what it was called didn't really matter. If I was understanding it correctly, the 51% under Power meant that time moved 51% slower while it was active. And if that was the case, then it also meant my 6-Seconds Uncompressed Time gave me just enough control over my ability that I could compress time for 6-Seconds for everyone else while for me it was roughly 9-seconds, just slightly more if I was being exact. In other words, Power let me do more while Time Compression was active, and Control made the Time Compression last longer. Now I understood what Light meant when he said that eventually I would want to emphasize one over the other. I would just need to see what getting to the next rank of each would do for me.

"Well?" Light asked impatiently.

"Time Compression," I said. "It says 51% under the Power side and 6-Seconds Uncompressed Time."

"That is amazing," Light said excitedly. "Imagine if you gain more Control over it, you could eventually get minutes of time compression. Do you know how much you can get done if you work outside of the constricts of regular time? By the same token, more Power and you can compress time even further. I guess you'll just need to wait and see which has the higher gains once you get a little further in the development." In other words, keep working on it.

I agreed with Light's assessment. And now that I knew more about my power and how it worked, I would have something to work on and practice. I already had an idea of how to take advantage of the time compression. But first, I would talk to Light and see if he had any recommendations.

"Okay, so what's next?" I asked.

"That's up to you," Light replied. "You can try to figure out what your Space ability can do."

I immediately shook my head on that idea. I didn't like the empty feeling my Nanos gave me when I felt the Space aspect.

Light nodded in understanding. "Sometimes, our abilities make us uncomfortable in the beginning. It's okay, but eventually you will want to at least see what it can do. If that's off the table, then the only other thing we can do is cultivate Nanos and practice using your Time ability."

I didn't argue with that. It was what I wanted to do. I had an experiment to complete.

I had come to really enjoy the atrium of the Hero Association building, even if it was starting to feel a little bit like a prison. I sat and closed my eyes. With a thought, I felt my Nanos wrap me in a blanket of compressed Time and I knew my ability was active. Immediately I started a mental countdown.

9 . . . 8 . . .

I didn't open my eyes. Instead, I felt for the wild Nanos that were usually moving around so rapidly, I could only grab one or two before having to search for more. This time, they were also slowed by my field.

7 . . . 6 . . .

I grabbed them, all of them, every single Nano that was within reach. Hundreds of them at a time.

5 . . . 4 . . .

I let myself be greedy and grabbed for more and more of them.

3 . . . 2 . . .

And before my counter hit '1', I released my Time Compression, letting my Nanos settle back into my Bioenergy Converter. I felt tired, but that didn't matter. I had in my grasp, 4,312 Nanos. I would have cackled like a mad genius if I wasn't afraid of letting them all go if I got distracted. Still, I must have been grinning like a loon, my face hurt from how hard I was smiling. This was guaranteed to get me to the 3rd Milestone and possibly even the 4th. I probably should have considered how long it would take to tame so many Nanos before I did it, but if this worked, I would be able to make up a lot of ground very quickly. But ground to what? I had no idea. For now, I was just enjoying the ride.

What was the gamer term I heard friends in High School say? Oh, right, DING!

8

Major Miracle sat in the center of one side of the table, flanked on either side by the other two permanent members of the council. Wet Work sat to his right and Mental Star sat to his left. Across from him sat Mechanic Parts, Hammer Jack, and Para-Hypno. Behind the three temporary council members sat Private Eye Light and Blue Ward. The topic of conversation was once again projected on one wall, though this time it was a still frame.

"So, Davis Malory is a genius, is that what you're telling me?" Major Miracle asked, his vision directed at the two guests.

"I'm not sure if he's a genius sir, but he's found a way to cultivate Nanos using his ability to compliment the process. Granted, he is using the most basic and simple cultivation method to do so, but it is somewhat astonishing what he's been able to accomplish," Ward answered. "His ability, Time Compression, allows him to slow time, which also slows the wild Nanos. With time slowed, he can seemingly grasp thousands of wild Nanos and begin cultivating them before he ends his Time Compression. Eventually, he will slow down just due to large volumes it will take for him to reach the next Milestone. And that is if he never learns another cultivation method."

"I told you this was a bad idea," Para-Hypno almost shouted. "Now you've got a guy that can stop time. Can you say 'assassin'?"

"Para, not now," Major Miracle stated firmly, silencing the paranoid investigator. "Is he dangerous?"

"Not really," Ward said. "Yeah, he can slow time for a few seconds. The problem is that he can't seem to move any faster than we can. In other words, he's as slow to move as he perceives us to move."

"Basically, it gives him time to think and apparently gather Nanos by the thousands," Light clarified, then blushed as he realized he was speaking to other heroes and not the oddity that was Davis Malory.

"What Milestone is he now?" Major Miracle asked, ignoring Light's odd clarification.

"By now, he should be around the 10th or 11th," Ward answered before Light could embarrass himself any further. "It really is quite interesting. A few more days and I imagine he will have achieved the 16th Milestone and brought his Time Power and Control both up to Average."

"What about his Space ability?" Major Miracle asked, seemingly satisfied with the explanation of Time.

"He has yet to work on it," Ward answered, causing Major Miracle to frown.

The frowning Major turned his gaze on Para-Hypno. "Para, share with the council what you have learned."

"Even . . . them?" Para asked, his had motioning slightly toward the back of the room where Light and Ward sat.

"Even them," Major Miracle confirmed. "They know him best. I want to hear what they are going to say after you give your report."

"Fine, but I don't agree," Para said, looking unhappy. Then again, he was never really happy anyway. Reluctantly, Para started, "So, I've been digging into the power source that Dr. Portal used. It was created by Verdant Labs. It took more than a week to get them to even admit anything was stolen and even then, they were very tight lipped about it. To make matters worse, the lab isn't able to provide us any specs on the device, because not even a day after the prototype was stolen by Dr. Portal, the blueprints and even the engineers involved were taken."

Wet Work spritzed his face with his water bottle then asked, "Two questions. First, how was Dr. Portal involved? Second, how were the engineers and plans taken?"

Para looked disgruntled by the interruption, but given Wet Work's status, he answered, "We don't have a lot of details. Dr. Portal somehow had knowledge of the device and where it would be. According to one of his henchmen, the late Dr. was hired to provide transportation by another villain. Instead, he stole it for himself, undercutting whoever hired him. That villain is now desperately searching for Dr. Portal, whether it's to kill him or to recover the device is undetermined. As to the engineers and plans, the plans were grabbed in a heist the next day, unlike Dr. Portal's heist, no alarms were sounded, and no heroes were dispatched to respond. And the engineers were nabbed from their homes the same night."

"What do you know about Verdant Labs?" Mental Star interrupted this time.

"Not enough. I'd never heard of them until this heist. I've been pouring through the company. I found a thread on an anonymous investor, I am pretty sure it's a front for a villain, but I'm not sure who," Para answered. "Honestly, Dr. Portal is probably our best shot at figuring out what was going on."

"Who's dead," Light commented.

Para snorted, then asked, "Is he? Are you sure about that?"

Light glared at the senior investigative hero. He was liking Para-Hypno less and less with every meeting. Light didn't hesitate to answer, he stated, "Yes, Portal never had Time powers. And the scans all confirmed Davis's Milestone and Body and Ability ranks before we began teaching him. And it isn't something that can be faked, a person just doesn't suddenly lose all their Nanos."

Para huffed and looked like he wanted to argue but a look from Major Miracle stopped him. The Major then firmly ordered, "Para, please, continue your report."

"The fact is, whichever villain is responsible, he or she is very careful. I don't see him or her making a mistake," Para said. "We need something to draw the villain out. And right now, that thing is Dr. Portal."

Light was about to state one again that Dr. Portal was dead when Major Miracle spoke, "You want to use Mr. Malory as bait."

"I want to use Dr. Portal as bait. Malory is useless to us," Para said, crossing his arms over his chest and looking very displeased.

Major Miracle finally turned to the two guests. He asked, "Light, Ward, with the rate at which Mr. Malory is progressing, can you make him a match for Dr. Portal?"

Light looked like he immediately wanted to say yes but hesitated. His hesitation gave Ward the chance to answer first.

Ward started, "Davis is hesitant to work on his ability to manipulate Space. First, he would need to overcome that hesitation. Second, if he overcomes that hesitation, we need to teach him to use his Space ability to open portals. And finally, if he did learn to make portals, we would need to build up his Milestone to even come close to Dr. Portal's ability. And if we raise his Milestone too far above Dr. Portal's, then there would be a lot of suspicion."

"Can you do it?" Major Miracle asked.

Ward thought for a moment then nodded. "I believe so, but we would need to take him into the wilds. With his cultivation technique, he would be able to gain a great deal of Nanos from fighting and defeating the various beasts there. It would also give us a chance to teach him to fight. Right now, he has no ability when it comes to combat. And with your permission, we could teach him a more advanced cultivation technique."

Major Miracle frowned at the last part but nodded his approval anyway. "I suppose we should ask Mr. Davis if he would be willing to try."

Light looked like he wanted to protest but held his tongue. He understood that sometimes, the greater good meant risking an innocent life. If Davis could somehow lead them to the villain trying to build the power supply, if they could put a stop to whatever this plan was, then wasn't it worth the risk? Even knowing that, Light didn't feel good about this plan. He finally spoke up, "I'll help train him if he's willing."

"Boy, you need the training almost as badly as he does," Para sniped, grinning when he saw Light tinge with embarrassment.

"Para, stop antagonizing him or I'll send you with them to babysit," Major Miracle threatened, silencing the shady hero in an instant.

"Who will you be sending?" Hammer Jack asked.

"Ward and Light, as you know him best, you'll be in charge of training Mr. Malory if he agrees to go. Hammer Jack, seeing as you like a good brawl, you can go along as well and make sure they don't get in over their heads.," Major Miracle ordered. "Now, if there is nothing else, I think it is time I meet Mr. Malory for myself. Light, Ward, an introduction if you will."

9

I was starting to love the sound of that chime and the message that followed.

> Congratulations! You've reached the 10th Milestone. The Nanos have accumulated within your body to a point in which it is now possible to enhance your Nano Evolved Body or Abilities. Be intelligent with your decisions as all choices are final.
>
> You may now open your Status and apply two points of enhancement.

A mental order to pull up my status and two more enhancement points quickly distributed. All in all, I was very pleased with my progress.

Davis Malory
Aliases: N/A
Occupation: N/A
Alignment: Neutral
Milestone: 10th
Nano: 176,227/275,000
Body
Athleticism: 1
-    Strength: Average
-    Agility: Above Average
-    Accuracy: Above Average
-    Speed: Average
-    Stamina: Average
Resistance: 1
-    Physical Resistance: Average
-    Energy Resistance: Above Average

- Mental Resistance: Above Average		
Recovery: 1		
- Physical Injury: Average		
- Nano Energy: Average		
Ability		
Power: 10		
- Time: Below Average (4/10)		
	o Time Compression: 59%	
- Space: Weak		
Control: 10		
- Time: Below Average (4/10)		
	o Time Compression: 14-Seconds Uncompressed Time	
- Space: Weak		

I was absolutely thrilled with the growth of my Time Compression. To be able to slow time so much for 14-seconds was incredible, especially with the increased compression which now gave me about 22-seconds. Though admittedly, I was starting to worry about the number of Nanos I would need to cultivate to get to the next Milestone.

I was about to close my eyes and start on another round of cultivation when I saw Light and Ward entering the atrium. With them was a large brawny looking man in a red bodysuit. Assuming they were coming to talk with me, I got up to meet them.

"Greetings Mr. Malory, I am Major Miracle," the man in the red bodysuit introduced himself before either Light or Ward could. I noticed the man didn't offer a hand to shake. As a matter of fact, I don't recall shaking hands with either Light or Ward. I would need to ask about that later. There were still so many cultural differences I was slowly but surely learning about.

"Pleased to meet you, Major Miracle," I replied, trying hard not to roll my eyes at the over the top comic book speech. It really was too much.

"How has your cultivation been progressing? I've heard you have made great strides thanks to your Time Compression ability," Major Miracle said.

"I just reached the 10th Milestone," I answered, more excited about telling Light and Ward than the newcomer.

"Congratulations, that is quite the accomplishment, especially in such a short amount of time. Most people these days don't go much past the 6th Milestone all their lives. Let alone the 10th. And in just two weeks at that," Major Miracle praised.

I couldn't help but feel like he was laying it on a little too thick.

"How can I help you today, Major?" I asked, getting tired of the small talk. This man was obviously there for a reason. And then I added, "And please, be direct. There is no need for that reassuring civilian talk."

"Ah, yes, Private Eye Light and Blue Ward mentioned you prefer direct speech," Major replied. "I shall do my best to accommodate."

I nodded, waiting for him to continue.

"We have a situation. It was one brought about by the way you arrived in this world," Major Miracle began, his speech drastically different from just moments before. It was also not nearly as loud. "Do you remember Dr. Portal?"

"How could I forget him?" I grumbled. My mind flashed back to that day, of seeing myself dead on the sidewalk. I mean, I know he wasn't me, but still . . . creepy. Seeing Major Miracle was waiting for an answer, I added a quick, "Yes, I remember him."

"His . . . arrival in your world occurred just after he stole some kind of experimental power supply from Verdant Labs, a Nano-Engineering firm. And while we haven't been able to get many details from the lab about the power supply, we have been able to piece together some of the details through other sources. For a start, Dr. Portal appears to have stolen the device from another villain, or rather just stole it first," Major Miracle began. "We're not yet sure who he stole it from, only that whoever it is, was very careful. In addition, this villain has now stolen the plans to the device and kidnapped the engineers involved with its creation. We believe the villain intends to rebuild the device."

This was the first time I had been given any more information about my situation. It was good to know that they hadn't forgotten about trying to find a way to send me home.

"Again, we don't yet know what the device does exactly. But for anyone to go through so much trouble, I can only imagine it is quite powerful. And in the hands of a villain, it could be even more dangerous. At this point, we believe our best hope is to locate this villain and put a stop to the organization behind him or her before the device is rebuilt," Major Miracle explained, pausing for a moment and taking a deep breath.

"We have also learned that this villain is now looking for Dr. Portal." The Major paused here and started looking at me expectantly, though I had no idea what he was expecting. "Your doppelganger, Dr. Portal. The man you are the spitting image of. He might be our only chance of finding this villain. Without Dr. Portal's help, stopping whatever plan the villain has concocted could very well be impossible."

I should have just said no right then and there. Instead, I feigned ignorance and asked, "But I thought Dr. Portal was dead?"

"According to you, he is dead, no one outside of the Hero Association is aware of this," Major Miracle stated, then added, "Just like no one outside of the Hero Association is aware of you, his doppelganger."

"I'm not sure I understand what you're getting at," I said. Oh, I definitely understood and there was very little chance I would accept. I hoped that if I continued to play dumb, they would think I was an idiot and come up with a different plan.

"We want you to take Dr. Portal's place," Major Miracle finally stated plainly and directly.

"Hmm, no," I said immediately and with a firm shake of my head. "I'm a doctor. I heal the sick and the injured. I'm not a superhero or a spy or anything else. Surely you have someone else that can shapeshift or something do it. Someone actually trained to do it."

"A shapeshifter can look like Dr. Portal but wouldn't be able to create portals like Dr. Portal. With a little training, you can," Major Miracle argued. Before I could reply, he pressed on, "And we would train you, first in portal creation and manipulation and then how to fight. And more importantly, we would help you get your Milestone up enough to pass for Dr. Portal in a very short amount of time."

"Training? That's your big solution? Training? Just how much training do you think you can give me and in how much time? I can't imagine you have years to get me ready before whatever this villain plans to do will be done," I replied.

Major Miracle finally cringed a little, then said, "Admittedly, time is short. But we wouldn't be asking you if the fate of the world didn't hang in the balance."

"Even more of a reason not to use me," I almost shouted. And fate of the world? Did he really want to put the fate of the world on an untrained civilian?

"Davis," Light finally interjected. "This device, it might be your only way back home."

Any more argument from me died in my throat. Home. I hadn't thought about home for a few weeks. I kept myself busy with my new superpower and cultivation. I kept myself . . . distracted. But hearing that word, a sudden rush of feelings threatened to overwhelm me. My sister

67

was back there. Oh man, I tried not to think about her too much. If I did, it would usually send my thoughts spiraling out of control with worry over her situation. Did she get evicted without money from me? Was she starving on the streets? Or worse, did she turn to selling- No, I cut that thought off right there.

"If I help, I'll get one of these devices?" I asked, looking at Major Miracle.

The Major looked uncomfortable but nodded. "I'll do everything I can to help you get back home. And if these devices are the only way to do it, then I'll make sure you get one as soon as possible."

I didn't necessarily like his word. As soon as possible could mean a lot of things. That said, he was a hero, a good guy, which meant I should be able to trust him at his word. Still, I looked to Light and asked, "Can I trust him?"

Light just nodded.

"Alright, I'm willing to try," I said, pushing down my reluctance and the feeling that this plan was going to go horribly wrong.

Major Miracle just smiled.

10

The wilds. As Light explained it to me, they were what was left of the world after the Nano-Virus changed everyone and everything. The Nano-Virus even changed plants and animals, enhancing them as much or more than humans. And unfortunately for humans, the plants and animals had a much higher survival rate. I guessed that the death rates I heard about following the virus had as much to do with the Nano infected beasts killing people and people killing people as it did the virus itself. Anyway, eventually the Fortress Cities were built to stand between the people and the wilds that dominated the rest of the planet.

Now, the wilds were a hunting ground for the more daring of ability users. Animals and plants with high Milestones were very valuable commodities. A 50th Milestone animal's pelt could be used to create Nano-Infused Armor, like the bodysuits all the heroes wore. Its meat could be eaten and the abundance of Nanos within it could be cultivated much more quickly than through standard cultivation. Same for plants and trees, different fruits, nuts, vegetables, and even flowers could be harvested and eaten to enhance cultivation.

And then there was actually hunting and killing beasts in the wild. Apparently, when a beast or person was killed, they released a large amount of their Nanos. Nanos that were extremely easy to cultivate as they were dazed and disoriented from the death of their host. A lesser amount could be gained from just beating them into submission or unconsciousness. Obviously, killing people was highly frowned upon and a quick way to get the heroes after you. Killing beasts, not so much.

Early on the morning of our planned departure from New Haven, Light, Ward, and myself were loaded into a windowless vehicle. I didn't get much of a look at the vehicle and there were no windows for me to look out.

The vehicle stopped about two hours after we left the Hero Association complex. When it did, I asked if we had arrived. Light informed me that it was just the New Haven Fortress City gates and that we still had a few more hours of travel before we would reach some sort of outpost. I was told it was unmanned and seldom used anymore. I was also informed it was a site the Hero Association once used for training purposes. And then that the Hero Association stopped using it because it became too dangerous.

I was honestly nervous as I felt the vehicle start moving past what I imagined where massive towering gates that kept the wilds out of New Haven Fortress City. I imagined mutated lizards the size of dinosaurs just waiting to chomp down on our transport, but no such attack came. In fact, it was boring. The transport was the smoothest ride I'd ever been on, not a single bump in the road. No rhythmic bumps of a highway to lull me to sleep. If it weren't for the acceleration, deceleration, and turning, I wouldn't have even known we were moving.

As Light said, a few hours later, the vehicle came to a halt and the doors were opened from the outside. It was another hero, or I hoped it was. He was dressed more dully than all the other superheroes I had met with his grey bodysuit. He had the image of a jackhammer on his chest with the letters HJ. He was large and imposing. If not for the ridiculous looking jackhammers that were strapped to his back, I might have been intimidated.

"Let's go," Light said, moving for the exit followed closely by Ward.

The outpost looked like a small fort with four thick metal walls, it was maybe 50-feet across. There was a single lookout tower at one corner of the walls and two buildings at opposite ends of the courtyard. There were no training dummies or targets for practice that I could see, so I wasn't sure what I was going to use for training, not that I had seen any of those things at the Hero Association Headquarters either.

I was barely out of the vehicle when my thoughts were interrupted by the new hero that opened the vehicle door and introduced himself. "Yo, I'm Hammer Jack," he said, his deep voice was gruff and unenthusiastic. Strangest of all, he spoke with a southern drawl. "I'm your babysitter for the wilds."

I wasn't sure how I felt about being told I needed a babysitter. Then again, I had no skill when it came to a fight, so maybe a babysitter was exactly what I needed. It still hurt to be told as much, and so bluntly. "I'm Davis, nice to meet you," I said, trying to keep the peace.

"Yeah, yeah, now, before we can start hunting the wilds," he said, pausing to point to the outside of the slowly closing metal gate, then continuing, "you need to learn some kind of attack or defense, preferably both, with at least one of your abilities. As good as I am, if we run into a pack of beasts, you might not have a choice but to fight or die," Hammer said bluntly. "Normally, a training expedition into the wilds would have at least ten heroes of the twentieth milestone or better. Due to the secretive nature of your mission, the four of us are it," he paused to motion between Light, Ward, himself and me. "And in reality, only three of us are really qualified heroes. However, if you can manage to learn some kind of attack, we will be able to start hunting and therefore rapidly increase your Milestone."

Hammer hadn't really told me anything I didn't know except for the current plan, which was simply for me to learn an attack or defense with one of my abilities. Once I accomplished that, we would start hunting. I didn't appreciate the jabs at how I wasn't qualified, but I let it slide. I couldn't afford to anger the man that was charged with keeping me alive.

"Now, I've heard what you can do with Time. I want to see what you can do with Space," Hammer said, brooking no room for argument.

I tried not to wince. I still didn't like the feel of Space. It was an empty, hollow feeling. Like if I let it out, it would swallow everything in an effort to fill in that hole.

"Shouldn't we get settled in first?" Light asked.

"No. We can get settled in once I know it's going to be worth settling in. And I won't know that until Dr. Portal here stops hesitating," Hammer snapped at Light. Then he turned to me and said, "It's your ability. Learn to use it and control it. If you don't, one day you might use it on accident and really hurt someone, maybe even kill someone, yourself included."

This time, I flinched. He was completely right. Blunt as hell, which I hadn't expected from the hero given how all the others tended to speak. I hated that I hadn't even considered that my lack of interest in exploring my other power could've led to someone getting hurt.

"Now, show me what you've got," Hammer ordered.

I frowned. I still didn't like being ordered around like that. And his expectation that I could snap my fingers and make my abilities work, really ground on me. I couldn't even use my Time Compression so easily and that was by far my best ability. Sure, it was my only ability but that wasn't the point.

Thankfully, Light chose to intercede. "Relax, Davis, just do like you did the first time you used your Time ability. Close your eyes and feel your ability. It will guide you on how to use it."

I nodded and closed my eyes. I had become very familiar with feeling the Nanos in my Bioenergy Converter, which, by the way, was the worst name for an organ ever. I mean, where was the beauty of the heart, the kidney, or pancreas? Bioenergy Converter sounded like some kind of high-tech garbage disposal.

Anyway, I took hold of my Nanos, just as I had done when I learned to use Time Compression. Only this time, I wasn't focusing on the fast and slow rhythm. I felt for the emptiness. I tried to understand what it wanted. It wasn't like Time. It definitely did not want to wrap itself around me. In fact, I felt like it would kill me if I did that. No, this was something . . . violent and dangerous.

I opened my eyes and looked around the courtyard for something to . . . project the emptiness upon. I was tempted to unleash, whatever it was my Space ability wanted to do, on Hammer Jack, but I didn't think the heroes would appreciate it if I somehow accidentally killed one of them. Instead, I picked a spot on one of the metal walls ten feet away from where I was standing. I picked a spot about 5 feet off the ground and about an inch in front of the wall, a mental target. I took hold of that feeling of emptiness again and the world turned black and white all around me as a ball began to form at my target. I fed power into it, eventually expanding the ball to about an inch in diameter. I tried to get a better understanding of what the ball was, but it was completely void. There was nothing inside it. No air, no moisture . . . just nothing. With a pop, the void burst and everything rushed to fill in the empty space.

Color returned to the world around me once again. The first thing I saw was a new black energy bar just below the gold bar. I also saw that the black energy bar was already half-empty. It told me that my ability did something, but I couldn't see anything at first glance. So, I approached the wall to get a closer look. The metal wall appeared to have warped slightly in the direction of where the small void I created was. It didn't sheer apart the wall or crush everything in the area. In fact, if you weren't looking closely, you might have completely missed it.

"An implosion. That is a very solid attack," Hammer Jack said from right next to me, startling me when he did. I had no idea when he'd come so close to me. Still, the man's nod of approval, as he looked at what my ability did, made me feel somewhat mollified, and then he spoke again, "It's weak, but still quite nice. At least it gives us something to work with."

I tried to ignore him. Which as it turns out, wasn't very hard. After using my new ability, I didn't feel as exhausted as I did after I used Time Compression for the first time, but I still felt slightly winded. That said, I was excited to see what my Status looked like now.

"Void Burst," I read aloud.

"Is that the name of the ability?" Light asked, having joined Hammer in examining the wall. Once again, I hadn't even noticed he moved over to check it. I really needed to be more aware of my surroundings.

Davis Malory	
Aliases: N/A	
Occupation: N/A	
Alignment: Neutral	
Milestone: 10th	
Nano: 192,704/275,000	
Body	
Athleticism: 1	
-	Strength: Average
-	Agility: Above Average
-	Accuracy: Above Average
-	Speed: Average
-	Stamina: Average
Resistance: 1	
-	Physical Resistance: Average
-	Energy Resistance: Above Average

-	Mental Resistance: Above Average	
Recovery: 1		
-	Physical Injury: Average	
-	Nano Energy: Average	
Ability		
Power: 10		
-	Time: Below Average (4/10)	
	o	Time Compression: 59%
-	Space: Weak	
	o	Void Burst: 2-Uses at Maximum Size
Control: 10		
-	Time: Below Average (4/10)	
	o	Time Compression: 14-Seconds Uncompressed Time
-	Space: Weak	
	o	Void Burst: up to a 20-Foot Range and up to a 1-Inch Diameter

"Yeah," I replied.

Light nodded. "Seems your Space ability is more offensively aligned. We'll need to do some additional testing to find out just how much damage you can do with it. Unfortunately, as great as the Nano Interface is, we don't get damage numbers. For example, the damage you did to the wall probably isn't enough to kill someone with one hit, but it can still do significant damage depending on where you target. A head shot has a very good chance of rendering someone unconscious, even a hero or villain."

"That would kill someone if I set it off inside their heads," I stated. I was a doctor, I understood just what kind of trauma an implosion could cause.

Hammer Jack snorted, then said, "Ha, you think you can just use an ability inside the body of another person? It doesn't work like that rookie. When you use an external ability, you are directing the Nanos that are part of your colony to act on a specific location. Unlike friendly healing Nanos, if you try to perform an attack directly inside the body of another person, those Nanos will be attacked and destroyed by the defending Nanos almost instantly."

"So, a body's Nano colony acts like an immune system where foreign Nanos are bacteria or a virus," I said, letting my medical brain take over.

Hammer just looked confused then shook his head and said, "Sure, go with that. Anyway, range abilities are either aimed and travel at a target like Light's Light Pistol or created near a target. And even then, you need to contend with resistances. Yours will probably struggle against people with higher Physical and Energy resistances."

I barely knew Hammer, but I could already tell we weren't going to get along very well if this was how he was going to treat my questions. I was glad to get the information. I just would have preferred a better delivery.

Thankfully, Ward spoke up. "That is a fair assessment. Also, something Hammer didn't mention, those destroyed Nanos are removed from you permanently."

That sounded bad. That meant I could potentially lose Nanos, which meant potentially losing Milestones.

"I understand," I said, swallowing thickly. I was very glad for the warning.

"Now, back to your new skill, Void Burst was it?" Hammer asked, no longer studying the wall.

"That's correct," I said.

Hammer nodded then followed up, asking, "How many times can you use it before you exhaust your Nanos?"

"It says I get two uses," I answered.

Hammer frowned then looked from me to the wall and back again. "You're Space ability is ranked Weak, right?"

I nodded.

Hammer's frown deepened. "That's a low number for a Weak ability. I would have expected you to have at least four uses."

Ward chimed in. "That metal wall is four-feet thick. The power required to warp it even that much is quite high. I do not believe his ability is as weak as you seem to think it is," he stated, looking at Hammer specifically.

"Humph, we'll see," Hammer said. "Alright, the bunk house is on the right, equipment shed on the left. Grab a cot and some equipment from the shed and set yourself up in the bunk house. I'm going on a quick patrol. I need to make sure you weren't followed."

"Light, get him settled. I'm going to put up some wards," Ward said, moving toward the gates, not far behind Hammer.

"Come on, Davis. Let's get you kitted out and settled in," Light said, motioning for me to follow him toward the equipment shed.

11

"Welcome to Nano Beast hunting for beginners," Hammer Jack joked as he held back an animal that at one time might have been a bulldog, if bulldogs were the size of horses, covered in porcupine spikes instead of fur . . . and was that acid it was drooling?

"This is a quilldog," Hammer Jack continued, ignoring the ineffective swipes from the giant animal. "It's only a 15th or 16th Milestone, no more than a juvenile at best. The quills make dealing physical damage nearly impossible without hurting yourself," he explained, then added, "unless you have some kind of skin hardening ability, which you don't." The quilldog tried to pull away from Hammer Jack but he just ignored it and held it firmly in place. "Alright, you've got two shots to kill it. If you do, all the Nanos are yours. Fail to kill it, and I'll kill it and keep the Nanos for myself. Good luck."

Just like that, Hammer expected me to kill the giant quilldog that looked like it could swallow me whole. And yet, Hammer was just nonchalantly holding the beast in place, like it was nothing.

"Look for a weak spot," Ward suggested from behind me. Both he and Light were there, and both had been instructed to stay out of it before we even left the outpost.

Still, I was happy for any help I could get. So, I studied the monster dog. The quills that covered it were tightly packed and covered almost every inch of the things body, including its face and chin. Even the space between its eyes had quills. However, the eyes seemed to be unprotected. I crouched down to get a look at the quilldog's belly. The spikes were shorter but still covered every inch. The nose had less coverage but that risked setting off a Void Burst inside its nose and that might be considered too close to inside the monster.

Hammer mock yawned very loudly, the threatened, "If you don't hurry up, I'm going to kill it myself."

"Fine," I said. That left nose or eyes. I think eyes were the best option I had. I concentrated on the monster dogs left eye and focused my ability. There was a pop of sound that accompanied my ability and a loud splashed that followed a very short-lived moan of pain followed by the quilldog going limp and falling to the ground with a heavy thud.

"Damn," Hammer said, sounding surprised. "Okay, that was a lot more powerful than I thought it would be. Still, not bad."

My Void Burst destroyed the monster's eye and seemed to have pulled part of the creature's brain out through the hole. I would be having nightmares about this monster's death for years to come.

"Never use that on another person," Ward said seriously.

I looked back to him and Light, only to find Light was gone. I was worried for a moment until I heard retching from some nearby brush.

I didn't think it was necessary for him to say that.

"At least, not at that range," Ward added. "You'll need to work on improving your control. Perhaps reducing the size of your attack until the damage is little more than concussive damage."

"I'll work on that," I said.

"Are you going to keep chatting or are you going to take in these Nanos before they all recover and float away?" Hammer asked impatiently.

"Oh, right," I said, quickly turning to look at . . . the quill monster. I activated my Time Compression as quickly as I could then reached out to grab ahold of all the Nanos.

For a moment I was stunned. There were so many. So many thousands of Nanos, some of them already trying to escape from the monster's corpse. I reached out to them. I grabbed onto them. Took them by the handful. Raked them in as fast as I could, trying to grab them all before my time compression ended. And then I reached my limit. I took hold of 34,566 Nanos. It was more than I had ever gathered at one time. I was disappointed I couldn't grab more with the limited time I had left. Trying to move past my disappointment, I sent the mental order to take them into my colony and convert them. It was almost instantaneous. There was no resistance. The Nanos just . . . changed. I was so stunned by how fast they changed that I didn't think to try to grab ahold of any more of them until after my Time Compression ended.

"Well, well, well," Hammer said, sounding a little impressed once again. "You managed to gather up a lot of them very quickly. Not bad."

I wanted to say I could have gotten more, but that would have just sounded childish.

"No sense in letting the rest go to waste," Hammer said. And even faster than I could have previously imagined, the remaining Nanos vanished. Thousands, hundreds of thousands of Nanos vanished. I hardly felt anything, but I knew that Hammer was able to cultivate them just that quickly. It was . . . unreal. Was everyone else able to cultivate that fast? Or was Hammer Jack really that powerful?

"You'll find that as you grow in power, you will be able to cultivate massive amounts of Nanos very quickly. That was barely a drop in the bucket for someone of Hammer Jack's Milestone," Ward said.

"Light, if you're done playing around, incinerate the body," Hammer yelled toward where Light had been retching.

"I don't have enough power to do that," Light yelled back.

"Fine," Hammer said, reaching behind his back to pull free one of his jackhammers. The machine was odd. It was actually a glove-like device where Hammer fit the jackhammer over one of his fists. He then reared back with the jackhammer covered fist and the hammer action started firing in and out rapidly until it was moving so fast, I couldn't see it. Hammer punched. It was like a cannon firing, louder than any bullet I'd ever heard. And the aftershock was enough to lift me off my feet and blow me onto my back rather painfully. When I looked up, the quilldog was gone. In fact, there was barely a blood pool from where I killed it.

"What happened to it?" I asked.

"I hit it so hard it disintegrated," Hammer answered as he slipped the jackhammer back in place behind him.

"No, really, what happened to it," I asked.

"No, really, I hit it so hard it disintegrated," Hammer replied. "Listen kid, in this world of people with abilities like Light or even you, but with power that is several magnitudes greater than you can imagine. How can someone like me compete if I don't have the ability to deal similar damage?"

"What is your ability?" I asked in awe.

Hammer grinned. "The muscles in my arms can undulate to create an effect similar to a jackhammer. With enough power and speed, I can create a shockwave that will disintegrate just about anything caught in its path."

I swallowed thickly. That was absolutely terrifying.

"Now, aren't you glad I'm a hero?" Hammer asked with a cackling laugh. "In this world, there are real monsters out there. And sometimes, it takes a monster to stop a monster."

My respect and fear of Hammer Jack grew in leaps and bounds in that moment.

"Now, let's see if we can find that little guy's pack," Hammer said jovially. "There might actually be a few alphas for Light or Ward to take on. Don't worry, I'll save a couple of them just for you. If you don't kill them with your two shots, you'll need to do it with your fists," he added the last part with a cackle of laughter.

I looked to Light and Ward then asked, "He's not serious about that last part, is he?"

Ward shrugged.

"Probably not," Light said, making us follow Hammer before the overpowered hero got too far away.

"Wait, what do you mean, 'Probably not'?" I asked, chasing after Light as he ran to keep up. "Light? Light!" I called after him but got no answer.

12

I easily broke through the 11th and 12th Milestones by the time there was a single quilldog left. It seemed Hammer Jack wouldn't be satisfied with hunting for the day until we killed every last one of them. And the sheer number of quilldogs in the nearby nest or burrow or whatever it was called was simply staggering. The number of Nanos I was able to cultivate after each kill might have been more so if I hadn't felt Ward and Light easily gobble up far more Nanos and far faster than I could, even when I doubled or even tripled my cultivating thanks to my Time Compression ability. Their ability to cultivate was simply overwhelming. Then again, given the sheer increase in Nanos required to move from one Milestone to the next at this point was beyond me. It really drove home how difficult progression was.

"Okay, last one," Hammer said, punching a much larger quilldog and knocking it a dozen yards back, this one's quills were dripping acid. Given their durability, I was surprised by the contradiction but then this was a world of superpowers. Hammer, looking none the worse for wear added, "Let's see if you can kill this one, Davis."

I swallowed nervously. Through the process of killing these monsters, I had learned that my Nanos recovered enough for one full strength shot every 15-minutes, though I could feel a strain on my system when I did. Currently, I had just one shot, and that was barely recovered from the last time.

I aimed for the eye on the still stunned quilldog and concentrated, calling up my ability. Before I could use it, the quilldog's eyes snapped back into focus, much faster than the others I'd killed previously. The beast charged back at Hammer. After the missed opportunity, I was ready and waiting for Hammer to stop the beast again. As soon as he did, I would be able to let loose with my ability. Unfortunately, that's not what happened. When the monster charged at Hammer, the large brute simply side stepped the monster, leaving it to continue barreling right at me, ready to bite my head off or impale me with its quills.

I panicked. I dropped to the ground and curled up into a ball, trying to minimize the damage I was about to receive. I hoped I would survive long enough for a healer to fix me up. Then I heard a heavy thud followed by a high-pitched rubbing sound, like skin on glass. After a moment of not being dead or injured, I peeked out, to see the quilldog had crashed headlong into a shimmering blue barrier and the monster was once again stunned.

"If you are going to do stuff like that, at least make sure he'll survive it first," Ward said, a hint of anger in his voice.

"I knew you would protect him," Hammer said. "Now we know how he'll react when his life is in danger. I'll give him another day, if he doesn't improve by the end of hunting tomorrow then I'm leaving."

"He's new at this," Light said. "You need to give him time to develop and learn. No one can become a combat veteran overnight. Not you. Not even Major Miracle."

"Which is why I said he's got until tomorrow," Hammer said. "Time is short, we can't wait until the end of the month to determine if he's got the will to go through with this. If he can't face down a simple alpha quilldog, then he stands no chance against the villains. If he stands no chance against the villains, then this mission is pointless. Now, Davis, kill that quilldog."

There was a problem with doing that. I was still petrified, curled up on the ground, staring at the massive monster just inches away from gutting me with one of its acid dripping quills.

Thankfully, Light did it for me. One shot from his finger into the exposed underbelly and the quilldog died.

Hammer scoffed, then repeated himself, "One more day."

"Cultivate what you can," Light said, looking to me now. "And don't worry about Hammer."

Except that Hammer was right. If I didn't improve, and improve quickly, then there was no point in this mission moving forward. I was slow to climb back to my feet. I felt embarrassed for panicking like I did. And especially for Hammer to call me on it. It was . . . humiliating.

"This time, don't focus directly on the quilldog," Ward advised. "Instead, stretch your senses out as far as you can."

I frowned. Wasn't that what I was already doing? Still, Ward and Light hadn't steered me wrong yet. I sat down and tried to sense for the Nanos coming from the quilldog, using it as a starting point. Then I tried to sense out further from it. Even just five feet away from the quilldog, there was a good number of tired Nanos. It wasn't as concentrated as it was at the corpse, but there was still a lot to be taken.

"Now, don't try to take everything from the highest concentration of Nanos, instead, try to take in the Nanos within range," Ward continued. "Start with those farthest away and work inwards. Build up momentum.

Within my range? I had a range? Once again, I tried to push out the range of my Nano-sense. Upon opening my senses, I found I could feel Nanos up to about twenty feet away from me. I activated my Time Compression and grabbed them. It felt slow at first because there were so few Nanos that I could feel at my outer limits. But as I closed in on my center, it was like he said, I picked up momentum, grabbing more and more, quickly surpassing what I thought was my limit. And when I got to the alpha, I was moving so fast I swept through the Nanos, grabbing most of them in one go. And then my Time Compression ended and within seconds I converted 312,983 Nanos.

Congratulations! You've reached the 13th Milestone. The Nanos have accumulated within your body to a point in which it is now possible to enhance your Nano Evolved Body or Abilities. Be intelligent with your decisions as all choices are final.

You may now open your Status and apply two points of enhancement.

I was dumbfounded. I had never been able to gather so many Nanos at once. It was slower than my usual cultivation, at least at first it was. But when I had momentum . . . I more than quadrupled what I thought was my maximum. Was that how everyone gathered Nanos? Or was that a secret of Ward's that he just shared with me? Did Light know this technique? I made a mental note to ask Ward about it later. For now, I satisfied myself by applying my two enhancement points. I know I was supposed to be improving my space manipulation, and both Ward and Hammer would probably be displeased, but I wanted to get my Time Power and Control both up to Average first, plus I was so close, 7 out of 10 on both. Just three Milestones to go.

A few minutes later, a seemingly satisfied Hammer grunted and said, "I'll start disintegrating the corpses except for the alpha, we'll take it back with us for dinner."

"Dinner?" I questioned, feeling slightly ill at the thought of eating monster dog.

"Yeah, quilldog isn't bad eats. Might even gain an enhancement point of Physical Resistance," Hammer said, then jabbed at me with the snide comment, "You'll need it if you want to survive this world."

Ignoring what I was sure was a jab at my cowardice, the statement confused me. Rather than ask Hammer, I looked to Ward. The man was as close to a scientist as I could find so far.

"When you eat certain Nano-Infused foods, there is a very slim chance you can carry over some of the strength of the Nanos being converted. Quilldogs have a very potent Physical Resistance. There is a chance, albeit very small chance, you will be able to gain an enhancement point," Ward explained. "You may have noticed that when you kill a beast, they only release a portion of their Nanos. Some of the Nanos are destroyed by the death of the beast. And finally, everything else is infused into the body. The quills, the skin, the meat, organs, and bones all have Nanos. Some of the parts like the skin and quills are used to create our bodysuits and armor. Some parts, like the meat and some organs can be consumed. The rest is . . . mostly unusable."

"Back up, the Nanos we absorb can carry over enhancement points from their host?" I asked.

Ward looked thoughtful for a moment, then replied, "Not exactly, at least I can't say for certain. It only seems to work with the Nanos absorbed during consumption. Hammer Jack for instance, eats meat from beasts known to have an abundance of Strength enhancements."

"Is it the meat or the Nanos in the meat that carry the enhancements?" I asked, excited by the information.

Ward blinked at me several times as if he was confused. That, or I just asked such a stupid question he didn't know how to answer. "The Nanos," he finally answered, then added, "I assume."

What did he mean 'assume'? I asked, "Haven't you ever studied it?"

"I haven't, no. But there are others that study Nanos extensively. They would know more," Ward answered.

That was frustrating. I would have loved to sit down and talk to these people that study Nanos. I really wanted to understand better how they worked. But if my mission was a success, I would hopefully be going home and there weren't any Nanos there for me to study.

"I would be happy to arrange a meeting with Mechanical Parts, he's probably the leading expert on Nanos in New Haven," Ward offered.

I shook my head. "I would, but . . . well, if we succeed, I'll hopefully be on my way home."

"You could stay, you know," Light said. "You could find a place in this world."

"My sister is back there. I need to get back to her," I said. "She depends on me."

"I didn't know you had a sister," Light said. "Is she also a doctor?"

"No, she's a student . . . was a student. She should have graduated by now," I said, thinking of the little girl I practically raised.

"What did she study?" Ward asked.

"Computer Engineering," I answered. "Just goes to show that she is so much smarter than me."

"And what's that?" Light asked.

"Computer Engineering?" I asked, getting a nod from Light. "Oh, well she's learning how computers work, everything from software to hardware. If I remember correctly, she's focusing on network engineering."

"I see," Light said, nodding. "But . . . uh, what's a computer?"

"A computer, you know, like a machine that can be used to process information using various software applications," I said, getting a blank look in return. "You don't have computers?"

Light shook his head and when I looked to Ward, he also shook his head.

I was perplexed by their responses. "If you don't have computers, then how do you-" I paused to think about how to ask this question. What is something that is done today that computers made easier or better. "Type a letter or write a paper? Or what about large mathematical calculations?"

"On a typewriter or with a pen," Light answered. "As for the math, I'm not sure," he added, looking to Ward for help.

"There are people with abilities that give them enhanced brain power. If there is a math problem, they can usually solve it," Ward answered.

I was stunned by the answer. A typewriter was such old technology. How in the world did they create a Nano-Virus so long ago without computers? Or was the technology lost after the Advent? And ability users had math powers? "Then how did that windowless vehicle fly if a computer wasn't controlling it?"

"Nano-Engineers build them. They are built with Nano-Infused materials and can be controlled by anyone using their own Nanos to control them," Ward explained.

"But how do they work?" I asked.

Ward shrugged, then said, "You would need to ask a Nano-Engineer. I don't know how they work, just that they do."

"And you're comfortable with that?" I asked.

"For the most part anyway. For me, as long as the Nanotech has been proven and properly tested, I'm comfortable using it. Some heroes love experimenting with Nanotech, but they risk their lives every time they do," Ward replied.

I wasn't satisfied. I thought about some other common things that would be used daily. I asked, "What about your power grid? How do you keep the lights on in the city?"

"Nanos," Ward answered again, leaving me completely dissatisfied with the answers I was getting. Worse, I was starting to get worried. It sounded like this culture was completely reliant on Nanos.

"Then what do you learn in school as children?" I asked, hoping to whatever deity ruled this world that they at least had some standard of education.

"Reading, writing, mathematics, history, and Ability Power and Control," Light answered.

"What about things like the sciences of biology, physics, and chemistry?" I asked.

"Those subjects are briefly discussed in History," Ward answered, then seeing my confusion he elaborated. "Who needs to study biology when people have the ability to heal others with a touch or a thought? What's the point in learning physics when there are abilities that defy those ancient laws with the snap of fingers? Same for Chemistry, what's the point when a person can use their ability to change lead into gold? Sure, some of that knowledge might help people with a power that relates specifically to their ability, but for the most part, the control of our abilities is instinctual."

I wanted to laugh when he equated Chemistry to Alchemy, but another more serious part of me wanted to cry. "What about the Bioenergy Converter? Has anyone ever studied that?" I asked.

"Nano-Engineers have tried to study the Bioenergy Converters found in animals, but they have never been able to adapt them to the Nano-Tech we use," Ward answered. "Most research into Bioenergy Converters is banned these days. The organ is too volatile outside of the body."

I wasn't satisfied with that answer. I needed more information, so I asked several questions at once, "I meant, how does the Bioenergy Converter work? How does it work with the other organs? How is it connected to the nervous system and other organs?"

Ward didn't look uncomfortable with the number of questions. He looked more like he just didn't know how to answer. And then he finally said, "I don't know. Never needed to know."

I was stunned. "Are you really telling me, no one has studied the Bioenergy Converter from the standpoint of biology?"

"Maybe in the past, but like I said, research is currently banned on anything to do with the human Bioenergy Converter," Ward replied with a shrug. He must have seen my disappointment with his answer because he added, "I suppose, maybe one of the old governments did some research right after the Advent, but if they did, I doubt any of that research still exists."

I still couldn't believe what I was hearing. How could a society become so dependent upon something they didn't fully understand? How could they trust in Nanotech when they didn't even know how Nanos worked? The doctor in me was starting to panic. I had these microscopic machines, if they were machines and not some kind of biological agent, infesting my body and no one could tell me exactly how they worked or what they were doing to me. And worse, no one seemed to care or want to find out. They just accepted that this was the way things were and that was the end of it.

"What's wrong?" Light asked.

The panic must have been clear on my face as I turned to look at him sharply. "I . . . I can't . . . this . . . How does a society trust so blindly in a technology they don't fully understand? I've been infested with these Nanos and no one can tell me exactly how they work, only that they can take on certain traits that enhance the body. Is it genetic editing? Or is it something else? Has anyone ever looked at a Nano under an electron microscope? Do you even know what that is?"

Ward and Light both looked at me worriedly before anyone spoke. And when someone did speak, I had the misfortune of hearing Hammer Jack's voice.

Dragging one of the alpha quilldogs behind him, Hammer Jack joined us, barely pausing to drop the corpse and cross his arms, he started talking, "Stop your belly aching. Sounds to me like you came from a world that relied on technology. Do you know how every technology in your world worked? Are you a master of those sciences you just mentioned? Ward already told you, we have people that study Nanos, but most of us just know that they work and that's enough. If you want more information, then stick around long enough to talk to someone that actually studies Nanos." With that, Hammer took hold of the alpha quilldog again and marched ahead, dragging the large body behind him.

"Wow," Ward said, staring after Hammer. "That was almost . . . eloquent."

Light seemed to ignore what Hammer said, or at least didn't let it get to him. He kept his focus on me. "Davis, I'm sure there is a lot you could learn from us if you give it some time. And I would guess there is a lot you can teach us. For now, I would suggest you focus on the mission. Just get through the mission then you can worry about everything else."

Light spoke sense. Unfortunately, it did little to assuage my issues with the current status quo. "Let's get back to the outpost," I said, not interested in talking anymore.

"Alright, let's go," Ward said, leading the way.

I nodded and followed.

"What's an electron microscope?" Ward asked surprising me slightly. Usually, Light was the curious one.

I spent the rest of the walk back to the outpost explaining what I knew of electron microscopes and some other earth technology, including a more detailed explanation of computers and the internet and finally video games.

13

The quilldog steaks did not reward me with any points of Physical Resistance. Not for nothing, I did gain a few hundred Nanos but that was it.

Davis Malory		
Aliases: N/A		
Occupation: N/A		
Alignment: Neutral		
Milestone: 13th		
Nano: 713,506/725,000		
Body		
	Athleticism: 1	
-	Strength: Average	
-	Agility: Above Average	
-	Accuracy: Above Average	
-	Speed: Average	
-	Stamina: Average	
	Resistance: 1	
-	Physical Resistance: Average	
-	Energy Resistance: Above Average	
-	Mental Resistance: Above Average	
	Recovery: 1	
-	Physical Injury: Average	
-	Nano Energy: Average	
Ability		
	Power: 13	
-	Time: Below Average (7/10)	
	o	Time Compression: 62%

- Space: Weak		
	o Void Burst: 2-Uses at Maximum Size	
Control: 13		
- Time: Below Average (7/10)		
	o Time Compression: 17-Seconds Uncompressed Time	
- Space: Weak		
	o Void Burst: up to a 20-Foot Range and up to a 1-Inch Diameter	

After dinner, I didn't much feel like talking to the others. I was too worried over the next day's hunting. I didn't know if I would be able to react fast enough. I didn't know if I would be able to use my ability fast enough to kill in a split second. I felt the fear of not completing the mission creeping in . . . the fear of not going home.

"Get some sleep," Hammer's voice rudely interrupted my thoughts.

I frowned at the man but didn't argue and began the walk toward the bunkhouse.

"You know, you've got the power kid. With time you might make for a great hero," Hammer said, surprising me.

Unfortunately, I heard what he wasn't saying. So, I said it, "But I don't have time."

"No," Hammer agreed, "You don't. Or do you?"

What did that mean?

"Anyway, get some rack, I'll be waking you up soon enough," Hammer promised, walking back toward the makeshift commissary. It was actually more of a campfire, but it worked just the same.

I jumped just before I entered the bunkhouse, a loud boom startling me. When I looked back, the rest of the remains of the alpha quilldog were gone, no doubt disintegrated by Hammer.

I would love to say I slept well that night, but I didn't. Every howl, growl, and cry of pain from an animal outside the compound had me on edge. And as promised, Hammer woke me up early. Early enough to see Light and Ward were both still sound asleep.

Hammer led me up to the top of the wall that surrounded the small compound, his eyes scanning the forest. I guessed he was looking for something, but I had no idea what, until his eyes narrowed and he grinned, pointing a finger at a small brown animal that had the upper body and head of a squirrel with the legs and fluffy tail of a rabbit, though slightly larger than both. It seemed all animals on this world were larger, some extremely so.

"That varmint is what we call a squirbit," Hammer whispered, then elaborated, "They are the fastest animal on the planet."

I looked back at the animal he was talking about. I was barely looking at it when it seemed to vanish, reappearing ten feet away from where it started.

"Teleportation?" I asked, looking back to Hammer.

Hammer shook his head. "No, pure speed," he answered, then continued, "They are sadistic little buggers, always dodging attacks, like it's a game. Taunting you when you miss. Anyway, you're going to kill it by the end of today, or we're leaving." Then with a heavy clap on my back that almost pushed me over the wall, Hammer walked away.

I looked back at the . . . squirbit . . . the little brown animal with super speed. It was just standing there, digging into the ground for a moment before standing to its hind legs with an oversized grub or worm in its mouth, which was struggling to get free of the squirbit only to be devoured in short order. And then the little guy vanished again, appearing a few feet closer to me and digging once more.

"Sorry little guy, it's either you or me," I said, taking aim and charging up my shot. Given it was a small animal, I didn't want to use too much power so I tried to make the Void Burst as small as I could, maybe half of a centimeter in diameter. As soon as the squirbit stood again with another insect in its mouth, I burst the miniature void next to its head. But there was no blood or guts.

Then I heard a chittering. Twenty feet away from where I attacked the squirbit, the little bugger stood, completely unharmed, a squirming grub clutched in its paws.

Okay, so maybe this wasn't going to be as easy as I hoped. I took aim and fired again, keeping the Void Burst small, and again, the little bugger dodged effortlessly. This time when I spotted it again, it was slurping down the grub like it was a noodle, then smacked its lips as though it was satisfied. Then it vanished again, this time appearing ten feet closer to me and once more digging into the ground for its next meal.

I tried using a larger Void Burst and another miss. I tried using my largest Void Burst and missed. I tried to vary my timing, using Void Burst right after it moved and missed. I tried hitting it while it was digging, and not only did I miss, but the squirbit still managed to get its food. After the first hour, I resorted to attacking the environment around it, trying to trip it up with divots in the ground or causing dirt to fly up into its face to blind it. I even tried dropping a few trees on it but stopped after one of the trees almost fell on the wall. Thankfully, Ward's barrier prevented that, and another Void Burst broke the tree in half so that the part resting on the barrier fell to the ground outside, but it was a little too close for comfort.

By this time, I was starting to see what Hammer meant about the little bugger taunting him. I swear, the chittering after the last tree fell almost sounded like laughing, but I was sure that was just my imagination. A delusion induced by frustration.

Having come to accept that none of my well thought out plans were working, I decided to try something else. I needed to be faster. I needed to form and collapse the void my ability created in an instant, and I needed to control it.

So, I tried again with the smallest Void Burst I could make. I just focused on making it much faster. My goal was to form and collapse the void in the time it took for me to snap my fingers. My first try took about ten snaps of my fingers. By my tenth attempt, I was down to eight snaps. At fifteen attempts, I had something of a breakthrough. I don't know if it was just gaining comfort with the ability or perhaps muscle memory, but I got it in three snaps.

I aimed for the squirbit with every attack, but, as I had come to expect by then, I missed every time. And when I got it down to a single snap, I still missed. But that didn't stop me, I kept at it. I tried to use them rapid fire, using three or four Void Bursts in a row, chasing the squirbit all over the field. Eventually, I used twelve of the minimum power attacks in a row, exhausting my power in an attempt to exhaust the squirbits power. The squirbit won that battle. It wasn't all bad news, I learned that if I used my minimum power, I could use Void Burst twelve times before I couldn't use it anymore, or at least until I rested and recovered. It suddenly made sense as to why Light was interest in increasing his Recovery.

Around noon, Light brought me some rations but didn't say anything about the squirbit hunt. He wouldn't even give me any advice on the matter. Just saying that it was something I needed to figure out for myself.

I spent hours more, trying to kill that furry little bugger to no avail. I was beginning to feel desperate to kill the thing, especially once the sun began to set. I started firing of Void Bursts again, trying to combine everything I had done earlier. I tried using the Void Bursts to drive it into a corner, but the thing was just too fast.

"Alright, times up," Hammer said, loudly from behind me.

"No," I said desperately turning to face him. "I need more time," I said, then froze. I needed more time. More time was something I could actually give myself.

I turned back swiftly toward the squirbit and activated my Time Compression. The squirbit was still faster than I thought possible while my Time Compression was active, but I could suddenly see it moving. I knew my time was ticking by, so I needed to act quickly. I saw the path it was taking. Without deactivating my Time Compression, I fired off a Void Burst. I saw the squirbit's eyes widen a fraction before its head nearly exploded in slow motion. Thankfully, my Time Compression ended suddenly when I ran out of power and time resumed its normal speed, preventing me from having the watch the rest of that in slow motion. I was more than a little satisfied when the little rodent from hell finally died.

"Yes!" I shouted, raising both hands, fists clenched, into the air in celebration, giving my best Rocky pose.

"What?" Hammer asked, sounding confused and pushing me out of the way. Much louder and with much more surprise, he repeated, "What? You . . . you . . . how the hell did you do that? I've been trying to kill that little demon for years . . . years I say. And you got it in just a day?"

Ignoring the fact that it sounded like Hammer had set me up to fail, I was overjoyed at my success.

Hammer though, jumped off the wall, landing effortlessly next to the squirbit. He knelt down next to it and picked it up, shaking his head in disbelief as he did.

Hammer grumbled something I couldn't hear. "Alright, cultivate your winnings. To the victor go the spoils. I'll cook this up for you. Too bad there isn't enough for all of us. I bet you'll get a few points of Speed from this thing."

I wasn't about to jump off the wall. I didn't have Hammer's strength. Instead, I ran through the compound and out the gates to where I killed the squirbit. Using Ward's cultivation technique, I quickly gobbled up the Nanos. I don't know what that little thing's Milestone was, but I was stunned by the number of Nanos it let loose into the atmosphere. I cultivated 537,441 Nanos. And if I would have had more Time Compression left, I would have gone back for seconds.

Congratulations! You've reached the 16th Milestone. The Nanos have accumulated within your body to a point in which it is now possible to enhance your Nano Evolved Body or Abilities. Be intelligent with your decisions as all choices are final.

You may now open your Status and apply two points of enhancement.

With that one kill, I jumped three Milestones. And more importantly, I had the points to bring my Time Power and Control both up to Average.

Davis Malory	
Aliases: N/A	
Occupation: N/A	
Alignment: Neutral	
Milestone: 16th	
Nano: 1,250,947/1,400,000	
Body	
Athleticism: 1	
- Strength: Average	
- Agility: Above Average	

-   Accuracy: Above Average
-   Speed: Average
-   Stamina: Average
Resistance: 1
-   Physical Resistance: Average
-   Energy Resistance: Above Average
-   Mental Resistance: Above Average
Recovery: 1
-   Physical Injury: Average
-   Nano Energy: Average
Ability
Power: 16
-   Time: Average
o   Time Compression: 65%
-   Space: Weak
o   Void Burst: 2-Uses at Maximum Size
Control: 16
-   Time: Average
o   Time Compression: 20-Seconds Uncompressed Time
-   Space: Weak
o   Void Burst: up to a 20-Foot Range and up to a 1-Inch Diameter

I now had 33-seconds to act while 20-seconds of uncompressed time passed. You could do a lot in half a minute while everyone else was moving in slow motion.

"Congratulations," Light said, running out to join me. "That was a 25th Milestone animal. Way to go."

"How do you know that?" I asked. I should have asked sooner. How was it that the heroes seemed to be able to tell what Milestone a person or monster was at, and with such ease.

"Do what? Tell what something's Milestone is?" Light asked.

"Yeah, that, how can you tell what something's Milestone is?" I asked.

"Oh, sometimes I forget that you didn't grow up here," Light said. "It's a feature of the Advent system. When you look at someone or an animal, just think scan. Your Nanos will send out a small pulse and contact your target's Nanos. Most heroes learn to do this automatically as part of our threat assessment protocols. You never know when a villain is going to attack."

"Huh," I said, feeling slightly annoyed. I looked at Light and thought Scan. I saw a 38 over his head for a moment before it vanished from view. "Is there a way to get a deeper scan?"

"There is Nanotech that can scan deeper. And there are probably some ability users that can scan someone more thoroughly, but those are rare," Light answered. "Anyway, let's get back inside before Hammer decides to eat your reward."

Light had a good point.

Inside the wall of the outpost, Hammer stood in front of the fire pit, slowly turning the skewered squirbit while the meat sizzled. He looked up when he heard me coming and said, "You'd better eat every last bite of the meat on those bones. If you let anything go to waste, I will be mighty displeased. And if I'm displeased, you can bet tomorrow's hunt is going to be unpleasant."

I nodded in understanding. Honestly, I didn't feel great about eating the skewered animal, but it really did smell good.

"Oh, and starting tomorrow, no more free Nanos. You'll need to fight for it like everyone else," Hammer added, rotating the skewered squirbit over the fire.

Twenty minutes later, Hammer seemed satisfied with the cook of the meat. He handed me a pair of potholders and walked away. I took the skewer from over the fire and dug in. As ordered, I left nothing behind but bones. By the end, I didn't think I would want to eat ever again. The meat was gamey and could have used some salt. Otherwise, it was edible. I thought or hoped there would be some kind of system message after eating but nothing appeared.

Ward looked at me expectantly.

"What?" I asked.

"Did you gain anything?" Ward asked.

"Not that I can tell," I said.

"Check your status," Ward said.

I checked but saw no difference. "Nothing."

Ward frowned, "I don't understand. Something like that squirbit must have had at least Master Rank Speed, it should have given you something."

I shrugged, I didn't know what to say and apparently neither did Ward.

But it was Light that recognized the problem and came up with a solution. He then asked, "Did you cultivate the food?"

"No," I said. "Should I have?"

"Of course," Ward said, slapping both open hands on his knees. "Of course, that's got to be it. I should have thought of that sooner. You're not from our world so you wouldn't know. Fresh meat and fruits, and I mean really fresh like the quilldog yesterday and that squirbit today, they need to be cultivated to absorb all the Nanos within the food."

"Why does fresh matter?" I asked, already feeling for the Nanos in my gut.

"After a day, the potency of the Nanos fades significantly. Often even turning inert," Ward answered.

For a guy who doesn't know much about science, he sure did speak like he knew a lot about it.

Anyway, I concentrated on the Nanos in my stomach. I could already feel the stomach acid starting to break down the meat. I could feel Nanos being destroyed. I couldn't help but wonder how many Nanos I wasted by taking so long. I took hold of the Nanos in my stomach, those that remained. There were only 8,543 left. I applied my rhythm to them and in short order they were mine and no longer being digested. I also notice that the food seemed to burn up in the process, leaving me feeling hungry again, which also explained how Light, Ward, and Hammer ate so much more of the quilldog steaks than I managed.

"Now check your status," Ward instructed.

Davis Malory
Aliases: N/A
Occupation: N/A
Alignment: Neutral
Milestone: 16th
Nano: 1,259,490/1,400,000
Body
Athleticism: 8
-   Strength: Average
-   Agility: Above Average
-   Accuracy: Above Average
-   Speed: Average (7/10)
-   Stamina: Average
Resistance: 1
-   Physical Resistance: Average
-   Energy Resistance: Above Average
-   Mental Resistance: Above Average
Recovery: 1
-   Physical Injury: Average
-   Nano Energy: Average
Ability

Power: 16		
-	Time: Average	
	o	Time Compression: 65%
-	Space: Weak	
	o	Void Burst: 2-Uses at Maximum Size
Control: 16		
-	Time: Average	
	o	Time Compression: 20-Seconds Uncompressed Time
-	Space: Weak	
	o	Void Burst: up to a 20-Foot Range and up to a 1-Inch Diameter

"Seven," I whispered, then a little louder, I said, "Seven. I gained seven points of enhancement."

"Goodness me," Light said.

"Don't tell Hammer," Ward warned, looking around for the brutish man.

"Think you could kill one of those again?" Light asked, a hopeful look on his face.

"Yeah," I said honestly. I could definitely kill one of those again. I would happily kill a hundred of those if it gained me seven points of enhancement.

"We need to find one first," Ward said with a sigh. "As you can imagine, they are a bit on the rare side. The one you got today has lived near this outpost for years. We liked to use it as a training tool. With its speed, it helped our trainees gain speed with their attacks."

"Does that mean Hammer was never going to leave?" I asked.

"Only if you failed to get faster. I don't think he ever imagined you would get that fast," Ward said with a laugh. "How did you get it anyway?"

"I hit it with Void Burst while my Time Compression was active," I answered.

"You can do that?" Light asked.

I shrugged, "I just did."

"You are quite the wonder," Ward said.

"Why is that?" I asked.

"Having multiple abilities is already rare. Being able to combine both abilities is even rarer," Ward answered. "Anyway, I'm going to cultivate. Can't let Davis get ahead of me, now can I?" He stood and stretched before walking off. As he did, I looked at him and thought Scan, causing a 44 to appear over his head briefly. I made a mental note to do the same to Hammer Jack later.

"I should do the same," Light said a minute later.

Sitting on my own by the small firepit, I closed my eyes and let my senses expand outward, feeling for the ambient Nanos in the air. Today ended up being a really good day, then my stomach rumbled reminding me that I was hungry . . . again.

14

Despite me eating every last bite of the squirbit, Hammer Jack still seemed to be rather displeased with me. I could only assume he was more than a little jealous. That or he found out I didn't know to cultivate the meat after eating it and he was punishing me for wasting the good Nanos.

The seven headed hydrasnakes he chose to hunt next was all the proof I needed to know that the man held a grudge. Thankfully, they were very different from the hydra of Greek mythology, they were neither gigantic nor did the heads regrow when you killed one. No, these were more snakes with seven heads and only about the size of a person when they reared up like a cobra to face an enemy. An enemy . . . like me.

I wished I had taken some time to learn to activate my Time Compression faster. As it was, the seven heads with deadly looking fangs dripping venom that were bearing down on me, promising a painful death, would have been the perfect time to slow time. Unfortunately, by the time I did, the serpent was less than a foot away from me.

I needed to stop the snake without putting myself in further danger. I created a half-inch Void Burst at the point where the seven heads connected to the body, and in an instant, I collapsed the void. Time resumed and the snake suddenly stopped its attack, looking kind of like one of those old cartoons. The one with the coyote that was always chasing that bird and always losing in humorous ways. Anyway, the snake heads suddenly stopped then reversed direction briefly before the seven heads were severed from the body. Thankfully, when they stopped moving backwards, they stopped moving.

With my primary target down, I looked for my next opponent. Light was easily sniping three different hydrasnakes from a fair distance away. As with each head killed, the snakes seemed to slow down.

Ward created barriers around a few of the snakes. I could see one or two fighting against the barrier and the other three were looking lethargic, hardly fighting back. I noticed the weaker hydrasnakes were slightly discolored, slowly turning darker blue with each passing second. It was about then I realized that Ward was suffocating them.

I couldn't see where Hammer had gone off to, but I assumed he was fine.

From the corner of my eye, I saw another snake trying to sneak up on me. This time, I was better prepared, so I activated my Time Compression before it was able to attack. I set off two minimum powered Void Bursts at the same spot but from opposite sides. The hydrasnake was suddenly and violently pulled in two different directions almost at once. It split and died with barely a death throw after the spine had been broken so thoroughly.

"I'm running low," I shouted, running back from the fight.

"I've got you, stay calm," Ward said, looking completely unperturbed. He held a hand up in my direction for a moment and over my shoulder, I saw a blue shimmer appear. "Stay behind the shield, choose your targets carefully."

I skidded to a halt and turned around, moving close behind the shimmering blue barrier.

We'd been killing these things for a while and they didn't seem to have an end. I learned early in the fight that these were ambush predators. They liked to sneak up and lunge from the flanks or from the branches of the trees above us. I needed to always be aware of that. With the barrier in front of me, I finally had a chance to look at one of the hydrasnakes and think Scan. I was unimpressed. It was only a ten. I checked another and it was also a ten. The next was a nine.

"Don't let their Milestone fool you," Ward warned. "They will still kill you in one attack."

"On your left," Light yelled out a warning.

I looked left, seeing the snake starting to rear up. I didn't use Time Compression this time, I didn't have the power for it. I let off two small Void Bursts where the necks all met. It wasn't as effective as when they went off at almost the same time, but it successfully snapped the hydrasnakes back . . . neck . . . body . . . whatever. I'm a doctor, not a veterinarian. When one of the heads kept moving, I used one more weakened Void Burst to kill it.

"I'm tapped," I shouted nervously. I didn't need to worry, Ward was on it, extending the transparent blue barrier around me. My health bar showed I was uninjured but the gold-colored bar that appeared after I unlocked my first Ability, Time Compression, was almost completely drained. I still liked that feature of the interface. I found it especially useful for when I lost count of how many Void Bursts I used.

"Start cultivating," Ward ordered. "If you don't start now, Hammer will take it all for himself."

"What about you and Light?" I asked.

"We'll still get some, but Hammer will take the lion's share. If you find yourself competing with Hammer and us, you'll get almost nothing. So, cultivate," Ward ordered again.

I didn't like the idea of cultivating like that. It almost felt like stealing. Still, if Ward was right, and he probably was, I really should just cultivate what I could now. Still not liking it, I did as Ward ordered. And given my Time Compression, like my Void Burst, was out of power, it meant I was doing it the slow way. I let my senses expand, pushing out to the farthest reaches and took hold of what I could, there were a lot more than I thought possible. Although, when I considered the sheer volume of hydrasnake bodies all around me, I shouldn't have been. It was harder to build up momentum as I pulled my Nano-senses inward. I barely took hold of 53,421 Nanos. Worse, it took almost ten minutes to grab that much.

Davis Malory		
Aliases: N/A		
Occupation: N/A		
Alignment: Neutral		
Milestone: 16th		
Nano: 1,342,118/1,400,000		
Body		
	Athleticism: 8	
-	Strength: Average	
-	Agility: Above Average	
-	Accuracy: Above Average	
-	Speed: Average (7/10)	
-	Stamina: Average	
	Resistance: 1	
-	Physical Resistance: Average	
-	Energy Resistance: Above Average	
-	Mental Resistance: Above Average	
	Recovery: 1	
-	Physical Injury: Average	
-	Nano Energy: Average	
Ability		
	Power: 16	
-	Time: Average	
	o	Time Compression: 65%
-	Space: Weak	
	o	Void Burst: 2-Uses at Maximum Size

Control: 16		
- Time: Average		
	o Time Compression: 20-Seconds Uncompressed Time	
- Space: Weak		
	o Void Burst: up to a 20-Foot Range and up to a 1-Inch Diameter	

I was so close to the 17th Milestone, but when I looked back up, the fight was over. I wanted to reach out again to try to grab more Nanos but when I reached out, there was nothing. All but a few hundred Nanos were gone. A quick look around showed Hammer was back and grinning at me like the cat that got the canary, which told me all I needed to know.

"You've got to be faster than that if you want to gather anymore Nanos," Hammer taunted, then pointed to what I thought was north and said, "I found their nest about a mile that way, let's go get us a hydrasnake queen."

"Great, more snakes," I groaned. I promised myself in that moment, I was going to get a lot faster at activating Time Compression. I looked to Ward and asked, "Please tell me the hydrasnake queen's meat is good for something."

"Agility," Ward answered. "But don't count on it. It is very rare that people gain anything from less than a Master or Grandmaster Body Rank."

"What about the quilldogs?" I asked.

"Below Excellent I think, but it might only be Above Good," Ward answered. "I don't think anyone has ever bothered to capture a quilldog alive to give it a full scan. In fact, I doubt any beast has ever been fully scanned."

I was bothered once again by the lack of scientific research. I didn't get the highest grade in pharmacology in medical school, but I did well enough. I knew that all manner of medications had been created from plants and even some animals. If Chinese medication was anything to go by, animal parts were able to cure everything depending on the part, even though there wasn't much for scientific proof. I had a feeling, especially after the effects of eating that squirbit yesterday, that the Chinese medicine might just work in this world.

Sighing, I shook the thoughts away. I couldn't worry about that right now. I needed to keep up. Right now, I needed to grow and increase my Ability points if I ever wanted to go home.

"What should I expect when we get to the nest?" I asked, running just behind Light and Ward.

"More swarms," Ward said.

"Hydrasnake royal guards," Light said, then added, "They are just a little bigger than the regular variety. And they are a darker blue color."

As we ran, I began to feel weariness seep into the muscles in my legs and my lungs burn with the effort. I was really wishing I had done more running and less cycling. It also made me understand Light's desire to boost his Stamina.

When I got my first look at the nest. It was chaos. Hammer Jack was standing in the middle of a hole in the ground with sloped sides and a few tunnel entrances going in various directions. It was about then I decided that Hammer could do with a psychiatric evaluation. He was punching seven-headed snakes and crushing them with a single blow, all while laughing and taunting the beasts.

"Come at me," Hammer shouted as a darker blue hydrasnake lunged from one of the caves. Hammer didn't seem to care as he swept a hand through the air, crushing or severing all seven heads in a single blow.

I stood at the top of the hole while Light and Ward both moved in without hesitating. Neither man was smiling, so I didn't think they enjoyed it. But they did it anyway. I didn't see any fear of death. I didn't see a risk assessment. I just saw . . . I can't say heroes because they weren't saving anyone. But I can say I saw two of the most determined men I've ever witnessed. It made me doubt whether or not I could ever live up to the expectations they placed on me. I really didn't know if I could.

"Are you waiting for a written invitation?" Hammer yelled up at me, snapping me out of my thoughts.

Right, battle. I rushed down the slope and into the hole to stand with the other three men. As I was coming to understand, slowly, very slowly, I couldn't afford to just stand around. I needed to act and not think so much. I picked my targets. I went after the ones that were preparing to pounce, trying to kill them before they moved. And when my Nanos got tired, I hid behind Ward's barriers until I could attack again.

I didn't understand how there could be so many hydrasnakes. There must have been a hundred corpses laying all around us. It was enough that Light and Ward both finally looked tired. Hammer looked bored and not tired in the slightest. I could only guess how high his Stamina was.

"Here, queenie, queenie, queenie," Hammer bellowed down one of the tunnels.

Ignoring Hammer, I finally had a chance to look at the tunnels closer. I could see they were much too small for a grown man, so there was no way we were going in after the queen. At the same time, I wasn't even sure how the hydrasnakes fit through them. And if the queen was larger than the other hydrasnakes, then I wasn't sure how she was going to be able to come for us.

There was a slight tremor under my feet that worried me.

I looked to Hammer, who was grinning broadly and said, "Here she comes. Don't wet yourself."

There was a heavier tremor and then another even stronger tremor and several after that, each one stronger than the one before it. The queen hydrasnake burst from the hole, sending dirt and debris through the air, stirring up a dust cloud large enough to obscure all but her shadow. A twenty-foot tall nine-headed hydrasnake.

Hammer punched and a shockwave followed. With it, the dust cloud was blown away, revealing the purple snake, which thankfully only looked twenty-feet tall in the dust. The queen was barely nine-feet tall when it reared up like a cobra, just waiting to strike. Then Hammer said something that I'll never forget . . . or forgive. "She's all yours, Davis, good luck!"

I gave the mental command of 'Scan', and over her head flashed a '19'. She was a full three Milestones above my own.

"Ha, just kidding," Hammer said, jumping ahead and punching one of the heads, crushing it in a single hit before the queen suddenly spun, her tail lashing out and swatting Hammer . . . who didn't even flinch. "Is that all you've got? Shoot, maybe Davis should take this one."

"Aim for the heads. We want to preserve as much of the meat as we can," Ward said, focusing on creating barriers in front of Light and me.

Light took a few steps to the left to put some space between us, firing light bullets from his index fingers as he ran. He seemed to be focusing his shots on the head to the farthest left.

Hammer was nonchalantly batting away the heads after he determined it wasn't much of a threat. "Alright, new plan. Davis, if you don't kill at least one of these heads, you don't get to eat any of it tonight," he said. I think he was trying to motivate me, but honestly, nothing about eating hydrasnake sounded appetizing.

Still, I knew I'd regret it later if I missed out on a chance at gaining a free enhancement point, though nothing about killing this thing was free. One wrong move and I'd be dead. I stopped that thought in its tracks. I needed to focus.

I activated Time Compression and picked out a head. I could feel I had just about enough energy for one full power Void Burst or eight, maybe nine, of the smallest ones I could make. With time slowed, though not for long, I needed to act fast. I was assuming the queen was going to be tougher than the regular or even the royal guard. I also needed to aim for the head which liked to move around. It wasn't very fast with time slowed the way it was, but it was still faster than I would have liked if I was going to pin all my hopes on a single shot. So, multiple shots. I couldn't count on the minimum damage shots to do enough damage either. I needed something in between my minimum and maximum. A half-inch diameter is what I settled on, and I used all four shots, surrounding one of the heads.

When time suddenly resumed and all four Void Bursts went off, I killed not one head but three.

"Well, well, well, looks like the kid has some teeth after all," Hammer commented. "But was that intentional, or just lucky?"

"One was intentional," I replied. There was no point in claiming otherwise. However, now that I knew the power of the half-inch Void Burst, I knew I could have killed four heads at once. Unfortunately, my Ability was out of power until my Nanos had a chance to rest and recover.

Hammer nodded. I couldn't tell if he was pleased or annoyed, but less than a minute later, the remaining heads were dead, and the cultivation began. And of course, competing against the cultivation monsters around me granted me just 57,423 Nanos. That was 1,399,541 out of 1,400,000 Nanos to my next Milestone. At least dinner should get me the last few Nanos I needed to reach my 17th Milestone.

15

"Okay, Light, shoot him," Hammer ordered calmly, sipping from a mug filled with what passed for coffee in this world.

Fun fact, remember how they said that even plants had been mutated? Well, Coffee apparently didn't grow in this hemisphere. And the area of the planet where it did grow was turned into a massive expanse of irradiated land after a villain . . . possibly a hero . . . either way, someone went nuclear . . . literally. Anyway, the coffee plant was now extinct. Part of me broke a little when I heard that.

"And what do you mean, shoot him?" I asked, staring wide-eyed at Hammer then glancing over to a just as surprised Light.

"I didn't say to kill you. I said to shoot you," Hammer said for clarification.

"But you're still asking him to shoot me," I protested.

Hammer sighed. "Listen Davis, we've been trying to get you to create portals for weeks. You seem to need a little motivation."

"We only started yesterday," I shouted. After killing the queen hydrasnake, which gave me nothing after cultivating the meat, Hammer decided it was time to start working on portals. The very next day, that was my instruction. Figure out how to make a portal. With no idea what I was doing, it made for a wasted day.

"Yesterday, a few weeks, same difference," Hammer said, waving away my concerns. "It doesn't change the fact that you need to learn faster. There isn't anything in the world that can get someone to learn faster than imminent danger."

"Says who?" I asked.

Hammer shrugged. "Anyway, Light, shoot him with your weakest setting."

Light looked to Ward for help, who replied, "It's worth a try."

I gave Ward the dirtiest look I could manage.

"Aim for the face," Hammer suggested. "Maybe you'll make him prettier to look at."

"You're supposed to be a hero," I shouted at the man.

"I am," Hammer said with a wide grin. "Just think of all the terror I'll be saving people from by making you prettier."

"You sick, sadistic-" I let the rest of my comments trail off. "I don't even know the theory behind portals."

"Portals are easy," Hammer said. "You open a hole to another location."

I glared at the man and said, "If it's so easy, why don't you do it?"

"Cause it's not my power," Hammer retorted. "Now, stop dawdling and shoot him already."

I was about to start yelling at Hammer again when I felt a sting hit my shoulder. "Ow!" I shouted, my left hand going to my right shoulder where I felt the burning sting. When I looked at where I was stung, there was a new hole in my shirt and a red welt on my skin.

Hammer laughed, then joyfully said, "Do it again."

At least Light said, "Sorry," before shooting me again.

An hour later, I was covered in welts and absolutely furious. I nearly shouted when Light seemed to finally run out of energy himself as he commented, "Obviously this isn't working. We need to try something else."

Hammer frowned. "Fine, take an hour to try and figure it out. We'll resume then," he said, walking toward the cookfire, probably to get more of the not-coffee.

"Ward, please, I need some science on this," I pleaded with the man.

"I wish I could help, but like I told you before. The science doesn't matter," Ward replied. "Use your instincts."

"My instincts only tell me there is a nothingness, which is what creates a Void Burst," I replied hotly.

"Then you need to listen deeper," Ward said.

"Stop with the wise old monk act," I complained.

"I'm not doing a wise old monk act," Ward replied, calm as ever. "I'm telling you what you need to do. By now, you should have developed your connection to your Nanos deeply enough to start feeling more from them. You might not get portals on your first try or even your second, but if you keep trying, you will not only get new abilities, eventually, you will get to portals."

I grumbled unhappily. Why couldn't the man have explained that sooner? Or did he, and I just didn't want to hear it? Whatever, that still didn't justify continually shooting me for the last hour, especially when I didn't yet have the ability to create portals or even the first clue of how to do it.

Light looked like he wanted to say something but refrained. Instead, he walked to the cookfire and poured himself a mug of the not-coffee.

I sat down in a huff, accidentally irritating one of the painful welts and wincing. I would have loved to complain more but there was no one to complain to as even Ward had moved off. I grumbled under my breath about the stupidity of it all. I was starting to feel like I was in some strange kung fu movie where I would learn to punch lightning, breathe fire, and stomp earthquakes.

"Listen deeper," I grumbled, trying to calm my breathing and close my eyes. Just as the first time I learned to make a Void Burst, I focused on the empty feeling my Nanos gave off, but nothing was any different. It still felt empty. It still tried to guide me to create a void away from my body and then collapse it suddenly. I tried to ignore what it was telling me to do. I tried to push past the Void Burst. But nothing happened and I let it go. Opening my eyes and sighing. I stretched a little, ignoring the sting from the welts that covered my arms and torso. I closed my eyes and tried again.

Once again, the Nanos guided me toward the Void Burst. In my frustration, I mentally yelled at them, 'I know, show me something else!'. And to my great surprise, they did. They showed me . . . everything. Not everything, as in the various skills I needed to learn, but everything as in everything around me. It was an . . . awareness. I could feel the air currents around me. I could feel something the size of my arm borrowing through the ground under me . . . a worm. I was now aware of all of it. I could feel the thick walls just ten feet behind me. I could feel the stress points where the wall had begun to weaken. I could feel exactly how much damage Light's shots had done, the cells that were damaged. I could feel everything up to about 20-feet . . . 21-feet to be exact. Then I felt the Nanos tire and the awareness faded. It wasn't completely gone, just muted. And yet, I knew, I could gain that awareness again with just a thought. I also knew, I just gained a new ability.

Davis Malory
Aliases: N/A
Occupation: N/A
Alignment: Neutral
Milestone: 17th
Nano: 1,410,987/1,675,000
Body
Athleticism: 8
- Strength: Average

- Agility: Above Average	
- Accuracy: Above Average	
- Speed: Average (7/10)	
- Stamina: Average	
Resistance: 1	
- Physical Resistance: Average	
- Energy Resistance: Above Average	
- Mental Resistance: Above Average	
Recovery: 1	
- Physical Injury: Average	
- Nano Energy: Average	
Ability	
Power: 17	
- Time: Average	
o Time Compression: 65%	
- Space: Weak (1/5)	
o Void Burst: 2.1-Uses at Maximum Size	
o Spatial Awareness: Passive senses may be enhanced for up to 5-Seconds	
Control: 17	
- Time: Average	
o Time Compression: 20-Seconds Uncompressed Time	
- Space: Weak (1/5)	
o Void Burst: up to a 21-Foot Range and up to a 1.1-Inch Diameter	
o Spatial Awareness: up to 21-Foot Range	

Spatial Awareness. That sounded extremely useful to me.

Then Hammer's voice cut in, saying, "I'm hoping that pleased expression means you've figured out how to make portals."

"Not yet," I said, cursing my lack of attention to my new skill. I literally felt the man move into my sphere of awareness. "I learned something called Spatial Awareness."

"Good skill to have," Hammer commented. "I have something similar but more of a motion or vibration sensor. Not everyone's abilities grant them any kind of extra senses."

"Is it that rare?" I asked curiously.

"Not so much rare as just something not everyone bothers to learn. Take Light for example. He could easily learn to sense light and the changes in light. But he hasn't. Why? Because being able to sense the changes in light can affect his ability to see. He'd be better off developing the ability to see the different light spectrums. But that is him and not you," Hammer explained.

There were times where I just couldn't figure Hammer out, like now. Most of the time he seemed pompous, rude, arrogant, and a host of other negative descriptors. Then there were the times where he was being helpful and offering advice and explanations.

Hammer continued, "Now, your hour is up. But seeing as you did manage to learn something. And something I deem valuable at that. I'm generously going to allow you another hour. Don't waste it."

I nodded, glad to avoid another hour of being peppered with stinging bullets of light. But before I started probing at my Nanos again, I needed to get up and stretch, maybe walk around a bit. And grab a bite to eat . . . a quick bite as I knew the clock was ticking.

Ten minutes later, I was back at it. Reaching out to my Nanos, which began showing me Void Burst again. I was about to try to ask them to show me something different again when a thought occurred. I wondered just how intelligent the Nanos were. Could I, for example, simply ask them to teach me about portals? I figured it was worth a shot.

So, I focused in on the feeling presented by the Nanos and sent a mental request, 'Teach me about Portals.' It didn't take long for them to respond. In my mind's eye, I saw two different places. There was nothing connecting them. But then I saw the Nanos concentrate on a spot between the two points. They built up for a moment then collapsed in a burst of light and somehow, the two different places were now next to each other, being held open by a ring of Nanos. It held for a few seconds and collapsed. Then it was gone, and I knew I had missed something. I knew I couldn't recreate what I just experienced.

I tried again, making the same request. I felt the same thing. And again, when it was done, I knew I was still missing something. It almost felt like I had skipped a step somewhere. I tried again with the same results. I tried three more times and still couldn't do it. But I think I finally understood why. My Space ability just wasn't strong enough yet.

"Times up," Hammer said.

"I need to get stronger," I said, holding up a hand and hoping to forestall any further shots. "I think I know how to do it now. But I'm not strong enough yet. Or, my Space ability isn't strong enough yet. We need to do more hunting. We can try again in four more Milestones."

"Four?" Hammer questioned. "That should put you at what, about halfway to Average. How do you figure halfway to average is going to give enough power to do it?"

I flinched, then, with great reluctance, I answered, "That will put me at Below Average. I chose to get Time up to Average first."

"You idiot! Of all the stupid things I have ever heard. Why in the hell would you go and do something so stupid?" Hammer yelled.

I didn't have a good answered. Boosting Time to Average was just something I felt like I needed to do. So, I said as much.

Hammer didn't look happy with my answer. Thankfully, he didn't yell at me any further. Instead, he looked to Ward and asked, "Ward, if we can get him up to the 31st Milestone, will it be enough for him to pass for Dr. Portal?"

Ward rubbed his chin in thought for a moment before answering, "We don't know exactly what Dr. Portal's Portal ability was. At the 31st Milestone, and if Davis puts all his enhancement points for the next fourteen Milestones into Space, he will just be at Average. Admittedly, he still would have only been halfway to Above Average if he put all his other points into the ability when we began."

"Can we get away with Below Average control and Above Average Power?" Hammer asked.

"Maybe, we'll need to wait to see what kind of portal size constraints he's under once he does unlock the ability. We might just need to try to get him another five Milestones above the 31st before time is up," Ward said.

"Won't that make the villains suspicious if he suddenly comes back stronger?" Light asked.

"Villains get stronger all the time, just like heroes," Hammer replied, crossing his arms and looking rather angry. Then he spat out a loud, "Damn it!"

"What's the plan?" Ward asked. "Do we abort?"

"No, we can still do it. We are just going to have to hunt tougher beasts. And teach him a more efficient cultivation technique," Hammer said, still looking angry. "If he wants to have any chance of surviving the villains he will be sent to infiltrate, then he'll need it. He'll need that experience to be able to compete with the two of you at the very least."

I wisely kept my mouth shut. I could clearly see I was already in trouble, there was no sense in making it worse. I was also surprised to find out that Hammer actually had a reason for making it more difficult for me to cultivate by competing against them.

Light cleared his throat and spoke up for the first time. There was a slight nervousness in his voice when he asked, "When you say, tougher beasts, what exactly do you mean?"

I expected Hammer to grin or show some sign of excitement. Instead, he looked . . . grim. It was far more unsettling.

16

Light was nervous as he approached Hammer and Ward. It was late in the evening after the training with Davis had come to an end. Light was not pleased with the way things were being handled.

"Do you have a moment?" Light asked, interrupting the pair.

"What's on your mind?" Hammer asked nonchalantly, all his heat from earlier absent.

"Davis," Light started.

"What about him?" Hammer asked.

Light hesitated for a moment before speaking. "You need to be gentler with him. He's barely more than a civilian. He hasn't had years of hero training schools plus years as a sidekick to learn how to do all this."

"And that is exactly why I can't take it easy on him," Hammer said. "Listen, I know you mean well but you haven't really considered the situation too closely. We're asking an untrained civilian to infiltrate an unknown villain organization. I don't know many heroes that would undertake such an operation. And now this with his enhancement allocation . . . I'm sorry, but I won't take it easy on him. If I do, he's as good as dead."

Light frowned, not liking anything that was just said, but not able to really disagree. Still, he could push to help Davis a little more. "Then you need to start explaining things to him better. You need to actually teach him how to fight. And you need to let him cultivate without fighting against us. Teach him to cultivate against others when his Milestone is higher, for now, he needs all the Nanos he can get."

Hammer frowned and worked his jaw side to side, producing an audible grinding sound. He finally ground out, "Fine, I won't cultivate. But you will, he still needs some competition."

Light was glad to have gotten at least that much of a concession.

"And let me be clear. If you do not give him honest competition then he'll need to compete against all of us again," Hammer stated firmly. "As to teaching him to fight, that's on you. You weren't just brought along to be his buddy. Your fighting style is the closest to his. You both fight from range and you have the experience to teach him."

Light couldn't argue with that, except that Light wasn't the strongest fighter. It was why he hadn't even tried. He thought that he really was just there to be Davis's friend.

Seeing Light wasn't going to say anything, Hammer said, "Now, get some sleep. We've got hunting to do tomorrow."

"About that," Light said, pushing for more.

"What now?" Hammer asked.

"I had an idea . . . about hunting," Light said.

Hammer quirked an eyebrow in interest, and asked, "And what is this idea of yours?"

"Warp hunters," Light said, causing even Hammer's eyes to widen in surprise.

"Are you insane?" Ward asked before Hammer could. "I wouldn't even attempt to hunt those with a full and experienced group of hunters."

"I understand," Light said. "But I believe Davis could do it. He was able to get a squirbit. The first killed in my lifetime . . . in any of our lifetimes. And with his new Spatial Awareness ability, he might actually have a chance. And they are solitary predators, which means he wouldn't need to worry about getting swarmed."

Hammer rubbed his chin in thought. "It isn't the worst idea I've ever heard. Craziest, maybe. But not the worst. And it might get him the enhancement points he needs in his Space ability."

"Are you both insane?" Ward asked. "I would expect something like that from Hammer, but not you, Light. Just what are you thinking?"

"I'm thinking Davis's only chance to get enough enhancement points in Space without over leveling, is to cultivate the meat of a warp hunter," Light answered seriously.

"And you understand that we wouldn't be able to help him with such a hunt?" Ward asked. "My barriers won't stop it's teleportation. We'd be vulnerable. I'm not even sure Hammer could stand up to their attacks."

"I know it's a risk. A very, very big risk," Light said. "But it's something we should at least offer to him. Give him the choice."

"And what happens if he dies?" Ward asked.

"Then the mission is a failure," Light replied. "And someone I am starting to count as a friend would be dead. But can you honestly say that he has a chance as things are now?"

"Yes," Ward said, then hesitantly added, "Maybe."

"I don't like the idea of putting him in danger . . . more danger. We're already putting him in plenty of danger just being outside of the fortress city," Light said. "If you can think of a better alternative that does not include increasing his Milestone above what Dr. Portal's was known to be, then please, tell me."

"Raising his Milestone will work though," Ward replied.

"Five additional Milestones?" Light asked. "Villains don't have the same level of access to cultivation that heroes do, I've never heard of a villain increasing that much in such a short window of time, have you?"

"No, but it could happen," Ward protested.

"It could. But I would bet anything, the villains would assume it was a setup by the heroes and kill him on principal. In that case, he has a better chance against a warp hunter," Light replied. "I'm open to alternatives, but as Hammer mentioned, time is short."

"Do you even know where to find a warp hunter?" Ward asked.

"Unfortunately, yes," Light replied. "It will take a few days to clear a path to its hunting grounds, but there is a well-known warp hunter a few miles from here."

"Now I know you're insane," Ward said.

"Maybe I am," Light agreed. "But it's the only one I know of."

Hammer just chuckled and grinned. He said just one word, "Shadowfury."

17

"Davis," Light said, drawing my attention away from my morning preparations. I say preparations but it was just making sure my boots were tied and my canteen was full. "Let's talk before we get to work today."

"Sure, what's up?" I asked.

"I had a conversation with Ward and Hammer yesterday. We're going to do things a little differently today. First, you won't be competing with all of us for Nanos today, just me," Light started.

"That's good . . . I think. What changed their minds?" I asked. It was good that I wouldn't need to compete with either Ward or Hammer. Still, I would need to compete with Light and he was no slouch when it came to cultivating Nanos.

"With the new issue you raised yesterday regarding your enhancement point distribution, we now need to push you to increase your Milestone even faster, especially if we have no choice but to raise you an extra five Milestones," Light explained. "You'll still be competing against me, but I'm actually going to teach you how to compete when cultivating against others, something you will absolutely need to be able to do once you're among villains. With that, I'll be teaching you the next step in cultivation."

"Why is that? I mean, why would I compete with the villains for Nanos?" I asked.

"Villains are for the most part . . . cowards. They are unwilling to brave the wilds to increase their Milestones and too impatient to do it the old-fashioned way. They prefer to attack the weak and steal Nanos from them. As a result, when they get access to a good number of Nanos, they fight over it like wild quilldogs. Not fight as in trying to hurt each other but fight to cultivate more than those around them." Light answered. "But we're getting off topic."

Light paused for a moment then continued, "Second, I have been derelict in my responsibility to you. I thought I was brought here so you would have a friendly face, someone to talk to as a friend. I didn't realize I was also expected to train you in combat. Specifically, in ranged combat. Something I know more about than either Ward or Hammer because of my ability."

I nodded in understanding.

"Third, for the next few days, we're going to be hunting, trying to get you a few more Milestones," Light said, but I could see there was something he wasn't saying.

"What is it?" I asked. "That was already the plan, why does it sound like that's a different plan from before?"

Light really needed to work on his poker face. Cringing all the time when ever he had bad news was a big give away. Eventually, he said, "We have an idea. Something for you specifically. But we need to clear a path to its last known hunting grounds. It's dangerous."

"How dangerous?" I asked.

"Very," Light replied. "But don't worry about that yet. We will evaluate how things go over the next few days before we make a final decision. For now, let's focus on your cultivation and gaining Milestones."

I really didn't like that answer. If they were going to put me in even more danger, I had a right to know . . . didn't I? "I'd like to know more about this danger," I said.

"Later, I promise," Light rebuffed my request. "For now, let's focus on cultivation."

I frowned. Relenting, I said, "Alright, what's next?"

"I know we've been pushing your cultivation technique very quickly. Normally, we learn as children and have years to get used to it," Light began. "I know this is getting repetitive, but time is short. You've had a few days to get used to starting at your limit and collapsing inward, building up momentum. Now, we're going to see if we can increase that momentum."

"And how do we do that?" I asked. I was also unsure why it would take time to get used to the different cultivation techniques they've taught me. So far, I hadn't really struggled with any of it, not with the aid of my Time Compression. Or was that the difference? They didn't have Time Compression to help them along. I found myself wondering just how powerful my skill really was.

"We pick a point out to our maximum limit. Then we spiral it. Rotate around the outside of your limit and spiral inwards," Light answered. "You may have noticed using your current method, that you tend to get slowed down by large swarms of Nanos. This method should allow you to run over those swarms with ease."

"And how does this let me fight for Nanos?" I asked.

Light chuckled, then said, "Learn this method first, then we'll get into fighting for Nanos."

I pushed down my desire to question him. The faster I learned what he wanted me to learn, the faster I would be able to move on to the next step.

I sat down on the hardpacked ground of the inner courtyard of the outpost and closed my eyes, only for Light to interrupt me before I could even begin. "On your feet, Villains aren't going to wait for you to sit down and get comfortable."

I stood back up again and closed my eyes, and Light interrupted me again, "Eyes open. I know I said that Villains won't fight you over the

Nanos but a Villain that loses to you might try to attack you immediately after. You would be better off seeing it coming."

Okay, that was different. "Should I learn to do it while moving as well?" I asked, half-joking.

"Eventually," Light answered seriously. "For now, just learn this step. Oh, and no Time Compression. You won't be able to use it to cultivate while you're around the villains or they'll know something is up. If we're lucky, you won't have to fight it out like this. But just in case, you need to be prepared." I really didn't like the restrictions, even if he had a point. I hadn't cultivated without Time Compression since I first activated the ability.

Trying to shake off my new doubts, I bounced on my feet a few times and shook out my limbs. "Okay, let's try this," I said. I wanted to close my eyes because it was how I was originally trained. I knew how my Nanos felt by now. That rhythm of fast and slow. The emptiness. I knew how wild Nanos felt. Their untamed, constant motion. Their restlessness. I just needed to figure how to feel for them without closing off my other senses. But I couldn't close my eyes. I needed to figure this out a different way. I activated my Time Compression, feeling the world around me grind to a crawl. I knew the Nanos were all around me, I could faintly feel them. I activated my Spatial Awareness and suddenly I was acutely aware of everything around me. Light's heartbeat slowly thudded in his chest right in front of me. Hammer and Ward were at the limit of my range.

And all around us was a sparse number of Nanos. I picked a spot at the limit of my reach and took hold of the Nanos. It was just a small bubble about three feet wide. There were maybe a few hundred Nanos. Then I moved my bubble of control, pushing it clockwise. It moved, slowly at first, but as it moved it pulled in more and more Nanos, until it was circling around my outer limits and no longer gathering Nanos. With a gasp, I dropped to a knee, my grip on the Nanos suddenly ending as I was out of breath.

"You alright?" Light asked, checking on me immediately.

"Yes," I said, feeling like I'd just run a marathon.

"What happened?" Light asked, sounding worried.

Panting and trying to catch my breath, I eventually answered, "I think . . . I think I tried . . . to do . . . too much."

Light looked confused and asked, "Too many Nanos?"

I shook my head. I answered, "Time Compression and Spatial Awareness. I think I held them both active for too long."

Light looked both relieved, upset and worried by my answer. He said, "You need to be careful with that. You can actually damage your ability that way. Overuse can cause Nano-Burnout. It's not good. And I said no abilities."

"Right, Nano-Burnout, got it," I said, shrugging off his reminder to not use my abilities. It wasn't easy to just not use them after I had gotten so used to it. "Okay, so I was able to rotate but it just spun at the outer reach, never rotating in. What did I miss?"

"How big of an area did you try to grab to start?" Light asked.

"About a three-foot diameter," I answered.

"That should be good to start. As soon as you've sent it around two or three times, give it a gentle, constant pull toward yourself," Light instructed.

I nodded and said, "Okay, let my abilities recharge and I'll try again." Fifteen minutes later, my energy bars were refilled, and the Nanos recovered from their previous exertion. I was ready to try again, this time with only my Spatial Awareness active. I figured it wouldn't hurt to just be more aware of where the Nanos were. I started my gathering bubble flying along the outer limits of my area of influence. As soon as I got two rotations, I started trying to pull the bubble toward me. I was surprised by the initial resistance. It didn't want to leave its orbit. I pulled a little harder and the orbit suddenly changed its trajectory, rotating just twice more before it reached me. I only gathered a few thousand Nanos, which was nothing compared to my previous methods. I believe that I pulled too hard, reducing the number of rotations and the number of Nanos I could gather at the same time.

"I need to rest again," I said, ending my Spatial Awareness early.

"How did it go?" Light asked.

"Better, but I pulled too hard on the Nanos," I answered. Eager for my ability to recover so I could try again.

"Okay, I'll leave you with this for now. I'm going to go give Hammer and Ward an update," Light said, leaving me to work on my cultivation.

I was surprised by how much more difficult this cultivation method was. Especially after I picked up the others so easily. It took a couple hours before I thought I had the hang of it.

"I think I'm ready for the next step," I said as I approached the cookfire where Light, Ward, and Hammer were sitting.

"Good," Light said. "Next step is to create another gathering point. Once you're up to ten gathering points, I'll fight you."

"Ten?" I asked. I struggled mightily just getting one gathering point and now he wanted me to make ten? "Is that even possible?"

Hammer snorted. "Ten is nothing," he said, then added, "I had over fifty gathering points when I was at that stage."

Fifty! I was shocked. No wonder he was able to gather up so many Nanos so quickly. And wait, did he just say 'had'? As in past tense? And what did he mean 'at that stage'? I had so many questions.

"What are you still standing around for? If we ever want to get back to hunting, then you need to learn this stuff. Now get to it," Hammer ordered gruffly.

Ten? I questioned in my head. How in the world was I going to get to ten? I suppose the only way I was going to find out was by doing it. I started with one gathering point. I spun it up and once I started pulling on it, I tried to create another point in the original starting spot only for the cultivation attempt to falter and fall apart. I tried a few more times but every one of them ended in failure.

"Okay, Davis," I said talking to myself. "You can't seem to create a new gathering point after you've already started. So, let's try creating two from the start." I reached an arm out to the left and the other out to the right. I visualized creating the two gathering points at opposite sides and it seemed to work. Then I spun them. I would have hoped that pulling two points was only slightly more difficult than pulling on one point. It wasn't. It was a lot harder. But . . . it worked. It was a struggle to spin them at the same speed. It was more of a struggle to pull them inwards at the same speed. But eventually, I got there. After that success, I added one more point of gathering with each attempt until I had ten perfectly spaced points of gathering rotating around me and collapsing inward until I was rewarded for all my effort. Pulling just the nearby Nanos, and doing it repeatedly granted me just enough to break into my next Milestone.

Congratulations! You've reached the 18th Milestone. The Nanos have accumulated within your body to a point in which it is now possible to enhance your Nano Evolved Body or Abilities. Be intelligent with your decisions as all choices are final.

You may now open your Status and apply two points of enhancement.

"And done," I said, feeling proud of my accomplishment.

"Good," Light said. "Now, you can compete with me for the ambient Nanos."

"Okay, how do I do that?" I asked.

"Do what you just did," Light replied. "I'll attack you so you can get a feel for it."

I didn't much care for the sink or swim lessons these guys liked to thrust upon me. Still, I complied. I felt my ten points rotate, each point picking up more and more Nanos. Then I felt a sudden drop in the gathered Nanos from one of my points. And then another, and another. Then I felt it, there were points of Nanos being gathered near mine, but they were moving faster, gaining on my points until they overtook them, stripping away thousands of my gathered Nanos.

I narrowed my eyes and glared at Light. I knew this must be his doing, especially after he smirked. Light never smirked, but now he was. I felt his points drawing closer to him, but also slowing down. I think that was when I understood. He moved his points faster to overtake mine and strip away Nanos. But now that he was ahead of me, he slowed down to increase the Nanos he gathered. I tried to push my gathering points faster, trying to catch up to Light's.

I can honestly say, I was . . . pleased when Light's smirk vanished, replaced by a look of astonishment as my gathering points tore through his own, pulling away thousands more Nanos than he took from me.

Light's smirk returned when he reversed the situation again.

"You may have won this round," I said. "But there is plenty of fight left in me. Round two?"

18

"Pick your shots," Light repeated for the fiftieth time. "Let Hammer get their attention. As a marksman, our job is to pick them off from a distance without drawing their attention."

I nodded absentmindedly as I targeted another Dungeness Spider, a cross between a crab and a spider and, as usual, bigger than both. It was more spider than crab except for the extra pair of appendages connected to its thorax in the form of pincers.

"We are going to eat so good tonight," Hammer crowed excitedly as he smashed another. And did I mention that these things are apparently a delicacy?

I collapsed a void next to one of the spiders that was trying to attack Hammer from behind, rupturing the carapace and killing the little beast. But more importantly, I didn't draw the attention of any of the other spiders.

Almost a week ago, we started moving through the wilds in an almost straight-line, northwest of the outpost, returning to the safety of the walled fort each night. Sometimes, we needed to clear out whatever moved in overnight. It was hard work and we were clearly moving toward a destination, but they hadn't told me much about it yet. Anyway, when we were out in the wilds, I was pushed harder every day.

Light focused on teaching me how to fight from a distance without my Time Compression. He taught me how to lead my targets and pick my shots. I was encouraged to increase the number of shots I could take with my Void Burst regardless of the number of enhancements I put into my Space ability. As a result, I was able to get my Void Burst down to a quarter of an inch in size, just large enough to knock out a human so long as it wasn't too close to the head. For something like these spiders that were the size of a small dog, they were the perfect weapon.

I killed two more spiders in rapid succession with each one receiving a Void Burst as they rushed at Hammer. I checked my Spatial Awareness, briefly enhancing it to check our surroundings. It was a habit by now. I found that a quick burst of enhanced Spatial Awareness was generally enough to let me know if there was anything I needed to worry about. "Second swarm incoming," I reported after sensing a few dozen of the things swarming toward us from deeper within the wilds.

"I'm aware," Hammer replied, punching a jackhammer into the ground and creating a fissure in front of him for about twenty yards, spreading the swarm to either side of him and slowing their progress. Through my passive Spatial Awareness, I faintly felt the new swarm's progress and how much Hammer was able to hamper it. They either fell into the fissure where they were crushed at the bottom by the rocks that fell in after them or they simply piled up on the far side. Hammer's solution did exactly what he intended, he slowed them down and gave us time to safely deal with them and not get overwhelmed.

I killed three more of the spiders in rapid succession as they crawled out of the woods and around the edge of the fissure Hammer created. That was something else that was great about my smaller Void Burst. It was so much faster. And as long as I picked my shots, I rarely ran out of power. It helped that I didn't panic like I did in the beginning. I was sure a psychologist would say I had become desensitized to the violence. That or I had some strange form of PTSD. As a doctor I really should have known more about this kind of thing, but psychology was not my field of study.

"Hey Ward, we've got butter back at the outpost, right?" Hammer asked, humming as he crushed one spider after another.

"I think so," Ward said, forming barriers around any of the spiders that started to move in our general direction. "If not, I'm sure we have something we can use on them."

"Might be worth freezing them until we go back to New Haven," Light suggested.

Hammer stopped punching spiders and turned to look at Light in disbelief. "Boy, if I didn't know for a fact that you're a hero, I'd arrest you for saying something only a villain would suggest."

In my peripheral, I saw Light roll his eyes. He ignored the comment as he fired off bullets of light rapidly in an attempt to keep them off Hammer. "Just, kill the spiders, you can comment on my commonsense later," he said, his rate of fire not slowing down as he picked them off.

Hammer quirked an eyebrow, surprised by Light's cheek. Then he snorted a laugh and turned back to killing Dungeness Spiders.

Not much later the last of the spiders were dead.

"On your marks," Hammer said with a grin, looking between Light and me. "Get set," he said, pausing to build tension. Then, after what seemed like an eternity, he shouted, "Go!"

In an instant I had twenty-five cultivation points spread out to my maximum range, pushing them to rotate and grab ahold of as many Nanos as I could. Trying to feel for Light's gathering points as I did. Over the last week, I also learned just how sneaky and conniving Light really was. "Got any tricks up your sleeve I haven't seen at this point?" I asked, increasing the speed of my rotation.

"A few," Light replied with a smirk.

Then, like a bowling ball, I felt Light's gathering points crashing through mine . . . in the opposite direction, completely breaking the cultivation for both of us.

"What was that?" I asked.

Light's grin widened, he answered, "Me winning. Better hurry and start your cultivation again or I'm going to get it all."

My jaw dropped slightly. I scrambled to spin up my cultivation again, this time watching for his rotation, but he was way ahead of me. I tried to rush up to speed but it was too late. I wasn't going to catch him at that point. I grumbled under my breath. I barely got anything from the spiders because of that.

"Better luck next time," Light replied.

I was about to say something witty, but Hammer spoke first. "Alright, let's get moving. It's still early, I want to try to get a little further today."

We cleared out a lot of beasts daily. They didn't always rush in to claim territory after we decimated the previous residents, but there seemed to always be at least one new group. Today, it was the Dungeness Spiders. Yesterday, it was a pack of quilldogs, and I even got a single enhancement point in physical resistance from cultivating the meat.

"What do the spiders give?" I asked.

"Nothing that I know of," Hammer answered, moving ahead into the brush, then pausing at the edge of the clearing, he added, "I just know they taste damned good. Ward, you want to collect the legs for us?"

Ward nodded and answered, "Yeah, I can do that, just be careful moving ahead. We've got to be getting close to its territory."

"It?" I asked, curious if this was the beast Light had alluded to.

"I suppose it's about time to fill you in on what we're after," Hammer said, turning back from the brush and moving closer to talk. "Alright, we're after a Warp Hunter."

"And what is that?" I asked.

"A teleporting beast and a very dangerous one at that," Hammer answered. "We need to get you enhancements to your Space ability. If you can kill a Warp Hunter and eat the meat, it should give you a hell of a lot of enhancements."

"Okay, I get the feeling you're leaving something out," I said.

"No, I just haven't gotten there yet," Hammer replied. "Look, this beast is dangerous. Like the squirbit, no one has ever killed one to the best of my knowledge. Unlike the squirbit, this one is a predator. And an ambush predator at that."

"So, what makes you think I'll be able to kill one?" I asked.

"Your Time Compression," Hammer answered. "Now that you're able to activate the ability instantly, you should be able to freeze time or whatever and kill it before it kills one of us."

Ward chimed in at this point. "It will create a distraction. I've heard it described as an unholy scream that could cause the most hardened hero to wet himself. The point is that it will draw your attention. And when you look away, it teleports in, kills, and teleports away with its food. It's done in less than 5-seconds from scream to the endless dream."

"And you're sure I'll be able to kill it with one hit?" I asked.

"Maybe, maybe not, but you should at the very least be able to daze it long enough for one of us to kill it," Hammer answered.

"And whose insane idea was this?" I asked, glaring at the smirking Hammer.

Light cleared his throat then said softly, "It was my idea."

"You?" I questioned, looking at my friend in surprise. "You suggested this?"

"Yes," Light replied. "I couldn't think of another way to get you the enhancements to your Space Ability. Without them, this plan of ours has little chance of succeeding."

"What about Ward's idea, getting more Milestones?" I asked.

"Villains don't gain Milestones that quickly," Light said. "It might have worked but there was a really big risk. I believe the risk to be too great. This is also risky, but at least, I believe, this has a chance to succeed."

"So, most likely death versus certain death?" I quipped.

"Pretty much," Hammer replied with a nod. "Anyway, keep on your toes. You hear the unholy cry of something from a hell dimension, you freeze time immediately and kill that thing before it kills one of us. This thing has been around for a long time and no one knows what its Milestone might be, it can probably even kill me. So, I say again, keep on your toes."

I swallowed nervously and nodded. Suddenly acutely aware of all the strange sounds of the wilds around me.

Thankfully, we didn't run into the Warp Hunter that day. The next day, we weren't so lucky.

Hammer laughed as I tried to extricate myself from the puddle of Bunk guts. What is a Bunk? If a bat and skunk had a baby, you'd get your Bunk. And they stink so much worse than any skunk I ever encountered.

"Tell me this at least washes off," I pleaded.

"I'm sure we have industrial sanitizer back at the outpost," Ward offered, not bothering to hide his smirk.

"Oh, ha ha, very funny," I said sarcastically. "Can we at least find a stream to try to wash some of this gunk off me?"

"Yeah, yeah, we passed one a mile or so back, we can go and take care of you there," Light offered.

"Thank you," I said loudly. "See, this is what a real friend looks like. You two should take notes."

Hammer laughed louder and even Ward let out a chuckle. Both men were silenced when a scream cut them off. It was the most horrid thing I had ever heard. I can't put into words exactly what is sounded like other than to say that if death had a sound, that might have been it.

Remembering Hammer's orders, I instantly activated my Time Compression but didn't see anything, but my Spatial Awareness could feel something was . . . coming? I enhanced my awareness and I could see a tube . . . no . . . it was a hole in Space. I could see something traveling through that tube and emerging on the other side, above and slightly behind Ward.

The beast that appeared was pure nightmare fuel. At first, I thought it was a monkey with razor sharp claws as long as its fingers. But that wasn't quite right. The head was something between a chimpanzee and a bobcat only slightly smaller with cat ears and long whiskers with a rounder mouth filled with sharp teeth. The head was attached to a cat's body. Then there was the tail. It was already moving toward Ward's neck as though to grab it. I think it was prehensile. And it was bald or almost bald with tightly stretched grey skin. If the Time Compression hadn't held me in place, I would have shaken my head to will the horror of it away, but I needed to act quickly, or Ward was as good as dead.

I formed my first Void Burst next to the beast's head and to my greater horror, its eyes flicked over to me. I felt it forming another warp tunnel. I knew I couldn't let it escape, I placed another Void Burst into the tunnel and collapsed both. I watched as the top half of the beast vanished while the lower half hung suspended in air.

Then time resumed suddenly. I was tackled painfully from behind. I felt something sharp dig into my back and I screamed in pain. I kept waiting to be teleported away and killed but it never happened. I felt the weight of the beast on my upper back and unmoving. In my periphery, the red bar that represented my health was steadily dropping. It had never even moved before. If the red bar vanished, would that mean I was dead? I didn't like that idea. Not even a little.

"Davis," I heard Light's voice and a rush of feet.

"Ward, are you alright?" Hammer asked with similar urgency.

Ward groaned. "What hit me?" I heard him moan and start to move.

"Oh no, Ward, get over here, quickly," Light said, sounding panicked.

"Don't move it," Ward said. "We need to be very careful removing those claws."

I wanted to ask if there were claws in me, but I was starting to feel woozy. Blood loss was my professional opinion. The red bar just crossed the halfway point.

"He's going to make it though, right?" Light asked.

"I don't know," Ward snapped back at Light. "Let me work."

I felt pressure on my back and heard a wet squelching sound that accompanied enough pain that I blacked out, thankful for the bliss of unconsciousness. Before everything went black, I thought I saw the red health bar starting to go back up, but I couldn't be sure.

19

A very angry looking hologram of Major Miracle demanded, "What were you thinking?" His image was being projected into the air in front of the three heroes using a common household Nanotech device called a holo-communicator or holocator for short. It was Planet Hero's version of a phone.

"Sir, I decided it was worth the risk," Hammer stated before Light could say anything or take responsibility. "The idiot civilian raised his Time ability instead of his Space. As a result, I needed to find a way to raise his enhancement without increasing his Milestones. Given he was able to kill a squirbit, I felt it was worth the risk." Hammer paused, watching the Major. As soon as the Major opened his mouth to speak, Hammer continued, cutting him off in the process. "And I was right. He killed Shadowfury. Yes, he got hurt in the process, but he knew the risks and went along anyway."

"Will he even be able to take advantage of it while he's unconscious?" Major Miracle demanded.

Ward jumped in, "I'll be waking him shortly. His wounds were deep but not life threatening. He passed out from the pain. I just wanted to let him heal a little more. As it is, we're just about done cooking so it will be just in time."

Major Miracle frowned. His jaw was clenched so tightly the muscles in his cheeks were flexing. Finally, he shouted angrily, "This had better work!" Which was immediately followed by him cutting the feed.

"He didn't sound happy," I said, enjoying seeing the trio jump in surprise.

"Davis, you're up," Light said first in surprise. "Are you okay?"

"I think so, my shoulders feel a little stiff," I said. "Not going to lie, that really hurt."

"You were stabbed through both shoulders with four-inch long claws," Hammer said, then laughed and added, "I would be more worried if it didn't hurt."

"We got it then?" I asked.

"Yeah, you got it," Ward said. "And you saved my life. I owe you . . . so much. Thank you."

I was embarrassed by the praise. It was unexpected. "I'm pretty sure I owe you for saving my life. Shoulders or not, there was a real chance I would have died from blood loss if you weren't there. Speaking of, how am I healed?" I remembered Ward was there when I was first affected by the Nano-virus, but I didn't think he did anything at the time. I also thought he was a medical professional and not a healer. This was before I knew anything about people having superpowers.

Ward smiled, "Then I suppose this bit of information will make us even. I have two abilities. One is Barriers and the other is Wards. I know it sounds strange to say they are considered different abilities given the words mean more or less the same thing. Except that my interpretation of the abilities is different. My Wards reject damage. Therefore, I placed a ward over your wound and the damage was rejected, effectively healing you. With my other ability, I use my Barriers to prevent damage."

Ward was right. It was strange. Intriguing, but strange.

"Alright, enough already, Davis has food waiting for him," Hammer said. "And you better cultivate every bite or I'm going to snap you like a twig. Am I clear?"

"Got it, cultivating every bite," I promised.

Focusing on cultivating every bite was probably the only thing that kept me from vomiting after every bite. It was nasty. The meat was tough as hell and tasted like a leather shoe coated in urine. Still, I cultivated every last bite. When it was done, I still wanted to puke.

Then came the moment of truth. I gave the mental command, status.

Davis Malory
Aliases: N/A
Occupation: N/A
Alignment: Neutral
Milestone: 18th
Nano: 1,763,471/1,975,000
Body
Athleticism: 13
-   Strength: Average
-   Agility: Above Average
-   Accuracy: Above Average
-   Speed: Above Average (2/10)
-   Stamina: Average
Resistance: 2
-   Physical Resistance: Average (1/10)
-   Energy Resistance: Above Average
-   Mental Resistance: Above Average
Recovery: 1
-   Physical Injury: Average
-   Nano Energy: Average
Ability
Power: 41
-   Time: Average
o   Time Compression: 65%
-   Space: Above Average

○ Void Burst: 3.5-Uses at Maximum Size	
○ Spatial Awareness: Passive senses may be enhanced for up to 5-Seconds	
Control: 64	
- Time: Average	
○ Time Compression: 20-Seconds Uncompressed Time	
- Space: Below Good (13/25)	
○ Void Burst: up to a 68-Foot Range and up to a 5.8-Inch Diameter	
○ Spatial Awareness: up to 68-Foot Range	

I was . . . shocked. More than shocked. How was this even possible? If I was reading this correctly, I just gained 24-enhancements to my power and 47-enhancements to my control. More, I got 5-enhancements to my speed as well, which explained how that little monster was able to react to me so quickly.

"What? What's wrong?" Light asked, shaking me from my study of my status. "Did you not get enough?"

I shook my head, not sure how to answer.

"Well, don't leave us in suspense," Hammer butted in. "Spit it out. What did you gain?"

I told them.

"You want to repeat that?" Hammer requested.

I told them again.

"Are you two hearing the same crazy numbers I am?" Hammer asked, looking to an equally stunned Light and Ward.

"It shouldn't be possible, right?" Light asked, finally saying something.

"I've never heard of the like," Ward replied. "But then again, how many bother hunting beasts specific to their ability."

"Okay, tomorrow we're going after an elequake," Hammer said instantly.

"What's an elequake?" I asked.

"A very large beast that can cause minor earthquakes with every step it takes," Ward answered, then mumbled under his breath about searching for something called an armadeer.

"Think we could find a phoenix?" Light asked, sounding hopeful.

"Phoenix?" I asked, that was something out of legend, wasn't it?

"Sometimes called the sunbird," Light answered not really explaining anything.

"Are these all rare and extremely difficult to hunt beasts?" I asked.

"Yes," Hammer replied with a nod. "Though, I'll need to get approval to change locations," Hammer mumbled and clicked his tongue, pouting he added, "Major Miracle will never approve it."

"I'm just going to go see if I can make a portal now," I said, slowly backing away from the crazy heroes.

I made my way to the top of the wall and had a seat. I may be able to cultivate with my eyes open now but trying to figure out new abilities required focus. It didn't take long to follow the path and feel out my Nanos. This time, portals came easy to me. I had more than enough power to tear a hole in space and step through unimpeded though I only went from one end of the wall to the other. I had a feeling I could go quite a bit further than that, but it was enough to test my ability.

Then I thought about what that warp hunter was able to do, which made me wonder if that was something I could do as well. And according to my Nanos I could.

Power: 41		
-	Space: Above Average	
	o	Portal: up to 3.5-Foot Diameter

○ Teleport: 3.5-Uses	
Control: 64	
- Space: Below Good (13/25)	
○ Portal: Travel 0.48-Mile Range	
○ Teleport: 68-Foot Range	

That made me grin. I could Teleport. I could use Teleport almost four times. That was incredible to me. Sure, it didn't have much range, but it didn't need a lot of range. I had Portals to travel distances.

And of course, now that I had a new toy to play with, I was going to enjoy it. Get down from the wall? No problem, Teleport. Move to the cookfire? Easy, Teleport. Scare Hammer in a way that makes him scream like a little kid? Unbelievably easy, Teleport.

I never slept so well as I did that night. I was regretting my actions the next morning when Hammer got a little payback.

"Well now that Davis is a master of his abilities, I figure we can let him do the heavy lifting from now on," Hammer said, smirking in victory. "Also, you've got about a week to get your Milestone up where it needs to be. Good luck, I'm going back to bed."

20

The windowless vehicle bothered me this time. I had spent so much time outside over the last few weeks, that being closed in was uncomfortable. I earned my 31st Milestone just that morning. I was as ready as I was ever going to be at that point. Between the food and tougher beasts, I had gained quite a few additional points, not to mention the enhancements I spent with each Milestone.

Davis Malory	
Aliases: N/A	
Occupation: N/A	
Alignment: Neutral	
Milestone: 31st	
Nano: 7,501,135/7,875,000	
Body	
	Athleticism: 25
-	Strength: Average (3/10)
-	Agility: Above Average
-	Accuracy: Above Average
-	Speed: Below Good
-	Stamina: Average (1/10)
	Resistance: 3
-	Physical Resistance: Average (2/10)
-	Energy Resistance: Above Average
-	Mental Resistance: Above Average
	Recovery: 6
-	Physical Injury: Average
-	Nano Energy: Average (5/10)

Ability		
	Power: 64	
-	Time: Average	
	o	Time Compression: 65%
-	Space: Below Good (13/25)	
	o	Void Burst: 5.8-Uses at Maximum Size
	o	Spatial Awareness: Passive senses may be enhanced for up to 5-Seconds
	o	Portal: up to 5.8-Foot Diameter
	o	Teleport: 5.8-Uses
	Control: 64	
-	Time: Average	
	o	Time Compression: 20-Seconds Uncompressed Time
-	Space: Below Good (13/25)	
	o	Void Burst: up to a 68-Foot Range and up to a 5.8-Inch Diameter
	o	Spatial Awareness: up to 68-Foot Range
	o	Portal: Travel 0.48-Mile Range
	o	Teleport: 68-Foot Range

Ward interrupted my review of my status, saying, "We'll be meeting with Major Miracle as soon as we get back."

I nodded in understanding, then asked, "How much have you told him about my status?"

"Not much," Hammer said. "Your growth is unusual thanks to the warp hunter you consumed. That beast must have been at least a 70th Milestone with probably a Master rank in its Teleport ability, not to mention its Speed."

"Will we be informing him of everything when we get back?" I asked.

Hammer shrugged. "It's up to you really. The only thing he's going to care about is that you now have the ability to create portals."

I nodded again and waited. Not fifteen minutes later the vehicle came to a stop and the door opened. It looked like an underground parking garage and based on the half dozen windowless boxes all around me, I assumed that's exactly what it was.

Further inside the building, I met Major Miracle and another man I didn't know inside of a conference room.

Major Miracle started with a simple, "Welcome back, Mr. Malory. I hope your time in the wilds wasn't overly harrowing."

Great, I thought with a roll of the eyes, we were back to what I had come to call 'Hero Speak'. Trying to suppress my annoyance, I said, "Those monsters will provide nightmare fuel for years to come, thanks for that."

The Major looked surprised by my reply, as if he expected me to alleviate his guilt in some way. "I am sorry for the circumstances that brought us to this point, I truly am."

Not wanting to go into it any further, I changed the subject. "What's next? The sooner this 'mission' is done, the sooner I can go home."

Major Miracle nodded. "I understand, allow me to introduce you to Para-Hypno," he said, motioning to the man next to him.

Para-Hypno was shorter than the Major by a head. He had a thick five o'clock shadow that could almost be called a beard. The rest of his face was hidden by a black body suit that covered his hair and eyes, not that you could see much of his eyes under the wide-brimmed brown hat. All this was finished off by a long brown trench coat. His look felt like something out of an old detective noir film.

I was about to greet him when he cut me off with, stating firmly, "Skip the pleasantries. I am here to prep you to become Dr. Portal. Starting now, that is what everyone will call you. Get used to it. If you don't respond immediately to that name, you're as good as dead. Am I clear, Dr. Portal?"

I nodded.

Para continued, "Second, if you're going to be Dr. Portal, you need to speak like him, walk like him, and if you can squeeze enough brain cells together, think like him."

I didn't care for his insulting me like that, but I accepted what he said. I asked, "And do you have any recording or video of him I can study?"

Para grunted, tilting his head to the side. "Well, you already sound like him, but I suppose that makes sense, you are his doppelganger. Alright, come with me," he said, walking to the door only to pause and look back, stating, "Only him."

I hadn't noticed at first but Light, Ward, and Hammer had all started to follow along. None of them seem to like being told to stay behind until Major Miracle said, "You three stay here, we have some things to go over."

I followed Para higher into the building and into a small office. "Alright, Dr. Portal. Before we begin, let me make a few things absolutely clear. I don't trust you. I think you might be the real Dr. Portal and you're just using us. I don't know how you lost all your Milestones or how you became younger, but I know it's you."

I was startled by the accusation. "But I'm not him," I protested lamely.

Para snorted. "So you claim," he said harshly. He took a deep calming breath before speaking again, "But I have my orders, even if they are a complete waste of my time. So, let's get to work."

I didn't have much choice in the matter.

Para set what looked like an old slide projector on his desk and aimed it at the wall. "This was your debut as a villain," he said, flicking a switch on the projector and a video came to life. It was me, a little older than I am now. I wore a light purple bodysuit with some kind of pistol strapped to my thigh. My head was uncovered, except for my eyes which had a simple domino style mask, at least I think that's what the mask was called.

"Greetings, citizens of New Haven," I shouted to a scared looking crowd of people, or the me on the screen shouted. Dr. Portal was standing on top of a counter and addressing a scared crowd.

"Is that a bank?" I asked.

"Yes," Para answered.

"Who's filming this?" I asked as the video shook.

Para sighed, sounding annoyed, but he answered, "We don't know. The video was handed over to the heroes after you got away."

I wanted to ask more but the me on the screen seemed to be done scanning the crowd. "I . . . am Dr. Portal," he shouted. "If you could not already tell, I am a villain . . . no, a supervillain. Today begins my bid to conquer New Haven, and you are but a steppingstone to taking over the world!"

"Do all villains sound so . . . cliché?" I asked.

"Yes, you do," Para answered. "It's good for scaring the citizens, makes them more compliant."

"It's ridiculous," I said.

Para snorted. "I agree, but the psychology of speaking this way has been ingrained into society. Heroes speak one way to reassure and calm, Villains speak another, though very similar way, to get a different reaction. It's something we learn as children. Now, stop talking and pay attention," he finished, pointing firmly at the screen.

One of the citizens stood up, looking angry, he shouted, "The heroes will stop you. You won't get away with this."

Dr. Portal grinned viciously and said, "They can try." Suddenly a portal opened under the citizen that spoke and the man fell through. Another portal opened near the ceiling and the man fell out, landing on the hard floor with a crunch and howling in pain, both of his legs clearly broken.

Looking back to the crowd, Dr. Portal asked, "Anyone else want to praise the heroes?"

The video cut off a moment later.

"Was the man okay?" I asked.

"He was fine," Para replied, ejecting something from the projector and replacing it. It looked like a cassette tape but more cubed.

Then I asked something I was afraid to ask, but it needed to be asked anyway. "Has . . . has Dr. Portal ever killed anyone?"

"Not that we know of," Para answered absentmindedly as he tried to force the square cube thing into the projector. He grumbled under his voice, "I hate this device. Damned cubes never go in right."

"Can you tell me more about him?" I asked.

"Don't know much about him. He appeared about five years ago. Never knew his real identity. He was probably from another fortress city and moved here. If he has any relations, he probably left them behind to keep them safe. He's never killed in the public eye, but that's not to say he hasn't done so in private. There are more than a few unsolved murders where we can't figure out how someone got into or out of a high-security area," Para answered, then sighed before continuing, "Look, Dr. Portal was a middling villain at best. But he was smart and careful. His ability to open portals made him popular with a lot of higher-powered villains. Still, he never partnered with any of the really dangerous villains, at least not that we know of."

"I see," I said slowly, digesting what I'd just been told.

"Ah, finally, stupid device," Para said triumphantly, flicking a switch and starting another video.

Hours passed with plenty of footage to be viewed. I got to see how Dr. Portal fought. I rarely saw him use the pistol and when he did, he wounded, not killed. He liked to use the portals . . . a lot. I noticed that when someone shot at him with something, be it a bullet or an energy projectile, he always teleported it behind himself and angled at the ground so it wouldn't carry further and possibly injure someone not involved. It was an interesting dichotomy. He was a villain, but it seemed like he did everything he could to avoid permanently injuring anyone.

"Alright, now we come to the most interesting footage," Para said with an excited grin as he exchanged cubes, this time without any fuss.

The screen flickered to life and there I was again. It looked like I was robbing some kind of an armored truck.

"This was about a year ago," Para said.

It looked like everything was going smoothly. Dr. Portal disarmed the guards, using their own cuffs against them. Then he opened a portal that led inside the armored truck and stepped through. He left the portal open as he moved back and forth through the portal, each time Dr. Portal came back with a sack of money. When he had it all piled up and in public view, which made no sense to me, he crowed loudly in victory, scaring the citizens even further.

"Thanks for doing the heavy lifting, Dr. Portal," a new voice said. It was a very large man wearing a black three-piece suit and dark sunglasses.

"What are you doing here, Fingers?" Dr. Portal asked, one of his hands moving toward his pistol.

"I think you know," Fingers replied. "Hedge isn't happy with the cut you've been paying to operate in New Haven. You've gotten a little too full of yourself. Hedge thinks a little time in the cooler might do you some good."

Dr. Portal just grinned. "So, Hedge finally made a move. I've been waiting on this for months."

Fingers didn't like that reply. The bulky man seemed to become bulkier, growing both taller and wider, his suit stretching with him. "If you knew this was coming," Finger said, his voice growing deeper. "Then you know, you can't win."

"I already have," Dr. Portal said, falling backwards into a portal he opened on the ground behind him, vanishing from view.

Fingers looked around confused. That is until a hero wrapped in golden energy flew down from the sky, landing a single punch to Fingers's face, knocking him to the ground and completely unconscious. When the light faded, Major Miracle remained standing and stated, "No Villain shall harm my people! Citizens, please return to your daily business."

The footage cut out a moment later.

I got two things from that last video. First, Major Miracle was a major powerhouse. Second, Dr. Portal set Fingers and his boss up. "It was a setup," I said, looking to Para for confirmation.

"It was," Para nodded in agreement. "It was a powerplay by Dr. Portal. It wasn't just catching Fingers like that either. In that footage, Fingers admitted that Hedge gave the orders. Hedge is now one of our most wanted. We'll catch him, it's just a matter of time."

"What happened to Dr. Portal after that?" I asked. "Do you have more footage?"

"That was the last time he was seen until the event that brought you to this world," Para answered. "Most likely, he was laying low until Hedge had been dealt with, either by us or another villain."

"I see," I said, nodding in understanding. If I had angered a boss, something I assumed Hedge was, then laying low was probably a good idea. "What about the cameraman? Did you ever find him or her?"

"No," Para replied with a frown. "And yet, somehow, our cameraman was always in the perfect spot to film Dr. Portal. I think Dr. Portal had some kind of sidekick or partner. It's the only flaw in this plan of ours. Anyway, let's watch them all again. This time, I want you to start speaking the monologues. Stand up as well and start trying to imitate his movements."

I stood and stretched a little after sitting for so long. Para slipped in one of the cubes and hit play. I had a lot of work to do.

21

Blake Avenue intersected with Rich Street in a seedy part of New Haven. And despite that area of town being considered a bad neighborhood, petty criminals and villains alike knew better than to start trouble. Not with the Joker's Wild Club entrance hidden away there. It just wasn't done unless you wanted to end up six feet under.

According to Para, all I needed to do was show up to meet with an information broker and let myself be seen. And being seen was apparently an art unto itself. I needed to be inconspicuous and suspicious at the same time. I needed to hide as much of myself from view while letting a few individuals catch a glimpse of something identifiable. And if the training for that wasn't enough, part of the process to get me ready involved a less than reputable asset of Para's. Someone that changed my appearance, aged me slightly, also added some scars, that kind of thing. Anyway, with my costume firmly in place, it was time to risk my life for a chance to go home.

I wore a dark long coat, with its hood up, I was covered from my head to just below my knees by the coat and thank goodness for that. I did not like bodysuits. They were far too tight and rode up in all the wrong places. And did I mention the color? What was Dr. Portal thinking wearing lavender? It just didn't seem very villainous to me. I couldn't wait until this was all over.

I looked around the neighborhood again and marveled at the state of the city. It didn't occur to me that I hadn't seen the city since I came to this world until Para started preparing me for this insane plan. Not a photo or an image or anything. Even the footage of Dr. Portal didn't show much background. Looking around now, I was still amazed. Some buildings were new and nearly pristine, while others were crumbling from Nano-Rot. It was shocking when I first saw it. Para explained that the wild Nanos needed to feed, and what better food was there than buildings to provide inorganic materials and normal bio-waste to provide organic materials. The result was a city that was half crumbling and constantly being rebuilt, though the rebuilding was also partly due to property damage when heroes and villains fought. It gave off a feeling of a post-apocalyptic cityscape and a futuristic marvel at the same time, often right next to each other. The result was a booming economy built on construction and Nanotech engineering. Both of which were used to pay the heroes that protect the city.

I turned the corner, moving from Rich Street onto Blake Avenue, pulling my coat closer just as a gust of wind turned the same corner coming straight at me. About a hundred yards down, I took a right down an alley. It reminded me of the alleys back home. Dark, dirty, and poorly lit. Poorly lit that is, except for a single light that shined over an unmarked door. The door was a dark metal color with rivets framing the door, giving me the sense that it was both thick and heavy, probably armored as well for additional security. The look was finished off with an eye slat that was currently closed.

I pounded my fist on the door.

The slat opened with a clank. Someone on the other side peered out and with a deep baritone said, "Password."

"Open the damn door," I snapped back, snarling in irritation, trying not to show any nervousness. Part of me couldn't believe I was actually doing this cloak and dagger craziness. Another part . . . well, I kind of liked it. Not getting a response or movement from the guard on the other side of the door, I opened a small portal, no bigger than my fist and threatened, "Or do you want to find out what happens if I pull your head inside this portal and close it with your body still on the other side of the door?"

The slat slammed shut and the sounds of locks being turned could be heard from the inside. When the door opened, I could faintly hear some music from far below.

"Don't cause any trouble," the beefy security guard ordered, though the way he looked at me told me he was clearly afraid of my threat. I felt kind of bad about that. Still, I didn't react, just moved past him and down the first flight of stairs.

It was just like Para had told me. Apparently, there were several passwords and none of them were necessary. There was one for tourists, people that wanted to get a thrill. There was another for 'delivery' people, and while he didn't exactly explain what was being delivered, I could have made several guesses. There were other passwords for different reasons, but they all changed regularly. The easiest method, especially for a villain, was always a threat. It helped that the guard was there more for show than as actual security.

It was five flights down to the actual club. I moved quickly, not checking my coat, not talking to the waitress that tried to take my drink order. I followed Para's instructions and went straight to the bar. At the end of the bar sat a very small man in a brown suit with a red and white polka dot bowtie, though man wasn't exactly right. It was actually a puppet. The puppet was the ability of someone, somewhere at work. According to Para, the man behind the puppet was an information broker. And one that, because of his network of puppets, was impossible to catch, even for the heroes like Para. However, as a villain, he should have no qualms about giving Dr. Portal information.

I sat next to him and pulled my hood lower. "I need information," I said just loud enough for the puppet to hear.

"Of course you do," the puppet replied, its voice sounding like that of a child. "What information do you need?"

"I need to know who's after me," I replied, looking around nervously. It helped that I really was nervous.

One of the puppets wooden eyebrows raised in curiosity, then it asked, "I see, and who are you?"

"Dr. Portal," I replied even more softly.

"Rumors say you're dead," the puppet replied.

"Tales of my death have been greatly exaggerated," I said, trying not to smirk. I never thought I would ever get the chance to say something like that.

"I see," the puppet replied. "It will cost, 1,000 Nano-chips and information."

Nano-chips were this world's currency. Chips of compressed Nanos, each one holding 1,000-Nanos. They were an interesting piece of technology. The small glass tile was about the size of the tip of my pinky. In the very center of the tile was a tiny glowing hollow that was filled with the Nanos.

"Done," I said, placing my hand on a plate on the bar top. Part of my education with Para included some basic lessons in banking. A person could contribute their cultivated Nanos to form Nano-chips which could then be traded for goods and services. A person could then cultivate the chips or use them as currency. Part of that was the use of the metal plate I just set my hand on. It was a device that was able to withdraw the chips from Dr. Portal's Stash. A Stash was what villains call their bank account with the Trust of Villainy. That's right, villains had their own banking system. Who would have thought? Anyway, as Dr. Portal's doppelganger, I was able to access his accounts. It made the 1,000,000 Nanos I just paid out hurt a lot less.

"And done," the puppet replied, seeing the transaction completed. "Hedge is still after you for setting him up and getting Fingers caught by the heroes. Verdant Labs has initiated a contract on you after their engineers went missing."

"And who's backing Verdant?" I asked.

"Unknown," the puppet replied. "If you want to find out, I suggest you start with the CEO of Verdant Labs, the man that issued the contract . . . Winston Bleak."

"I have shared what I know. Your turn," the puppet said, "What happened to you?"

"The device worked, at least at first it did. Then it malfunctioned. I ended up near Wu-Shan Fortress City. It took a while to work my way back here," I replied.

The puppet followed up with the expected question. It asked, "And the device?"

"Self-destructed," I answered.

The puppet remained silent for a moment before saying, "Transaction complete. Have a nice day."

That was my signal to leave. I stepped back from the bar and the puppet. I turned, ready to leave before someone found me. Of course, when I turned, it was to see three men in matching black bodysuits and masks spread out before me.

The one in the middle spoke first, "Dr. Portal, we need you to come with us."

"And who would you be?" I asked, mentally commanding a scan as I looked at each of them. The one on the left was 25th Milestone and the one on the right was 28th Milestone, which I thought I could handle. Then there was the one in the middle, he was 35th Milestone. And while it was great to find out their Milestones, it didn't really tell me anything. That said, I felt like I should be able to handle all three, or I would if my only attack weren't going to cause me even more trouble. Still, I had the pistol at my side that Dr. Portal was known to carry.

"Who we are does not matter," the one in the middle replied. "What matters is that you will come with us."

"No, I don't think I will," I said, pulling the pistol from my leg holster and aiming it at the head of the one in the middle. And yet, none of them reacted.

"Your weapon is useless," the one in the middle said. "We were chosen for more than our uniforms."

So, high energy and or physical resistances?

I smirked, "Who said I was going to shoot you?" I aimed slightly higher and pulled the trigger. The chandelier I aimed at exploded in a shower of glass, sparks, and Nanos. All three men jerked back in surprise from the flash of light and then from the swarm of cultivation attempts by the patrons of the club, some of which physically rushed the epicenter, knocking into the three wannabe kidnappers. It wasn't going to buy me a lot of time, but it would be enough. Copying a move, one I had previously seen from Dr. Portal, I opened a portal on the floor behind me and fell back into it.

I emerged on the street outside the club. The portal opened vertically so the momentum of the fall continued to push me backward. I was forced to take an awkward step back, so I didn't continue to fall. It was kind of awesome. I would have bet money it looked really cool. The portal closed in an instant. I counted to ten to see if anyone was able to follow me. But when no one appeared, I pulled my coat and hood tighter around myself and walked into the night.

An hour later I was meeting Para in an abandoned building that I required several portals to reach, all in an effort to ease the paranoid man's paranoia.

"So, how did it go?" Para demanded as soon as I stepped out of the portal.

I told him what I had learned.

"Didn't know about the contract. I'll start working up a plan for you to grab and interrogate the CEO," Para said.

"What about those three weirdoes?" I asked.

"Kidnap, And, and Ransom, they don't kill, not that we know of anyway, but they have no problem handing you over to someone that will. Kidnap is the leader of that little trio. Ransom is the muscle, lots of resistances. The third is And, not much is known about him," Para explained.

I wanted to ask more about the trio and their very strange names, but it was more important to ask, "So what do I do about them?"

"Nothing," Para replied. "If they show up again, find a way to escape. Or, you're a villain, you could just kill them."

I glared at Para, not at all amused by the suggestion. "No, really, what do I do if they show up again? I can't guarantee I'll be able to escape like that again."

"Then be a villain. Do what a villain would do. I'm not here to hold your hand. It's bad enough I'm working logistical support for you. The sooner you start thinking and acting like a villain, the better," Para complained. "For now, make your way back to the safehouse we set up for you. Meet me back here in two days. I'll have a plan for you by then."

I didn't like that it would take so long, especially now that it was known that I, as in Dr. Portal, was still alive. Unfortunately, it wasn't like there was much I could do about it.

22

"And you're sure this will work?" I asked, looking at Para once again. I still wasn't comfortable with playing the villain.

After two days of waiting in my safehouse, I had started to go a little stir crazy. So, when I finally got to meet with Para, I was excited. Then he told me the plan.

Para rolled his eyes and grunted, "Yes, this will work."

I took a nervous look over the side of the skyscraper we were both standing on. Verdant Labs occupied four of the twenty-eight floors of the building including three subterranean floors where the actual labs were located. The other floor they occupied was an executive floor near the top, where they met with investors and ran the business side of things. This also included the office of the CEO, Winston Bleak.

"He just entered his office," Para said softly before ghosting. And when I say 'ghosting' I mean it as in he literally turned into a ghost and then went invisible.

I gave it a ten count before I opened a portal just large enough to see through. The other end opened inside of Bleak's office. I watched him move with purpose to his wet bar. He looked frazzled, nervous even. He kept looking around the room, checking the dark corners as if he expected to be attacked at a moment's notice. Clearly, he heard I was still alive . . . Dr. Portal was still alive. Never mind, the point was he had a reason to be afraid.

Winston moved to his wet bar and poured himself a healthy amount of a brownish gold liquor before moving over to his desk and sitting heavily in his oversized luxurious executive office chair behind his massive desk. He pressed a button and the doors and windows were slowly covered by thick metal plates. They were obviously meant to keep everyone out. Unfortunately for Mr. Bleak, they wouldn't be enough to keep me out.

Just as the man relaxed, I opened a portal under his chair, opening the other end a few feet above and in front of me. He dropped from the portal, still in his chair and now looking quite terrified to be sitting in front of me.

"Hello Winston, you don't mind if I call you Winston, do you?" I asked, standing in front of the terrified CEO. I kept my posture relaxed but the black coat and hood kept me mostly covered from view.

"P-P-P-P-Portal," Winston stuttered.

"Mind explaining why you decided to put out a contract on me?" I asked, nonchalantly.

Winston swallowed nervously, slowly starting to speak, "You . . . you stole the device. If I didn't . . . he would know about our deal."

That caught me off-guard. Before I could stop myself, I asked, "What deal?"

Winston looked confused. Then he started leaning closer to me, trying to look under my hood. Surprise evident in his voice, he said, "Our deal, you steal the device to keep it out of his hands. Don't you . . . you don't . . . remember?"

Uh oh. I needed to think quickly. Come up with something. Some reason I wouldn't remember.

Thankfully, Winston did the thinking for me when he asked, "You used it? You used the device, didn't you?"

I nodded, not trusting myself to speak.

"And you lived?" Winston asked, sounding even more surprised.

Now I had a plan. I knew exactly how to play this. "I don't remember. My memories are all . . . messed up. I woke up near Wu-Shan with no idea how I got there. There was something charred and melted that looked like it might have been a device, but I couldn't be sure. What happened to me?" I asked, grabbing Winston by the lapels of his jacket and pulling him close to my face so I could look him in the eyes, and he could get a clear look at me.

"I warned you not to use it. It was too unstable," Winston tried to defend himself, shying away in terror. "I still don't understand how you're still alive."

Good, one gap closed. Now I needed to press for more information, especially if he expected the device to kill me. But why would I . . . erm, Dr. Portal use it if I . . . he knew death was a likely outcome? I pushed him back into his chair which rolled closer to the edge of the roof. "Why? Why did you think it would kill me?"

"The other test subjects," Winston started, finally looking ashamed and guilty. I knew I wasn't going to like what he was about to say. "They . . . it was too much power for their bodies to handle. They . . . just died not long after use. Their bodies shut down rapidly."

I now had my answer as to what happened to the original Dr. Portal. The device he used to come to my world killed him, not some mysterious disease. "Then why am I alive?"

"I don't . . . I don't know. I would need to run some tests," Winston said.

"No!" I snapped, acting angry for him even suggesting it.

"But . . . we need to understand why you lived when all the others didn't," Winston tried to protest starting to stand from his chair.

I pushed him back into his seat and off the roof. He fell, screaming. And before he hit the ground, I opened a portal under him. The man shot upwards from the portal's other end that was level with the roof in front of me. He went up a few feet before his ascent arrested and began to fall back toward the rooftop. I closed the portal and let him smack bodily into the roof. I didn't like this particular part of the plan. Para insisted it would keep Winston talking. Keep me in control of the conversation. I was more worried about him having a heart attack from the fall.

Winston laid on the roof, breathing rapid, panicked breaths, clutching at his chest. I gave him a quick check to make sure he wasn't having a heart attack, and once I was sure he was good, I slapped him, bringing his attention back to me. I was also hoping the sudden pain would keep him from going into shock.

"Now, why did I steal the device? Who is this he? Why does he want it? Why would I agree to try to keep it out of the hands of whoever he is?" I asked rapidly while I had Winston's undivided attention. I really wish I didn't need to scare him like this. But Para's whole 'be a villain' speech kept running through my head.

"T-T-T-T-Terminus," Winston eventually stuttered out. His whole body was shaking in a way that made me worried he was about to go into shock anyway, if he wasn't already there.

I stopped myself from asking who that was. I was sure Para would inform me. "What did Terminus plan to do with the device?"

Winston looked up at me slowly, his eyes wide. "To bring about the end of all abilities."

Okay, that was going to take some explaining. "Explain," I ordered.

Winston swallowed thickly, then said, "With that device and his ability, he could permanently, take away everyone's abilities."

There was just one question left on Para's list, I asked, "I assume, he took the engineers that made the device? To rebuild it?"

Winston just nodded.

Satisfied and unable to think of anything else to ask, I opened a portal under him again. I set the other end to spit him back out in his office.

"Is that what you wanted?" I asked, knowing Para was still nearby.

When Para reappeared, he looked as if he'd seen a ghost. He was sickly pale and his hands were trembling. "What? What is it?" I asked, feeling very worried to see the seemingly unflappable paranoid hero was that terror stricken.

Para took a minute to gather himself. Then, his voice shaking, he said, "We need to go, right now. Get us back to the safe house as fast as you can without being seen. We need to warn Major Miracle, now! Hurry, before it's too late!"

That sounded really ominous to me. Still, I wasn't going to argue. I opened a portal that was nearly at my maximum distance and followed the still shaken Para through. I had a really bad feeling about this.

23

Major Miracle was silent after hearing the report Para just finished. He sat on the opposite side of the conference table from Para and I, his hands steepled in thought. For a moment, I thought I saw a small tremor in his hands, but it was gone too fast to be sure. I didn't like the long silence, it was awkward. And of course, there was nothing I could say to break the silence. Not that I had any idea what to say.

Finally, Major Miracle broke the silence, "And you're sure about this information?"

"As sure as we can be," Para answered.

Major Miracle closed his eyes and sighed. "So, Terminus did survive."

Now, I did have something to say, or rather a question to ask. "Who is Terminus?"

Major Miracle opened his eyes and leaned forward, then answered, "He is what a civilian would call an arch nemesis, my arch nemesis to be exact."

I nodded. That explained some of Para's panicking. "And what did you mean 'survive'?" I asked.

"A few years ago, Terminus attacked the Hero Association in force. Thirty-three villains against nineteen of us. Ten heroes . . . ten great men and women, including my mentor died that day. Six more chose to retire when it was all done. I fought Terminus myself. Fought him without any abilities, that was his power you know. He could stop the Abilities of others from working." The Major got a faraway look on his face, caught up in the memories of the past.

Major Miracle took a deep shuddering breath and refocused on me. "I was losing. I was going to die, and I knew it. Then I tripped over something. It was the body of a villain. And then I saw it. A weapon, a gun. I took the gun from the body of the fallen villain and I shot him. I shot him repeatedly, I continued to shoot him even as he ran. A normal man would have . . . should have died."

"When the fighting was done, I tried to follow after Terminus. His blood trail led to the New Haven aqueduct and ended there. It was assumed he fell in and drowned. We could never confirm it," Major Miracle finished his story.

"Why did he attack?" I asked. "Why would he attack the heroes back then? Why would he want to get rid of all powers now?"

"Why does any villain attack heroes? Because the heroes stand between them and whatever they want. I have no idea what Terminus wanted then, and I still don't. I'm not sure why he would want to eliminate all abilities. It would make more sense if he just wanted to eliminate my powers, or the powers of all the heroes," Major Miracle answered.

Silence returned to the room.

This time, it was Para that broke the silence. "Do we keep going?"

Major Miracle looked to me. "That is up to Davis," he said.

"If he gets rid of all powers, that means I'll never go home, right?" I asked.

Major Miracle frowned but nodded.

"Then I'm in." I was scared to death of facing a villain like this, but I was more terrified of never being able to go back home.

The Major nodded once and said, "Good, that's good. Para, what are our next steps?"

"We let Davis get captured," Para replied.

"Excuse me?" I said, hoping I just misheard him.

Para smirked, then sounding far too pleased, he said, "If Kidnap, And, and Ransom are working for Terminus, then letting them grab you is the best thing we can hope for."

"And if they are working for the other guy, what's his name?" I asked, trying to remember the name. "Hedge," I said as it came to me. "What if it's him?"

"You'll just need to ask the trio who hired them? If it's Hedge, you run. If it's Terminus, you cooperate," Para replied.

"This seems like a really bad idea," I said. "And what happens if they don't want to answer the question? What happens if I can't escape?"

Para shook his head. "Don't worry so much, it'll be fine. We've got your back."

I really wasn't feeling good about this plan.

Before I could protest further, Para continued, "I'll start floating word to some of my contacts about the safehouse you're hiding out in. It might take a few days, but they'll show up."

"And I, what? Sit in this safehouse waiting for them to show up and hope they feel like talking?" I asked.

"Yes," Para replied. "Anyway, I have work to do if we're going to pull this off."

I looked to Major Miracle hoping he would have something to say. "And you're okay with this plan?" I asked.

"I don't much like it myself," Major Miracle replied. "But if you've got a better plan, I'm all ears."

That was a problem in itself, I didn't have a better plan. I didn't know enough about this world to be able to make anything even resembling a plan.

"Davis, I know you're nervous. But try to have a little faith in us. We can, and will, help you through this," Major Miracle promised, failing to reassure me. "Anyway, Ward is waiting for you in the hall."

Seeing I was dismissed, I left the conference room. Ward was waiting for me in the hall as promised.

Ward spoke first, "Davis, how are you? How has the mission been going?"

"I don't want to talk about it," I said. It wasn't that I didn't want to talk about it. I just knew that if I started talking about it, I might breakdown. I couldn't have that right now. I could breakdown when this was all over.

"I understand," Ward said, nodding solemnly. "Anyway, I was able to get you some of the early research notes on Nanos and a few autopsy reports from people that died during the transition and those who died later. Unfortunately, the data is old and might not be accurate."

I happily accepted the thick stack of papers, stopping myself from thumbing through them immediately. Instead, I asked, "What about that lab equipment I asked for?"

"I needed to call in some favors, but I was able to get you an antique microscope. I asked a Nano-Engineer who owes me a favor if she could make a modern version, but it will take a few weeks, same for the centrifuge you described," Ward answered. "As to the samples you asked for, I was able to get a few for you to examine."

It was something. And it gave me something to do while I waited for my inevitable kidnapping.

24

My safehouse was a simple apartment in a rundown, nearly unoccupied apartment building. It had everything I needed, bathroom, bed, kitchenette and a fully stocked refrigerator. Other than that, there was my makeshift lab which consisted of a few beakers, a brass microscope with some glass slides, a scalpel, and a small cooler with the samples I requested. The only thing I really wished I had was a centrifuge. This world might not believe in using science, but I still did.

I had spent most of the first day reading and rereading the various reports and autopsies, Ward was able to make copies of for me. At least, I think they were copies. Anyway, the autopsies were about what I would have expected from something out of the dark ages of medicines. Okay, maybe not that archaic, but still very dated. And the methodologies were . . . not good. Honestly, some parts of it read like 'it's magic, just accept it', which obviously, they did.

Still, there were some interesting tidbits. One of the first real researchers into the bioenergy converter organ had determined that it was far and away the largest source of Nanos in any body. It was also extremely toxic, which wasn't clearly explained. And it was also combustible . . . very combustible when exposed to excessive heat, around 156^0F.

It was about then I checked the thermostat in my safehouse. It was a simple dial device, dated like many things in this world were. That wasn't the interesting part. The interesting part was the temperature. It was set to 63^0F. I should have been cold at that temperature. But I wasn't. I was in fact, very comfortable. Now I had one more thing on my list, a thermometer. If I was comfortable at this temperature, my body must have been running hot.

Then there were the samples Ward provided. The samples were bioenergy converter organs from a handful of beasts. None of them were really fresh, as they were all frozen and could have been that way for a long time, but they gave me something to analyze. That is, if I could ever get a proper sample to look at under the antique microscope.

"Okay Dave, slice this one even thinner," I said to myself. I was preparing another slide with a cross-section from a sample labeled doose, which I thought was some kind of a duck-goose hybrid based on the name and small size, but it could have just as easily been some kind of dog-moose hybrid. Whatever it was, it was small, and considering the size of the slide and the microscope, it was exactly what I needed. As carefully as I could, I sliced into the frozen organ, trying to cut a thin, very thin sliver of the organ. As the almost paper-thin bit of organ peeled away, I groaned in frustration. In spite of it being the thinnest slice so far, it was still too thick. I supposed that was another tool I would have liked to have, a microscopic specimen slicer. A person just could not do such fine work by hand . . . unless there was someone out there with an ability to do it.

Still, I would try. I would see if it was thin enough for me to view under the microscope. I put the slide into the holders of the microscope and turned on the light under it. I leaned down, and turned the nobs, adjusting the resolution. I got an image. It was rough and there were too many layers, but I could actually see the dead cell structure and unmoving dots that didn't appear to be a part of the cell. I supposed they could have been the Nanos. Dead and floating there, barely moving.

I jerked away from the microscope, blinking a few times before looking again. The dots, they were moving. Barely but they were. No, no, that couldn't be right. Nanos would have been smaller. I shouldn't be able to see individual Nanos even with this microscope. But . . . what if they weren't individual Nanos? What if they were clusters? Or colonies?

I reached out with my Spatial Awareness, pushing my energy to get the most out of it. I could feel Nanos within the organ slice. There were barely any of them, but they were there. Sluggish and unresponsive, but they were alive. They were also unwilling or unable to move from the organ slice. It felt like they were suspended in molasses . . . or fossilized tree sap like those prehistoric mosquitos.

Still, there must be a way to get to them. It would just take a lot more work . . . and a centrifuge.

I sat back from the microscope and sighed when I felt someone enter my passive Spatial Awareness . . . three someone's to be exact.

"Took you long enough," I said, writing notes on what I'd learned so far.

One of the three asked, "You are ready to come with us?"

"It depends," I said. "Do you work for Hedge? Or Terminus?"

My question was greeted by silence, so I turned on my stool to look at the trio.

"We do not work for Hedge," the one in the center finally said.

"I need you to confirm, you work for Terminus?" I asked.

All three frowned, looking from one to the other. The one in the middle eventually nodded.

"Excellent," I said, moving toward the door where my coat was hung. As I pulled the coat on, I asked, "Where are we going?"

One of them produced a black bag, most likely meant to go over my head, to which I responded with a firm, "No, that won't be necessary."

"We have orders," the leader of the trio said.

"Look, I think I've proven that I can leave anytime I want. Your hood doesn't really matter," I said. "So, either we go, or I leave. The choice is yours."

They shared looks again before the hood was put away.

"Good," I said. "Lead the way. Oh, and who's who? Are you Kidnap, Ransom, or And?"

"I am Kidnap," the leader of the trio replied.

"Well then, Kidnap, lead the way," I said, opening my front door and motioning for them to go ahead.

Kidnap nodded just once. I followed him and his cohorts to the roof where a car was parked. I wanted desperately to ask why there was a car parked on the roof, but I didn't want to sound like an idiot.

Ransom or And opened the rear door and motioned for me to enter the vehicle, I still didn't know who was who. Still, I was cooperating. I just really hoped Para and the rest of the heroes were tracking me, or watching me, or . . . something.

The car, lifted gently, silently from the roof and flew rapidly across the city.

"Won't the heroes see us?" I asked, curious.

Kidnap gave me a clipped one-word answer, "Invisible."

An invisible flying car. The five-year-old in me was over the moon. The scientist in me wanted to start asking questions about how it worked, but I kept my mouth shut. Instead, I tried to lean back and get comfortable.

"How long until we get to wherever you're taking me?" I asked.

"A few hours, no more questions," Kidnap replied snappishly.

A few hours seemed like a long time. I tried to look out the windows to get a clue as to where we were going but they were blurred out. There was no way I was going to be able to see where we were going.

"You still haven't told me where we're going or why," I protested. "Let's start with that."

Kidnap huffed in irritation, "We are not permitted to say."

"Then what are you permitted to tell me?" I asked.

"We have already said too much," Kidnap said.

Part of me wanted to be a petulant child about this whole thing but felt that approach could very well lead to them 'accidentally' pushing me out of the invisible flying car from a few miles up.

Ignoring the impulse to play it safe, I grinned and asked, "Are we there yet?"

I could feel Kidnap getting annoyed with me. I still wanted to push it, but I felt I had done enough, at least for now anyway. It was just a matter of waiting for us to arrive wherever it was they were taking me.

25

Travelling for hours in the invisible flying car was annoying. The zigzag path they took was even more annoying. And none of it did anything to hide the fact that we were flying above the wilds, the green of the jungle below us was something even the blurred windows couldn't block out whenever Kidnap banked to the left or right.

When the vehicle finally stopped, evening had set in. I also noted that when we stopped, we were still rather high up in the air. The windows unblurred at last, finally giving me a darkened view of where I was, right up until intense light spilled into the night, completely filling the sky and blinding me momentarily. Ahead of us, a very bright slit of light had appeared and slowly began to part. After blinking a few times, I was impressed to see the opening in the sky led to some kind of hangar bay.

With a small surge the car began moving again, into the hangar where it parked next to three matching cars. I could only watch as the giant doors slid closed behind us.

A loudspeaker announced, **"Beginning Pressurization!"**

I started to ask, "How long-" when I was interrupted by the same loudspeaker.

"Pressurization Complete!"

The doors opened and I followed Ransom, or was it And? Anyway, I followed one of them out of the vehicle. I still didn't know which was which. For now, I decided I would call the bigger of the two Ransom. Neither of them said a word during the trip and eventually Kidnap raised a divider between himself and the backseat.

Finally breaking the silence, Kidnap gave me a simple order, "Follow," and began walking.

As we walked, I paid attention to my surroundings, not that there was much to see. A single long hallway and the occasional closed door. "It's a bit of a ghost town," I commented, hoping for a little information.

Kidnap just kept walking.

I tried to listen for any signs of people but there was nothing. I couldn't even hear the sound of fans circulating air or the hum of engines like I would have in an airplane. And of course, my Spatial Awareness was limited by the hallway and couldn't find any gaps aside from a few small vents. It was frustrating.

Kidnap eventually entered an elevator and inserted a key card.

"Ooh, can I get one of those?" I asked. I really hoped that my act as Dr. Portal was working. A lot of this was guess work on my part. One of the things I noticed from watching Dr. Portal on film, he never seemed to take anything seriously. He was ostentatious to the point of almost being comical . . . very comic book like.

Kidnap still didn't respond as the elevator began moving up. It wasn't long before the elevator stopped, and the doors opened to what could only be called a throne room. The room was long and empty, aside from an unoccupied throne. At least, the room appeared . . . empty. At the very limit of my awareness, I could sense someone.

"Am I late?" I asked. "Or did you take me to the wrong throne room?" While I could sense someone, they didn't need to know that I sensed whoever it was.

"Leave us," a surprisingly female voice ordered, though I couldn't see her. I only knew that she was behind the throne, leaning against it.

Kidnap bowed and slowly backed up into the elevator, disappearing from view behind the closing doors.

"Dr. Portal," the still hidden female said. "I was surprised you came so willingly."

"I have questions," I said. "If I was going to get answers, this is where I needed to be."

"Interesting," she replied. "And what questions do you have?"

"My questions are for Terminus," I said, crossing my arms.

The woman's voice rang out with laughter that echoed all around the throne room.

"What's so funny?" I demanded, halting the woman's laughter.

Finally, the woman stepped out from behind the throne. She was young. I put her in her early twenties. She wore a skintight black bodysuit with a silver T spanning across her collarbone and down to her belt. "You are," she said lightly, her hips sashaying from left to right as she moved to sit in the throne. "I heard your brain got scrambled by the device. I suppose I shouldn't be surprised you would confuse the former Terminus with his successor."

"You?" I asked, trying to get a better look at the young woman.

"Me," Terminus replied with a wicked grin and amusement dancing in her eyes.

"And who are you?" I asked. I didn't know what the original Terminus looked like. And I didn't know if the woman in front of me was related to him. But based on her age and the timeline I got from Major Miracle, she could have been his daughter or niece.

"I'm the daughter of a murdered genius," Terminus declared proudly.

"Murdered genius? So Terminus really did die?" I asked.

"Precisely," Terminus replied. "And now, I intend to finish what he started. But to do that, I needed my power amplification device. A device you stole."

"Did I steal it?" I asked, trying to play dumb.

Terminus's amusement vanished. "You know you did. You can stop playing dumb."

"That's the funny thing," I said. "I really can't be sure if I did steal it. Did I steal it for you? Was I forced to use it to escape? Or did you force me to use it as a test, expecting me to die? I really don't remember. So, help me understand. What exactly . . . did I do?"

"It is very simple. You stole the power amplifier I spent billions of cubes developing. You ruined years of my hard work and careful planning," Terminus paused as a rage briefly overtook her features. "Because of you, I was forced to drastically change my plans. Because of you, the heroes are now aware there even is a plan."

"What plans would those be?" I asked. Another bit of Para's coaching encouraged me to get villains to monologue. He said it was because all villains seem to like the sound of their own voice. I suspected it was more due to a superiority complex and a compulsion to prove how much smarter they believed themselves to be than everyone else.

"With that device, I will finally tear down the hero association that murdered my father. The same association that oppresses non-heroes and treats them like slaves. I will change the world for the better. And I'll start by permanently stripping away the Ability of Major Miracle, the false king of New Haven. The butcher who murdered my father," Terminus boasted.

"And you would rule this world once the heroes were gone?" I asked.

"Of course, I will. I'll create a utopia. Everyone will be truly equal. Once abilities are gone from this world, when everyone is truly equal, there will be peace," Terminus said.

I could hear the belief in her voice. She truly believed that if there were no abilities, then everyone would be equal, and then peace would be achieved. There was only one problem. As Earth's history had taught me time and again, there was no such thing as a utopian society. Even without abilities, people were never equal. Even in my country, a place that espoused equality for all, no one was truly equal. All it ever took was one corrupt person to destroy peace and prosperity, thus allowing all manner of evil back into society. And let's be honest, with so many villains running rampant in this world already, there was already more than enough corruption and evil to go around.

"But now, because of you. I have been forced to adjust. I needed to take the engineers before the heroes could get to them, small grace though it was," Terminus continued. "They are here, rebuilding the power amplifier in secret. Still, the heroes are on to me, even if they do not know who I am or what exactly my plans are."

"And you still haven't said exactly what your plan is?" I asked, getting an angry glare. "Don't glare at me. So far, your plan sounds overly simple. Where is the flare? Where is the twist? Where are the timetables? Blueprints? Maps? It seems clear to me that you have none of that. But . . . maybe I can help you."

"You? Ha!" Terminus laughed a clearly fake laugh. "As for my plans, you don't need to know anything about them."

"Okay, then why am I here? Was it just so you could gloat and then kill me? Or did you actually need something from me?" I asked. "Or . . . did we-" I started to ask, pointing from her to me and back again.

Terminus grit her teeth. "I am going to kill you," she said. "But first, the engineers want to know how you survived using the device."

"And how would I know that?" I asked. I was sure that if I had actually survived using the power amplification device, I could have eventually figured out how I survived with ample use of the scientific method and experimentation. I might have even been able to help them figure out how to increase the survival rate, if given enough time and the right tools.

"If you are saying you are not useful, then I will kill you now," Terminus said, licking her lips in anticipation.

"I didn't say that I wasn't useful," I said. "I only said I don't know how I survived."

"Oh, and just how do you think you can be useful?" Terminus asked.

"How much do you actually know about me?" I asked, curious about what another villain knew about Dr. Portal.

Terminus narrowed her eyes, judging me. "You are a middling villain of the 31st Milestone. Violent but not deadly, a weakness that would have gotten you killed one day if I wasn't going to kill you today. You're clever but not devious, another weakness that would have gotten you killed one day. You've never been caught. You're a planner, which means you think you have an escape plan, or you would never have come along so willingly. Let me assure you now, your portals won't open while you're inside my negation field. And my negation field covers the entirety of this fortress."

I hadn't tried opening a portal since I'd been 'captured', but if she said I wasn't going to be able to open one, then I was inclined to believe her. I tested it anyway, and just as she said, nothing happened.

"Oh no, I'm caught," I said, putting both hands on my face and acting shocked. My portals might have been sealed off, but it didn't seem to affect my Spatial Awareness. I could still feel everything around me, including a subtle wave of energy that was pulsing outward from the woman. I could feel the energy pass out of the maximum range of my senses. More importantly, I could sense gaps in those energy waves.

"You are also strange," Terminus added. "You should be terrified right now, but you're not. You're not even taking me seriously. It is . . . both insulting and infuriating at the same time."

186

"Oh no, you saw through my act," I said, pointing a finger at her. "Whatever shall I do now?"

"Stop that!" Terminus shouted, standing from her throne. "Stop treating me like I'm some random civilian. I am a villainess of the 88th Milestone. I will not be looked down on by you or anyone else!"

"But . . . you're so short. If I do not look down on you, how will I see you?" I asked.

"I'll kill you!" Terminus shouted, storming across the room until she was standing in front of me. "How dare you treat me this way!"

I grinned. Her anger was making her sloppy. The gaps in the waves of energy were getting larger. I could have tried to attack her then, but at the 88th Milestone, there was no telling just how tough she was.

"It's been fun. It's been real. But it hasn't been real fun," I said, giving her a brief farewell wave before opening a portal under my feet in time with one of the larger gaps in her negation waves. I smiled a little wider when I heard her cry of disbelief before my portal fizzed out above me.

I landed on the other side of the portal with a thud and pain shooting up my legs, which was accompanied by a very small dip in my red health bar. Her negation field did manage to throw off the trajectory of the portal's other end. Still, I was in the hangar, exactly where I wanted to be. Or, I thought I wanted to be. Facing the surprised looking Ransom, at least I thought it was Ransom, was definitely not where I wanted to be.

I ran at him, using my Below Good Speed to close on him very quickly. I punched him and felt two cracks, his nose and my fist, which also included another dip in my health bar. Thankfully, the punch did its job. The large goon was unconscious.

"Now, I just need to steal one of these invisible cars and get out of here," I said to myself just in time to see red lights start flashing.

The loudspeaker crackled to life again. A robotic voice booming out, **"Lockdown Procedures Now Activated!"**

Which was followed by a loud metallic clank. The hangar doors now had another door covering it from the inside, giving me the impression, I wasn't going to be getting out that way.

I supposed I could have tried opening a portal to the outside, but my Spatial Awareness was telling me that the erratic gaps were fixed. I could still do something between the gaps if I used my Time Compression, but it wouldn't be enough time to open a portal and go through the other side.

I looked around the hangar for a way to escape, any way to escape, but other than the door I came in, and the door that led to the hall and back to Terminus's throne room, I was coming up short. Then I saw what I needed. Just above the door was a vent and beyond the vent was an airduct just begging to be crawled through.

I waited for a gap in the waves of negation to activate my Time Compression, then I used Teleport and put myself safely in the airduct . . . that was way too small. I barely fit. It was a struggle even to breathe. And there was no light. There was no way I was going to be crawling through the airducts.

I used my Time Compression again and teleported further into the ventilation system, this time to an intersection I could barely see in the dark of the ducts. Then again to another place in the ventilation system where I felt a small room was located. I was very thankful my Spatial Awareness still worked, or I would have gotten well and truly lost in that place. And finally, into the room where I gasped for breath and tried to get my heartbeat to calm down. I was never affected by small spaces before, but after that experience, I might have become a little bit claustrophobic. At least I was safe for the time being.

I really wished I could open a Portal, but the waves of Terminus's negation field made that all but impossible. As it was, I was going to need to rely on Teleporting to get around and even that would only be useful with Time Compression active so I could Teleport during the small gap between the negation waves.

26

Supply closets are not the most comfortable place to hide out. More comfortable than an airduct but not by much. I tried to make the best of my situation. Using a combination of my Time Compression, Spatial Awareness, and Portals, I began opening and closing several keyhole-sized portals. Just little holes in space that were just large enough to look through. I considered using my time while I waited for my ability to recharge to cultivate, but someone might notice the absence of Nanos, which would not be good for me if someone followed it to the source.

My goal was a simple one, figure out where I was inside the fortress and then try to figure out a way to escape. In the process of my exploration, I discovered the fortress was flying, slowly moving above the wilds. I had no idea where it was moving to or how long it would take to get there. And while the fortress was nowhere close to the size of a fortress city, it was large enough that it could house hundreds of people, probably a lot more. I also discovered that the whole ship was pressurized after I opened a small portal outside and almost got my eye sucked through. Thank you, Time Compression, for giving me just enough time to close the portal before it was too late. Unfortunately, it made it pretty clear that I would not be using a portal to get outside due to the pressurization differential. If I wanted out, I was going to need to commandeer one of those invisible flying cars . . . after getting the place out of lockdown . . . and opening the doors . . . but most importantly, not getting caught while doing any of it.

In the meantime, I was trying to build a map of the place . . . or find a map of the place. So far, I hadn't found anything resembling a command center or control room. I feared that it was someone's ability that made the place fly and move. And if that were true, then it also meant Terminus had enough control over her negation field that she could choose whose ability she negates. I really hoped that wasn't the case.

I spotted the first place of interest, the cafeteria, about an hour into my exploration. There were maybe a dozen people in the cafeteria, most of them wore uniforms that suggested they were guards or soldiers. Then I spotted Kidnap and his cohort. The big guy I punched out had his mask slightly off kilter. I guessed his nose was very swollen under his mask. I would have bet he had two black eyes as well. I gleaned one other important detail from looking at him. He wasn't healed. This fact suggested Terminus didn't have a healer on the ship. Either that or the guy was being punished for failing to catch me.

I continued my exploration, hoping to find something more useful than the cafeteria. After a few fruitless hours of searching, I was ready to groan in frustration, but any noise might have given my location away. There were too many variables that went along with a flying fortress populated by villains and henchmen. Which brought up another mental point. Just where were the heroes? I thought they were supposed to be tracking me or something?

My shoulders sagged then tensed as I heard the door to my room start moving. I quickly activated my Time Compression and used Teleport to get back into the very cramped and uncomfortable airduct. I made a note to sue Hollywood when I got home. Talk about false advertising. The airducts that heroes are always crawling through in the movies are just not that big or as clean in real life. That or Terminus saw large airducts as a weakness and purposely put in smaller ones.

"All clear," I heard a voice say from the supply closet followed closely by the door closing. Another Time Compression and Teleport put me back into the supply closet, breathing easier.

My stomach chose then to remind me that I hadn't eaten in a while, my mind briefly going back to the kitchen. There was no telling how long I was going to need to hide out and sneak around. I was going to need food soon enough, but I would wait until it was safer. For now, I needed to keep up my search of the flying fortress. What I really needed was to find the control room . . . if there was one. And barring that, I needed to find the person with the ability that was controlling this place.

I settled down in my little supply closet and went back to opening and closing keyhole-sized portals in the small gaps in the negation waves that were still covering the entire structure. If I was lucky, Terminus would tire out soon and I would be able to freely use my abilities. Even an 88th Milestone would get tired eventually, right? I sighed and leaned back in the cramped closet. I couldn't count on that. I went back to trying to map out the fortress.

In the late hours of the night, with the damnable negation field still active, I checked the kitchen again and found it empty. Then I needed to map out the airducts to find a path through the vents from my current location to the cafeteria. Eventually, I was able to teleport my way through the painfully cramped airducts until I was in the airducts above the kitchen, which now had a midnight-snacker raiding one of the industrial sized refrigerators. Naturally, he seemed to be in no hurry, like my time meant nothing to him.

I laid in the vents, trying to control my breathing and checking in on the guard regularly when something caught my eye. The guard had a keycard that looked a lot like the one Kidnap had. It gave me an idea. A very risky idea, but one that might be worth that risk, especially as the guard was completely alone.

I waited for him to bend low and took that moment to Teleport right behind him while he was so distracted. I set off a very small Void Burst next to his head to knock him out. Then I put my plan into action. On top of the refrigerator was a very large, very heavy looking, cast iron pot. With a little careful planning, I took the pot down and set the scene. I needed to smash him with the pot once to make it look real, but I was careful to not cause permanent damage. After that, I took his keycard. I knew it would eventually be discovered that I took the keycard. Hopefully by then, it would have been too late, and I'd have already escaped. On the other hand, I could have just taken the keycard from the idiot guard that only had access to the storage rooms and the bathroom. And speaking of bathroom, it had been a while.

Luckily, I spotted the bathroom connected to the cafeteria and made use of it. And thanks to the newly acquired keycard, I didn't even need to teleport through the vents to get to it.

After that, I raided the pantry, focusing on dried meats and cheeses and even some fruit. I knew well enough that I wouldn't be able to raid the kitchen daily. My only problem was storing all the food. I was worried about my sack of loot getting stuck in the airducts or getting squished against me. I ran out of time to ponder when I heard the guard groaning.

Not wasting anymore time, I used Teleport to return to the airducts. Thus, I began the long trek back to my storage room. I made a mental note to look for a vacant room closer to the kitchens. Especially if it seemed like I was going to be stuck here longer.

I tried to keep my eating light, making sure I didn't leave any crumbs or trash behind. Then I leaned back, and closed my eyes, hoping I could get a little rest before the new day came and I would need to resume my search for an escape.

Sleep didn't come easy inside my supply closet. It was cramped and I was forced to lean up against a cold metal wall with my knees bent uncomfortably. No, it was more that every creak or groan of the metal and every footstep passing the door brought me back to full alertness. I think I got some sleep in there, but it was not restful.

I spent another day stuck in that closet. Even after I found a vacant room not too far from the kitchen. I gave it that day just to make sure it was truly unoccupied. I could have given it more time, but I knew that the longer I took to escape, the more likely it would be for me to get caught.

I searched through a great deal of the flying fortress as well. I found more supply rooms. Various occupied bedrooms and a few more hangars, though the hangar doors were still sealed up tight. I checked on Terminus regularly, mostly just to see if she was getting tired. She wasn't. I did discover another elevator behind her throne. It wasn't exactly hidden, but it wasn't easily seen from the rooms entrance. Unfortunately, that was all I discovered. The elevator shafts were also pressurized, differently from the rest of the fortress but still an issue. Other than that, I figured out that the fortress was saucer shaped with five floors above me and three below me. It was also larger than I originally assume, at least over the 0.48-mile range of my portal ability.

On day three, after I finally decided to relocate to the unoccupied bedroom, the one I discovered the previous day. From there, I continued my search through the facility. I even found a room with a view outside. I couldn't see anything but the wilds for miles around, but it did give me the direction the fortress was travelling. Which gave me another idea. What if the fortress's direction of travel indicated the front of it? And what if the control center was located in the front of the ship? I mean, they did need to see where they were going, right?

So, with a destination in mind, I started trying to find my way to the front of the ship. The airducts and I had become well acquainted over the last day. I learned how to contort myself in just the right way that allowed me to breathe more easily. Unfortunately, my shoulders and neck did not appreciate it.

The 'front' of the ship wasn't exactly what I was hoping for. The saucer shaped ship had a bubble on the underside. A bubble that hosted almost a dozen people manning various stations that told me nothing about what any of them did. Though I suspected this was the command center I was looking for.

Refraining from sighing, I settled in to my cramped airduct and started using keyhole portals again to start looking over the various terminals, looking for the button that would turn off the lockdown. I found the flight control systems, and communications systems and made a mental note of where they were located. I identified the captain of the ship, a 32nd Milestone elderly woman with silver hair. She didn't appear to be much of a threat, but I still had no intention of tangling with her. In fact, most of the bridge crew were around the same Milestone. I was sure I could hurt a lot of them and do a lot of damage to the various systems. Unfortunately, it was just as likely I would crash the fortress as stop them.

As I was scanning the machines, I saw a monitor that gave me pause. It looked like a security station with live camera images being cycled through on four different screens. I didn't pay attention to the screens though. My focus was on the big red button that was currently depressed with a label below it that read 'Lockdown'. All I needed to do was depress that button and I would be able to escape. Then I remembered the button was in a room filled with villains . . . henchmen that would need to be dealt with first. I supposed I could have opened a small portal and stuck a finger through very quickly in the hopes that I could push it before the portal got cut off and my finger with it. After that, a sufficiently sized Void Burst could destroy the terminal. If only I could move fast enough. Where was a squirbit when I needed one?

Another look around the room again showed me there were two entrances. I could collapse the hallways outside of the room. But that would just trap me in the room with the henchmen. So, I would need to deal with them first. I had enough power to knock them all out, except that one or more of them might have enhanced physical resistance.

What I really needed was a way to convince them to evacuate from the bridge of their own accord. Like a radiation leak or gas leak or something like that. It always worked in the movies. Though, this wasn't exactly a movie as the airducts proved repeatedly.

There must be something else I could use.

I looked again at the security station. As I did, one of the screens caught my eye. The images were focused on one room, flipping through different angles. It was a lab with six haggard looking people in lab coats. They looked absolutely exhausted. They were completely unwashed and looked like they had barely eaten in days. One of the women looked like she was about to keel over. She looked like she was suffering from dehydration in addition to the starvation. If she didn't get medical help soon, she was likely to die.

And then I saw it. The most terrifying thing about the room was the device hovering above a centralized table. It was the same device that brought me to Planet Hero. It was the power amplification device I saw on Dr. Portal when he appeared in my world. It looked like it was completed . . . or almost completed. I was little comforted by the fact that they still didn't know how to make it safe. Hopefully, that would slow Terminus down.

I wanted to tell myself that those engineers would be fine. That I could leave them there. That if I got to the heroes, they would be able to come and save those people. But I was a doctor. I could see the signs plain as day. Those people weren't likely to live long enough for help to come. I gave a mental sigh. Apparently, I wasn't quite ready to escape after all.

27

I really wished the display in the command center told me where the lab was hidden away. I had yet to find a map of the fortress printed anywhere, which also made me wonder how the guards never got lost. I focused in on the images of the lab. Specifically, I was looking for windows, but they showed nothing of exterior facing windows if there even were any. I was starting to suspect that the lab might be connected to the not quite hidden elevator in what I was calling the throne room.

Even with my suspicions, I spent a few hours scouring as much of the flying fortress as I could. And sadly, I found nothing.

I was out of options. I needed to get into that elevator and get up to those engineers, which meant I needed to actually get eyes on the elevator.

First, I opened a keyhole sized portal outside of the elevator. There were no buttons to push to call the elevator. No visual keycard reader either. I didn't even see a motion sensor.

Closing the portal, I frowned and hummed in thought. I didn't like the idea of opening a keyhole portal on the other side of that door without knowing where the elevator was. I had a bad feeling the shaft would be pressurized differently from the rest of the fortress to allow for it to travel faster. That didn't change the fact that I would need to check.

Mentally bracing myself, I waited for a gap in my Spatial Awareness and activated Time Compression. Once again, the world crawled by. I opened the small portal, orienting it upwards, hoping I would be able to get at least a brief glimpse.

Blackness and a very powerful vacuum froze the air in my room as it whistled through the small Portal. I quickly cut off the Portal and let go of my Time Compression. I decided to give my Abilities at least a little time to recharge after glancing at the black and gold bars that indicated my energy levels. I was stalling opening another portal into the darkness. Unfortunately, I still needed to see where the elevator was. And more importantly, I needed to see the inside of it.

I vaguely remember seeing flashlights in the storage closet I first hid inside of. Unfortunately, that would require a lot of teleporting through the airducts. Not that I had much of a choice in the matter. It was what I needed to do.

Once I acquired the flashlight and seeing as the supply closet was actually closer to the throne room, I sat down and opened a new portal. This time with the flashlight directed at it. Again, I felt the freezing of the air in the room as it was escaping into the vacuum of the elevator shaft. However, this time I was able to see the bottom of the elevator about fifty feet above the portal.

I quickly cut off the portal and opened a new one, this time inside the elevator car. Just like the door to the shaft, the elevator car had no visual buttons or access panels. There was nothing I could see.

Closing the portal again, I frowned more deeply. There must be a way up there. And it seemed that only Terminus knew what it was. That would mean watching her. A lot.

After determining I wouldn't be able to access the elevator with my portals, I moved on to watching Terminus. I peeked in on her every few minutes, just waiting for her to move. To do something. But she just sat on her throne, unmoving. My Spatial Awareness was always active if weakened by her Negation Ability. I kept trying to figure out what Terminus was doing. She never ate. Never slept. Eventually, I figured out she was cultivating, but I couldn't understand what exactly she was doing.

It almost felt like she was destroying her own Nanos as she drew more in . . . or she was feeding the new Nanos to her old Nanos . . . then it hit me. She was consuming the Nanos in the atmosphere to sustain herself. Or that's what I thought she was doing. I couldn't exactly be sure of what she was up to. I would ask Ward or someone else about it later . . . if I escaped.

Still, I watched, hoping she would eventually move or do something.

Finally, something happened. It was late afternoon and I was about to teleport to somewhere with a little more space to get something to eat when the elevator opened with a whisper. Someone came out of the elevator. I immediately teleported back into the airducts and then through them until I got to the vent that hung high above the throne room. It wasn't the best view, but I could see the newcomer and more importantly, I could see directly into the elevator.

The man who exited the elevator wore a butler's uniform. His hair was combed crisply, and his face was completely clean shaven. He bowed low remaining silent.

Eyes remaining shut, Terminus irritably snapped, "What do you want?"

The butler straightened and said, "Madam, they believe they are done."

Terminus's eyes snapped open, a cruel smile on her lips. Her impatience was obvious when she demanded, "Have they tested it yet?"

"No, madam, they asked for a test subject," the butler replied.

"Test it on one of them," Terminus snapped back.

The butler cleared his throat then replied, "If madam recalls, your previous instructions included the direction that we were not to test the device on the engineers as they are necessary to ensuring proper functionality. As such, I believe it might be best if we refrain from testing it on them until we are sure it will work."

Terminus frowned, eventually saying, "Fine, fine, test it on one of the guards. They are easily replaced."

"If madam wishes it," the butler bowed again and turned back to the closed elevator doors. He then pulled something from his pocket. It looked like a remote control. He lifted it toward the closed elevator door and a moment later, the doors slid silently open.

This was it. This was my chance. But I needed to time it just right.

The butler entered and turned to face the entrance. There was just enough space behind him. I waited until the door had nearly closed, then I activated my Time Compression once again. There was maybe a gap of a centimeter, maybe less and it was still closing even with time being slowed down. I teleported, appearing silently behind the butler. Time Compression cut and the doors closed with him none the wiser.

I didn't dare breathe or move. I needed at least a few seconds to be able to get a short burst of Time Compression.

As the elevator moved up, I almost gasped when my Spatial Awareness felt something . . . unexpected. The Negation field suddenly came to an end, and I was free. With barely a thought, the butler was unconscious after a well place Void Burst did its job to perfection. I considered trying to grab what Nanos I could from him, but I had other priorities and I didn't know how long I would have before someone sounded the alarm.

I quickly went through the butler's pockets for the remote to the elevator. Once it was in hand, I examined it closely. There were three unmarked buttons and no clear indication which was the top and which was the bottom, but it didn't matter because at the moment, only the one in the middle was lit up green.

I wasn't sure how long it would take the elevator to reach its destination, so I figured I really shouldn't let the Nanos go to waste. Naturally, that was when the elevator door slid open, revealing a single guard who looked rather surprised to see the unconscious butler and me. As soon as the barrel of his rifle began to raise, I hit him with a Void Burst from behind, slamming him into the wall. He was unconscious before he hit the ground.

I knew immediately that I used too much power and quickly rushed to check on him. He was still breathing which was good. I then checked the back of his head and neck, looking for fractures that should have been there after such an impact. Thankfully, I didn't detect anything, either with my hands or my Spatial Awareness.

Then he groaned as if he was already waking up. I wanted to curse at my own stupidity. It was easy to forget that this was a world where people had superpowers. If this guard was already waking up, then he probably had increased physical resistance of at least Above Average, maybe even Below Good. I quickly hit him again with my weakest Void Burst right next to his temple. This time when I checked him over, I was confident he was unconscious and would remain that way for quite a while. I did feel a little bad about the concussion I just gave him.

Finally, I looked left and right, down each side of the curving hallway. There was no sign anyone heard or saw me. I didn't see anything immediately to either side and it didn't seem like my very quick scuffle was noticed.

I was strongly tempted to grab the Nanos I could from the two unconscious men, but once again, I wasn't in any kind of position to be able to relax. I needed to take advantage of the freedom afforded to me before Terminus found out what I was up to. That is if she didn't already have some idea. I shook the thought away. No, if she knew I was up here, she would have extended that field of hers to cover the area. I hoped she assumed I wouldn't be able to get up here. And given she had no idea about my other abilities, that wasn't hard to believe. Still, it would only take one radio call or whatever the equivalent was to let her know I was up here.

I quickly started opening and closing keyhole portals, exploring the floor I was on. It didn't take long to figure out I was on the lab floor. Their appeared to be five labs in total. I needed to get into the largest of them, which was located on the other side of the elevator, the entrance located at the opposite side of the circular hallway. It was also the most well-guarded. Two men stood at every door between the labs and me. That meant there were four doors on the exterior walls that I would need to clear before I got to the door I actually needed. That made ten guards in the hallway and two more inside the lab that I could see with my keyhole portals. I also imagined they were all going to be as tough or tougher than the first guard. I also assumed I was going to be under a time constraint.

"Five doors, ten guards, half to the left, half to the right, and two more inside," I mumbled to myself. It was strange to hear my voice after so many days of silence. So many days of being afraid to speak for fear of being caught.

It was time to free those people. Then I could figure out how to escape.

28

First things first. I needed to disable the fortresses lockdown and destroy the security terminal in the bridge. Hopefully, I was close enough to do it. Which gave me something else to consider. I still hadn't figured out how to press the big red button in the command center that would disable the lockdown without risking a lost finger. And even if I did break the system, I still needed to figure out how to get the scientists through Terminus's negation field and into the hangar.

Then I had an idea. I looked down at the unconscious guard, or more specifically, his rifle. Its barrel should do the trick. I grinned, it was still very risky, but I had nothing to lose at this point . . . other than my life . . . or the lives of the engineers . . . I needed to stop thinking about these things.

I activated my Time Compression and opened a small Portal just above the lockdown button, it wasn't much bigger than the barrel of the rifle. Or I tried to. It opened and fizzled immediately. Apparently, while the negation wave couldn't reach me up here, it was still able to reach the other end of the Portal to disrupt it. And worse, I couldn't quite time the gaps in the negation wave from here. I ended up opening almost a dozen portals trying to guess at the gap. The eleventh portal held, and I jammed the rifle through, hoping my enhanced speed would be enough.

As soon as the barrel of the rifle cut off, I knew I was out of time.

The loudspeaker boomed, **"Lockdown rescinded!"** It worked. The barrel of the rifle depressed the button before it was cutoff.

I activated my Time Compression one more time. I opened a portal just behind the security terminal and formed the fastest Void Burst I could in the short time gap before the portal fizzled out. But it didn't matter, it would still go off.

I opened another portal to see if I did enough damage. I might have overdone it. The terminal was scrapped as were the terminals to either side of it. And the man that had been working the terminal didn't look like he was in good condition.

The loudspeaker crackled to life again a moment later, **"Cloaking disabled! Security protocols disabled!"**

Okay, that was a happy accident. Unfortunately, Terminus would definitely know something was up now.

The time for being careful was over. It was time to act. I ran left down the hallway. I hit the first pair of guards, detonating multiple small Void Bursts next to them until they fell unconscious. I kept running, keeping one eye on the black energy bar that was steadily falling and not getting the chance to refill. I repeated the process, taking out eight more guards, until I was back to the elevator where I started at. Yes, I ran past the door I needed but it was better to eliminate the guards first, then worry about rescuing the engineers. This also gave me a few minutes to recharge. The black energy bar was almost completely depleted. Still, I couldn't wait too long, so as soon as I had about a quarter of my bar refilled, I moved on to the last door.

With the security protocols disabled, the door opened with ease.

As soon as I entered the lab, I saw the six engineers were huddled together in fear. A pair of nervous looking guards were threatening them with rifles. A pair of small Void Bursts near each guard's heads and they were down for the count.

"Alright folks, time to go," I said. I was tempted to give them a classic movie line but knew it was pointless as none of them would even get it.

One of the engineers collected himself and spoke, "And who are you?" The older man was malnourished and looked extremely weak. His hair was a dull brown with the occasional grey hair mixed in.

That was a fair question. None of my planning with the heroes ever accounted for me attempting a rescue or theft of the power amplifier in question. And call it a hunch, but I didn't think introducing myself as Dr. Portal would go over well. "I'm . . . the Physician. I'm here to rescue you, now let's go before Terminus figures out what I'm doing."

The same engineer asked, "Go where?"

"Away from here," I said.

Then the man asked, "And how do we do that?"

"I . . . haven't quite figured that part out yet. But there must be another way out of here," I said.

The woman I saw on the monitor, the weakest of them spoke up, "Then we'll all die here." She was a petite woman with dark brown, almost black hair, like her counterpart, there were a few strands of grey mixed in. As a doctor, I wanted to start diagnosing everything that was wrong just from looking at her poor state, but this was neither the time nor the place.

"Maybe we will, but I don't intend to die without a fight," the man that first spoke said, looking with hard eyes at the device that was suspended in midair above the workbench, held in place within an energy field of some kind.

The power amplifier looked just like the one I saw on Dr. Portal. It was a sleek tube, maybe a foot and a half long. It had softly glowing blue indicator lights but nothing that told me anything about how it worked. No buttons or switches, just . . . nothing.

I couldn't let him use the power amplifier, especially if it might kill him. It wouldn't end well for anyone. I did the only thing I could think to do. I surrounded the floating device with dozens of small Void Bursts and collapsed them all at once. The machine was shredded, pulled apart so violently that I was forced to open several small portals to divert the shrapnel.

"No," the man said, dropping to his knees. "That . . . that was our only hope."

"Nonsense," I said, trying to think of what to do next. I had a feeling that going down would be a bad idea. But going up was no guarantee we would be able to escape either. "Does anyone know how this remote works? I mean, how do I get the elevator to go up?"

The weak woman I saw in the monitors, the one I thought didn't have long to live, stepped forward and said, "Up? Let me see it?"

I handed the remote to her, placing it in her shaking hands. Her eyes glowed briefly then she tapped on one of the buttons. It was the one at the bottom as I was holding it. "This one," she said.

"Great, thank you," I said. "Sorry, I didn't catch your name."

"Sam, Samantha Greer," she said.

"Okay, Sam, let's go," I said, leading the way back to the elevator. I was hoping that guard reinforcements weren't already on their way. As we moved, I quickly learned the names of the engineers, the only one I really took note of was Nick, the man that wanted to use the device.

Thankfully, the elevator was empty, and the ride up went without a hitch, even if it was a tight fit with the six engineers and me. As soon as everyone was out of the elevator, I created the largest Void Burst I could and closed the doors and sent the elevator all the way down. A few seconds later there was a very loud boom as my control of the Void Burst was suddenly cutoff, which was followed by the elevator tube crumpling inward with sudden force.

"And now we're trapped up here," Nick said, he was the man that first spoke to me.

"No, now they are trapped down there," I said, looking around for a way out. I seemed to be in a bedroom, a very large bedroom with expansive windows that looked out over the uncloaked fortress. This was a tower, a spire of some sort. Terminus really did think of herself as a queen.

Thinking of Terminus brought me back to worrying about her extending her negation field up here now that she knew where I was, but nothing happened. Even after a few minutes, she did nothing. I needed information. I opened a small portal in her throne room, hoping I would catch a glimpse.

It was utter devastation. When my Void Burst collapsed, the resulting implosion was much worse than it should have been. It didn't take me long to see the elevator shaft was crumpled like an empty soda can, except for a large torn out section near the ceiling of the throne room. That was the spot where the connection to my Void Burst was most likely severed. What I didn't account for was the vacuum already inside the tube, suddenly empowered by my Void Burst weakening the integrity of the structure, such that it magnified the collapse and causing it to implode inward like a giant Void Burst. The implosion tore through the throne room, obliterating the throne and tearing up the walls and floor.

Terminus appeared to have been flung into the collapsed elevator with such force that there was an impact crater above the elevator door where she hit. The woman was laying on the floor, partly covered in rubble. She had scrapes and cuts and hopefully a few broken bones, but she was still breathing. And I now understood why she didn't extend her negation field. She was blissfully unconscious. Unfortunately, I also knew I couldn't count on it to last very long.

"Okay, we need to go quickly," I said, looking up as I closed the keyhole portal. I opened a much larger portal to one of the hangars that I found while conducting my search of the fortress. The important thing about this specific hangar was that it contained a pair of larger flying vans. "Hurry through before she wakes up and cuts off my power again."

The engineers looked at me dumbfounded but it didn't last long as Sam shambled through the portal without questioning me. The others quickly followed suit until I joined them, closing my portal behind me.

I tried to open the door of one of the vans, but it didn't budge.

"You need one of the security cards," Sam said helpfully.

I grinned. Hopefully, the card I stole a few days ago was still active. I touched the card to the door handle and the familiar sound of automatic locks disengaging followed.

"Now, does anyone know how to drive one of these things?" I asked, opening the door for everyone to enter.

Nick volunteered.

"Get us in the air," I said, taking the seat next to him.

"What about the doors? They're still closed," Nick said.

"I'm going to make us a door," I answered.

Nick nodded and started the engine, lifting us into the air a moment later.

Then it was my turn again. I opened the largest portal I could. I just hoped it was large enough to fit the van through. Not that Nick had any control over that. As soon as I opened the port, the hangar depressurized, and we were almost instantly sucked through the portal and spat out just outside the flying fortress.

"I can't believe that worked," Nick said.

My eyes were looking out the back window where the now visible flying fortress could easily be seen. The entire structure was painted white with large splotches of rust infesting the surface. I also noted that it had guns. Some of which were starting to move in our direction.

"Drive!" I shouted urgently, already mentally preparing to start opening portals behind us if the fortress started firing on us.

Nick didn't hesitate. The vehicle suddenly jerked forward, and I sank back into the passenger seat.

"Anyone know if this thing has a cloaking device like the cars?" I asked, opening my first portal behind us as the first shot was fired. I redirected the shot back at the cannon that fired on us, feeling satisfied when there was a small explosion from the weapon emplacement.

"Sam, get up here and help me look," Nick shouted urgently. "Physician, just do what you can to keep us from getting shot out of the sky."

I didn't need to be told twice. I gave up my seat to Sam, doing my best to slip past her without knocking her over. I might have teleported if energy wasn't a concern, my energy bar well below the half mark. I had a feeling I was going to need every last drop of energy I could muster and more if we didn't get out of range of the fortress fast.

Two more of the big guns fired at the same time. I repaid them with redirected shots, taking out two more weapon emplacements. But the size of the weapons being fired were significant. I wouldn't be able to redirect many more shots.

"How's it going up there?" I yelled.

"Slow," Nick shouted back.

Another shot and another redirection. "Please hurry, I can't redirect many more of these shots."

"We are hurrying," Nick shouted back.

Three shots and three redirections at the same time and the black energy bar was almost completely drained, no more than a sliver remained. "That's it, I'm out."

"Hold on," Nick shouted, suddenly diving the van toward the ground. And it was just in time, six shots went off at once, all of them missing thanks to the sudden dive.

"Got it," Sam said.

Nick suddenly leveled out the van and I fell to the floor rather painfully.

"I can't believe that actually worked," Nick said, his shock evident in his voice.

"Straight to New Haven and the Hero Association, if you please," I said, still laying on the floor of the van and completely unwilling to move. Everything ached. I was pretty sure I overused my ability and was now suffering the Nana-feedback Ward warned me about.

We were free. I actually managed to escape. I stopped Terminus's plans, rescued the kidnapped engineers, and I wasn't even a hero, just a civilian. Not bad Davis Malory. Not bad at all.

29

The flight back to the city was easy. The flying van cruised above the wilds and was never attacked by any of the beasts. Given the size of some of the birds that we occasionally saw as we flew over, I hoped the invisibility cloak, or whatever it was, that kept us out of sight would keep us alive. I truly believe it was the main reason we made it back alive.

When we landed at the Hero Association New Haven Fortress City branch, things got a bit messier. First, I needed to convince the hero on duty that I wasn't Dr. Portal. Then I needed to convince the hero's supervisor, another hero, that I wasn't Dr. Portal and that I was on a mission from Major Miracle himself. Unfortunately, I, along with the engineers, were all taken into custody. Me as a villain and them as my victims. And despite the engineers all vouching for me, the hero still didn't believe me, stating I could have hypnotized them. After that, I really did not appreciate being associated with Dr. Portal. It might have been fine for the mission, but the mission was over.

They held me for three days. I was interrogated multiple times by heroes I had never met. Heroes who also refused to reach out to any of the heroes I knew. And when I asked them why they wouldn't reach out, the only response I got was that they were all away on a mission. My guess was that mission was an attempt to rescue me. Joke's on them.

When they did return, it didn't take long before Major Miracle, Para-Hypno, Private Eye Light, Blue Ward, Mental Star, and Hammer Jack all found me locked in an Ability proof cell. Was it so wrong that I enjoyed the look of absolute disbelief on Para's face when he saw me sitting there looking bored? Or Hammer Jack's for that matter?

After that, I finally got the chance to debrief. I made sure to complain about the hero that arrested me, but it wasn't like there was much I could do about it. Major Miracle did gently chide Para for not setting up some kind of emergency passphrase.

"And then you came here?" Major Miracle asked after I told the story for the second time.

"Yes," I answered. "And then I came here. I came with the kidnapped engineers who should be around here somewhere, unless the idiot hero that arrested me sent them all home."

"I'll go look for them," Ward volunteered.

"Make sure they got proper medical care," I said before he left the room. "They were all malnourished and probably dehydrated."

Ward clearly didn't understand what I just said and yet he nodded anyway and went on his way.

"Don't worry, I'm sure our healers did good work," Major Miracle tried to reassure me. "But back to the matter at hand. Terminus, he died and left his mantle to his daughter?"

"That's what she claimed," I said. "Her Ability was similar to what you described. She didn't exactly give me a DNA test to prove it, but I had no reason to doubt her. And Terminus had no reason to lie if she was planning to kill me anyway. It's like Para said, villains really do love to monologue. She was no exception."

"It sounds to me like you did one hell of a job," Hammer said, slapping me on the back with far too much strength.

"Thanks," I groaned out in response. "But what's next? I can't imagine she's just going to let me go after that. Especially after I destroyed her power amplification device."

"No, I doubt she will let it go," Major Miracle said. "But that is a worry for tomorrow. Today, we celebrate your resounding success."

"If possible, I would like to check in on the engineers," I requested. I felt responsible for them. I wanted to know they were okay. That they were going to be okay.

"Of course," Major Miracle replied. "Occasionally, I will check in on the first man I ever saved. A lot of heroes do the same kind of thing, at least, the good ones do."

But I wasn't a hero . . . I mean, I might have saved those people like a hero, but I was not a hero. I was a doctor, the kind that helped to heal people. I was also leaving this place as soon as the heroes figured out how to send me home.

Major Miracle clapped me on the back, then asked, "I'll arrange something for first thing tomorrow morning, does that sound acceptable?"

"Yeah," I said, "That sounds fi-"

My sentence was cut off as an air raid siren suddenly filled the building.

Major Miracle's good humor and mood vanished almost instantly. He ran out of the room, followed quickly by Hammer Jack, Para-Hypno, and Mental Star, leaving just Light and me.

"What's going on?" I asked, hoping Light could tell me.

"It means the city is under attack," Light replied.

"Under attack?" I yelped. "What do you mean under attack? I thought this was supposed to be a Fortress City. Doesn't that mean it's highly defensible?"

"Don't panic. It's probably just a beast horde migration," Light said, trying and failing to reassure me.

"And if it's not?" I asked, feeling a pit form in my stomach as I had my own suspicions.

"It could be war with another nation," Light said.

That gave me something new to worry about. I asked, "Does that happen?"

Light grimaced. Again, the man was completely lacking a poker face. Still, he answered, "Not really."

I gave him a flat look.

"Or . . . it could be Terminus," Light finally relented, stating what I suspected to be the case.

"Okay, so what do we do?" I asked.

"We do nothing. You've already done more than enough to help," Light said. "For now, stay here, stay safe. We'll take care of the rest."

Somehow, that did nothing to reassure me. "And what about you?" I asked.

"I'm here to protect you," Light replied.

"And how much protection do you think you'll be against an 88th Milestone villain who seems to be capable of blocking powers?" I asked.

Again, with the grimace. That was something Light was really going to need to work on in the future. "I was ordered to protect you, so that is what I'm going to do."

"And who ordered that?" I asked, then added, "And when did they give the order?"

"It's a standing order," Light replied.

I was about to reply when I felt the building shake. "What was that?"

"An impact tremor," Light said.

"That seemed awfully close," I said. I was starting to feel claustrophobic again. I didn't like the idea of having a building crash down on me, trapping me.

"It was miles away," Light said, putting a hand on my shoulder in an effort to calm me down.

Another impact tremor followed his statement, this time it felt much closer. I asked, "Still miles away?"

Light grimaced.

"Stop with the damned grimacing all the time. You want to be a hero and reassure me then you can start by not doing that," I snapped. I took a few calming breaths, which were interrupted by another impact tremor, this one shaking the lights above me. I took a few more. "How close?"

"Too close," Light said, finally looking worried.

"Where can we go?" I asked.

"This is the safest building in town," Light said.

"Until Terminus's flying fortress hammers it into the ground," I said, feeling panic start to creep in.

Another impact tremor hit. This time drywall dust fell from the ceiling followed by a long crack running along the wall and across the ceiling.

"Okay, maybe we should relocate," Light finally said.

I agreed with him whole heartedly. "What are we waiting for?"

"Follow me," Light said, moving to the door and out into the hall.

I was right on his heels.

We ran down the hall and then down a flight of stairs. I wanted very badly to ask him about going deeper into the subbasements, but he was moving too fast.

Ward's familiar voice called from up ahead of us, "Light, what are you doing?"

"Moving Davis somewhere safer," Light answered. "What are you doing with those people?"

The engineers I rescued were cowering behind Ward, looking frightened but significantly healthier than when I last saw them.

"The same thing you are," Ward replied as another impact shook the building above us, which was quickly followed by a second and a third impact tremor. The last of which caused part of the hallway behind us to collapse.

"We need to get out of here," Nick said. The engineer wasn't nearly as gaunt as he was a few days ago but he was still thin. At least he had a healthy pallor to his skin, and he was now clean shaven.

"We're moving you all someplace safe," Ward said, attempting to reassure them.

"You don't understand," Nick protested. "She isn't going to stop until she gets us back or she kills us. You need to get us away from here. As far away as you can."

"I'm sorry citizen, but I cannot safely move you to another location at this time. I assure you that you are perfectly safe within the confines of the Hero Association Headquarters," Ward said, his voice taking on that tone I had come to think of as 'Hero-Speak'.

It surprised me when it actually worked to a small extent. The six engineers calmed slightly. Only for five consecutive impact tremors to hit the building at once. I could even see Light and Ward were starting to panic.

"You need to get us away," Nick pleaded this time.

Ward took a moment to master his expression before he spoke, but I could still tell even he was unsure of what to do. "There are safe bunkers further down. You'll be safe there until the heroes have resolved the situation."

Nick didn't believe him. Then he spotted me. "You, you're the Physician, right. You can make a portal. You can get us out of here, right?"

Ward and Light looked at me slightly confused. I had completely forgotten that I had given them that name. "I . . . I-" I didn't know how to answer.

"You can at least get us to the next building over, right?" Nick asked. "Maybe even two or three buildings over."

I looked to Ward and Light for help but neither of them seemed to know what to do.

"What about the van?" Sam asked. I was glad to see the woman was in much better health. "We can use the van's invisibility mode and fly far away. You can get us there, right?"

Now that was an idea. I just hoped the van hadn't been moved or towed away by that incompetent hero that arrested me. Still, I looked again to Ward and Light for confirmation. Light grimaced again, looking even more unsure about what to do than I was. But Ward . . . Ward looked conflicted only for a moment before slowly nodding.

I closed my eyes and pictured the flying invisible van. I pictured the inside of the van. The spacious compartment inside. With a mental command, I opened a portal. I peeked through one eye first to check the portal and to my relief, the other side was indeed just inside the van.

"Alright, everyone through," I said, stepping aside and waving everyone in, including Ward and Light. When they were all through, I joined them on the other side, closing my portal behind me.

The van looked to have been untouched and unmoved, though only by sheer luck if the outside was any indication. As the van began moving, I got a good look outside. There were craters pockmarking the streets all around the Hero Association. There were bodies lying unmoving in the street. Worse, there were moving bodies, many of which were injured, some probably dying. Part of my training to become a doctor involved crisis work. Emergency room rotations and the like. Part of me demanded I go out there and start triaging the wounded. Doing everything I could to help. Another part of me was terrified that I might end up just like them. Then I saw a crying child, she was trying to drag her unconscious mother or sister and I knew I needed to help.

I made my choice and I was about to teleport when there was a cry of frustration from the driver seat. The van was moving but it appeared Ward had no control over it.

"Can any of you engineers disable this autopilot?" Ward yelled into the van, finally sounding panicked.

Sam and Nick both rushed forward.

"Where are we going?" Light asked.

"Up there," Ward said, pointing to the flying fortress that was still bombarding the Hero Association and its surrounding buildings.

"That's bad, right?" I asked, forgetting about the people on the ground. I could still go but that would mean abandoning the engineers.

"It's certainly not good," Ward said.

"Okay, I'm opening another portal," I said. I finally had good line of sight down a street. It looked untouched at the distance I was capable of opening a portal. "Everybody, move through, quickly," I said.

Four of the engineers went through followed by Ward and Light, but Nick and Sam were still in the driver seat and passenger seat.

"Come on you two, let's go," I said, watching with worry as we got closer to the fortress.

Nick didn't wait another second. He almost ran from his seat toward the Portal. Only for the Portal to fizzle out before he could cross the threshold.

"No," Nick's panicked voice said. "No, no, no, no, no, no, no," he kept repeating to himself as a full-blown panic attack settled in. I wished I had a sedative I could give him. Sadly, I had bigger fish to fry as Terminus's flying fortress loomed ahead of us, the hangar door waiting to swallow us whole.

30

The hangar doors closed with a sense of finality. And while I may have escaped once, I honestly wasn't sure I could do it again.

The loudspeaker boomed once again, **"Beginning Pressurization!"**

I waited, knowing it wouldn't be long until the process completed.

"Pressurization Complete!"

I looked outside the van, specifically at the doors. I was afraid guards were going to storm in by the dozens. Unfortunately, what happened might have been worse. Kidnap, And, and Ransom entered.

Kidnap yelled, "The boss wants to kill you herself, Dr. Portal. If you really are Dr. Portal. Personally, I wouldn't mind killing you myself after what you did to Ransom's nose."

I know it was inappropriate, but I couldn't help but celebrate a little, saying, "Ha, I was right, the big one is Ransom."

"Do you really think now is the time for this?" Sam suddenly asked from right next to me. I completely missed her moving to look out the window with me.

"Probably not," I replied. It might have been a little flippant on my part, but when you're staring death in the face, one of the first things I seemed to lose were my inhibitions.

Kidnap seemed to be getting impatient as he yelled, "If you don't want to come out on your own, we can come in after you."

"To hell with it," I mumbled. "You two stay here."

"What are you going to do?" Sam asked.

"I'm going to deal with them," I said.

"But the negation field," Sam protested.

I cocked an eyebrow and gave her my best lopsided heroic grin. I winked at her then vanished. I used Teleport to move near the door that led into the fortress, thus putting myself behind the trio. With my Time Compression still active, I created three Void Bursts just in front of each member of the trio.

I dropped my Time Compression in an effort to conserve some of it, I would need it if this didn't stop them. Instantly, all three voids bursts at once. The trio were suddenly and violently torn off their feet. Propelled forward by the sudden suction of the voids collapsing, the trio flew through the air and bounced off the side of the van, cracking a pair of the windows in the process.

"Ooh, that must hurt," I said confidently, believing all three were down for the count. I would have put money on it that all three were down between the concussive force of the Void Bursts and the impact with the van. I would have lost that bet.

All three were definitely hurt, but they still climbed back to their feet.

Ransom put a hand on the van as he did and shoved, sending the van skidding across the hanger. It told me he was strong and that his strength was probably Ability related if he could move the van so easily. On the bright side, his nose was bleeding again, which suggested he didn't have a lot of physical resistance. On the other hand, he was able to get back up again. So . . . maybe he did have a high physical resistance and I was hitting him just hard enough? As a doctor, I knew there were places I could hit them to do the maximum amount of damage. Unfortunately, it would require the perfect shot and probably more power than I was comfortable using against another human being, superpowered or not.

Kidnap was the slowest of the trio to stand. It looked like his shoulder was dislocated and his arm was bent the wrong direction. I knew he must have been in tremendous pain. I could hardly believe he was standing with such injuries. And then with a few sickening snaps and pops, the damage reversed. Kidnap seemed to have the ability to heal. Painfully heal, but still heal. That or his Body Recovery to Physical Injury was through the roof.

And then there was And. And was the one that disturbed me the most. He was almost folded in half from the combination of impacts, and yet he didn't appear to be broken, just . . . bent. When he sprung back up to his feet looking completely uninjured, I wondered if he had healing like Kidnap did. Then he punched at me from across the hangar, his arm extending like rubber. Only my Speed saved me, and even then, I just barely dodged as his fist grazed my cheek.

It also made me very aware that none of the Abilities these three used were blocked, whereas my ability needed to be used between the waves of Terminus's negation field. It told me that either Terminus really did have that much control or that these three had some piece of tech that preserved their abilities.

"It was only a request, she didn't say we were *required* to take you alive," Kidnap said, cracking his knuckles, an action mimicked by Ransom.

And leaped at me, his rubbery legs propelling him at me faster than I thought possible. I activated my Time Compression just before he reached me. I used my Teleport to cross the hanger then created a few Void Bursts where I had been just a moment before.

As time resumed, the voids collapsed, pulling the rubberized villain in multiple directions but doing nothing to really injure him. Though I did take note that he wasn't snapping back to form as quickly. Then I remember one of the important lessons that had been drilled into me by Hammer, Light, and Ward during training. Everyone had a finite amount of energy to use their Abilities. Once someone used it up, they would have no choice but to rely on their Body enhancements. And villains . . . villains had a bad habit of being one trick ponies, going all Body or all Ability. Not that I was much better, but it still gave me hope, especially when I looked at my own energy bars. They were just over half full.

My distraction from watching And to see how long it took for him to return to his normal form almost cost me everything as Ransom and Kidnap moved suddenly enough to get on either side of me. I barely got Time Compression activated fast enough to Teleport away again, leaving behind a Void Burst in the space I just occupied.

The void collapsed and the pair suddenly and violently collided with each other. Ransom's elbow collided with Kidnap's head and his neck twisted with a sickening crack. With his healing ability, I wasn't sure if it would keep him down. Not that I had time to worry about it as And was back after me again.

I ducked one punch but didn't sense the punch coming from behind me until I was punched in my kidneys. I felt pain shoot through my gut, burning my insides. I felt like I couldn't move. I couldn't breathe for fear of the pain it would induce if I did.

Reflexively, I activated my Time Compression, which in hindsight might have been a bad idea while I was in so much pain as the slowed down time seemed to magnify the feeling. I felt every second of it. Still, I needed to act before And's head impacted with my face. I wanted to Teleport but at some point, And grabbed my shoulder. If I teleported, there was a chance he would just come with me. Instead, I created a Void Burst just behind his head.

The Void Burst went off and And was suddenly whipped back the way he came, and lucky for me his grip on my shoulder slipped free. I took the opportunity to Teleport to give myself a little breathing room, which I would need. My golden energy bar was almost depleted, and the black energy bar wasn't much better.

"That . . . hurt!" Kidnap yelled angrily as he climbed back to his feet.

"Oh, you've got to be kidding me," I complained. Okay, maybe I wasn't going to be able to beat them. Maybe I did overestimate myself. Given their seemingly indestructible nature, I was starting to get the picture that I was outgunned. That, and I had low energy bars that were beginning to wane from continued use every time I needed to Teleport or use a Void Burst. "What the hell are you three made of?"

"Power," Kidnap answered. "And you are lacking enough power to really do us any harm."

I looked around the hangar, desperate for a solution when I saw the large hangar doors. Sometimes, I was too smart for my own good. If they wanted to see my power, then I supposed I would need to oblige. I may have grinned a little as I teleported back into the van.

"It doesn't seem to be going well," Sam commented as soon as I appeared.

"It's not," I confirmed. "But I just realized something. I've been thinking about things like a doctor. I need to think more like a hero with too much power and not enough commonsense."

I moved to look out the other side of the van. Specifically, at the hangar doors. The hangar doors which did not have the lockdown doors engaged. I waited for the next gap in the negation field and slowed time. With the little bit of time I had, I opened the largest Void Burst I could right next to the hangar doors and let it rip.

I should have warned Sam and Nick to buckle up. Heck, I should have buckled up myself. The hangar door burst inward with a gaping hole only to get sucked right back out again from the sudden change in pressure. Pressure that sucked the trio straight out into the open air. Unfortunately, the pressure was also enough that the van got sucked toward the hole as well. Thankfully, the van hit the hole on its broadside, thus preventing it from being sucked out with the villains, which actually wouldn't have been the worst thing in the world. Eventually, I would have gotten out of range of the negation field and could have opened a portal or maybe even just teleported us away. Still, because of the sudden tumbling of the van, we got tossed around pretty good. It was sheer luck that the cracked windows didn't shatter.

A moment later the pressure normalized with the outside and the van slid down the hangar wall then rocked onto its side.

"Ow," I groaned. I was definitely hurting, bruised ribs at the very least, and I would no doubt be urinating blood after that hit to the kidneys from And. A quick look at my health bar confirmed I was hurt. Still, I was alive, which was more than I could say for the villains . . . who still might have survived that fall given their abilities. With my mind working again, I started a self-assessment. Nothing broken from what I could tell from a cursory examination, my ribs were definitely bruised. Otherwise, I was uninjured.

Once I was sure I was going to be okay, I painfully climbed back to my feet. Nick appeared to be unconscious, but he was breathing. Sam managed to stay conscious, but it looked like her arm was broken.

I rushed to her side. Her arm was fractured and would need to be set, and with the way her lower arm was turning purple, the fracture was cutting off circulation. "Your arm is broken," I started. "I need to set the fracture, or you risk losing your arm."

"What? What are you talking about?" Sam asked, then she looked at her arm and her eyes went wide, and I could see the panic setting in.

"I'm a doctor, let me fix your arm," I said.

"A what?" Sam asked.

I would have groaned if time wasn't of the essence here. "I'm a healer . . . sort of," I said.

"Oh," Sam replied.

"Lie back," I said, helping her to lay on her back. "I won't lie, this is going to hurt."

"Wait, what do you mean sort of?" Sam asked, but it was too late. I was already pulling her arm straight, getting a few pops and grinding sounds from the bones in her arm being forced back into position.

"There, all done," I said, looking around for something to splint her arm with.

The movement of the van had opened several compartments, shifting contents all over. I found something that looked like a wrench, a screwdriver, and duct tape, or this worlds equivalent of duct tape.

"You're insane," Sam shouted at me, fighting back tears of pain.

"Maybe, but your hand and wrist are back to a healthy color already. That means your circulation is back to normal, which means your arm won't die if it takes too long to get you to an Ability healer," I said, bracing the wrench and screwdriver on opposite sides of her arm then duct taping them in place. "It doesn't look pretty, but it should keep the bone immobilized."

With her settled, I moved to check on Nick. He was unconscious but breathing. I gave him a cursory exam, checking his neck and limbs for breaks. He was fine except for a large contusion forming near his temple. More than likely he was concussed.

"Great," Sam said, sarcasm clear in her voice.

"It is," I said, matching her sarcasm with seriousness. "Now to get out of here," I said, looking at the still cracked window. I sat down and started kicking at the window.

"Wait," Sam said urgently.

"What?" I asked, halting my second kick before it could hit.

"What about the pressure, won't we get sucked out?" Sam asked.

"Not with the little bit of pressure in here, we'll be fine," I said, resuming my kicking at the window. When the crack finally broke there was a slight suction but that was it. A few more kicks, and the window was opened.

I crawled out first to get a look around. I didn't recognize the hangar, but then all the hangars pretty much looked the same. Except this one was empty aside from the now upside-down van.

I heard the sound of glass crunching and turned to see Sam trying to crawl out of the van.

"Be careful of the glass," I warned her.

"No, really?" Sam replied sarcastically.

"Sarcasm really isn't helpful," I said.

Sam looked like she had another sarcastic retort prepared when the lockdown doors finally closed over the gap in the original hangar door and the loudspeaker buzzed to life once more.

"Great, now what?" Sam asked.

"Now . . . now I figure out how to get us out of here, preferably alive," I said.

"I won't be much help. This negation field just makes me even more useless," Sam said, starting to cross her arms then wincing as she remembered her broken arm.

"You're not useless," I said. It was such a reflex from my world to say something like that. But if I understood her ability correctly, she could analyze and scan Nanotech. Not exactly useful in this situation, however, she was an engineer. Hopefully, that meant she knew how to work with the machinery of this place. "In fact, you are exactly the person I need."

"Oh yeah, and why is that?" Sam asked.

"You're an engineer. You understand all this Nanotech, right?" I asked, waving to the area around us.

Sam nodded, then said, "Yeah, what about it?"

"That means you know how to stop those weapons, right?" I asked.

"In theory," Sam answered.

"Good, then you're going to help me stop those weapons," I said.

"And then what?" Sam asked.

"I'll let you know once I've figured that out," I said. If I was stuck miles above the city in a flying fortress surrounded by hostile enemies, then I might as well make the best of a really bad situation.

31

I released the smallest Void Burst I could through the keyhole portal. The tiny implosion crumpled the nano-control box with ease, unleashing sparks of electricity before that also fizzled out as my portal closed. I opened a new keyhole portal a moment later when the next gap appeared. I watched for a second as the generically uniformed soldiers began moving around frantically when the weapon they had just been firing suddenly cut out.

From what Sam had told me, these nano-control boxes were vitally important to the function of the weapons. They were also extremely difficult to install, taking hours to remove the one I just destroyed and hours more to replace it due to the sensitivity of the Nanos that ran the machines.

With my job in this control room done, I began teleporting back through the fortress until I returned to the supply closet Sam and I chose to hide in.

After everything in the hangar, we both figured it would be a good idea to relocate, even carrying Nick with us. Thankfully, the halls seemed to be vacant and no alarms sounded as we passed by a security camera, or viewer as Sam called it. It suggested that the security station on the bridge I had destroyed during my previous escape had not been replaced. This was also probably why no one had come busting down the door of the supply closet Sam and I used as our temporary base of operations.

When I appeared back in the closet, Sam spoke, "That should be thirty-two down."

"How many more do we need to take out?" I asked.

"A few hundred more," Sam replied. "But that should have taken out the forward battery, which is something. Unfortunately, they will rotate the fortress and resume firing soon enough, if they haven't done that already."

"We just needed to open a gap for the heroes to approach," I said, reminding her of the plan. "Speaking of, are there any more on that approach we need to take out?"

Sam frowned at me, then shook her head. "That should clear a few degrees of approach where the overlapping fire won't be able to hit. It will still be dangerous, but you've at least opened a path," she said, then added, "Assuming the heroes are smart enough to see it and use it."

I really hoped they were. Unfortunately, I couldn't count on it. "Okay, let's assume the heroes don't figure it out. Is it enough for us to escape?"

Sam shook her head. "I would need to get into the hangar and start reprograming one of the vehicles, so we didn't get caught in another one of those autopilot situations as soon as we left. And without my ability, there is just no way." Sam's Ability, as she explained it, was the ability to scan and understand Nanotech. I asked her about non-Nanotech and she just gave me a confused look.

"Okay, other options?" I asked, hoping she had some ideas.

Sam hesitated for a moment before reluctantly saying, "We could crash the fortress."

I gave her the flattest stare I could muster.

"No, really," Sam said. "We could orchestrate a controlled crash. If the fortress isn't too far over the city and if we strategically disable about two dozen of the engines, we could set it on a glide path to crash outside of New Haven."

I nodded along with her. No matter how strategic she made it sound, she was still talking about crashing a flying fortress that was larger than a few city blocks.

"There is only one problem," Sam continued. "I need to know which way to send the fortress crashing."

"So, I need to find a window," I said.

"I need a window. I might need to send you to destroy a different engine if the pitch or yaw are off even a little. That means I need to see . . . I need to see where we're crashing," Sam explained.

"You want a front row seat for the crash?" I asked, shocked by her request.

"If everything goes right, we'll be long gone by the time the fortress actually crashes," Sam tried to reassure me.

I couldn't exactly argue with her about it. She was the engineer. I was just a doctor whose brain was working through the possible collision injuries. I was well aware, that even if we managed to bring the fortress down gently, we were still planning to crash several hundred thousand tons of metal and other materials onto an uneven surface with innumerable obstacles, many of which would probably be able to tear through the hull of the fortress like a hot knife through butter. The point was, even if I did get us away from the crash side of the fortress, it didn't guarantee anywhere else on board would be any safer during a crash landing.

"Okay, give me a few minutes to find a room with a view," I said, hunkering down against one of the walls of the small storage room. I let my Spatial Awareness find the gaps in Terminus's negation field and activated Time Compression. From there I opened dozens of keyhole-sized portals. I had a general idea of where I needed to go, but I still couldn't just randomly open a portal and hope for the best.

I worked through the vast duct system, moving in one direction until I found a room with a window . . . that was covered from the outside with an armored plate. With a sigh, I tried opening a Void Burst on the other side of the metal plate without being able to see it. It didn't work.

Letting go of my Time Compression, I looked to Sam and said, "The windows are covered by some kind of metal plate."

Sam clicked her tongue and looked down, then grumbled, "Defensive measures. If I had my Ability, I could probably figure out a work around."

Then I had a thought. "What about the gunnery stations? They have a view outside, right?"

Sam looked up and smiled. "They do."

"Will the ones in the stations I destroyed still work?" I asked.

Sam shook her head immediately. "No, with the control panel destroyed, everything in there should be shut down, including the viewers."

"Okay, then I better start looking around for one with the view we need," I said, slipping back into Time Compression. With a goal in mind, I started moving through the ducts again with keyhole portals to watch where I was going.

I opened a keyhole into a gunnery station with a familiar looking guard. It was the same guy I stole the keycard from. Part of me was surprised to see he was still alive. Didn't the villain always kill the henchman that screwed up? Not that it really mattered. This was the one I needed. He was on his own, the view from his terminal was looking at the wilds outside the walls. This was exactly where we needed to go.

The dangerous part now, was getting Sam there safely. I couldn't Teleport with her. I discovered that I wasn't strong enough to Teleport more than myself. I also discovered that trying to do so would cause the attempt to fail and for me to black out from the strain. It was a good thing I didn't try to do that when And had a hold of me in the hangar or I would probably already be dead.

I backtracked through the halls, trying to be very aware of anyone wandering around. But just like when we ran to this storage room, they were eerily vacant.

"Okay, it looks like the halls are still empty. We should go before that changes," I said.

"What about Nick?" Sam asked.

I frowned, then said, "I don't like it, but we'll need to leave him here."

"Let's hope he doesn't wake up," Sam said.

I knelt down next to him and gave him a once over. The bruising on his head worried me a lot. The bruising on the outside wasn't what worried me. If he was that bruised on the outside, I worried just how much he was bruised on the inside. Still, without a CT scan or an MRI I wouldn't be able to tell for sure. For now, at least, I was confident he would remain unconscious for some time.

"Let's go," I said, moving away from Nick and out into the hallway, followed closely by Sam.

We were able to run the same path I saw through my keyhole portals. I wanted to stop at every intersection to check for guards, but time was already against us. And if anyone did come, I could use my Void Burst to knock them out . . . hopefully.

When we reached the door to the gunnery station, I was annoyed to find it locked.

"We need the keycard," Sam said, pointing to the pad outside the door.

With a grumble, I timed it just right and teleported inside the gunnery station.

"I'm so bored," the seated gunner complained. "Why is my cousin such a pain? Oh, I'm the Terminus. Oh, I'm a super villain. Oh, I look really good in a super suit. So what if my keycard was stolen? He did escape from her unescapable fortress and Ability. So why did I get the worst assignment? It's just so unfair."

"I hear you, buddy," I said, startling the gunner. The man swiftly turned around, a look of utter panic on his face.

The man . . . boy really, his voice tinged with worry, asked, "Who are you? How did you get in here?" He couldn't have been more than 18 or 19 years old.

"That's a bit of a long story and I really don't have time for it right now," I said. "So, you have two choices. You can open the door and let my associate in and then go sit quietly in a corner, or, I can knock you out, take your keycard and let my associate in myself. Which do you prefer?"

The guard slumped in his chair. "Awe man, this is so unfair. My cousin might actually kill me this time," he said with a heavy sigh. "I'll open the door, but you really should knock me out afterwards. It is probably the only chance I'll have of keeping Terry from killing me."

"Very sensible choice," I said, patting the young man on the shoulder.

"Names Mitch," the boy said, moving from his station to the door.

"So, Mitch, why become a henchman?" I asked.

"My mom was on me about getting a job. Terry said I could come work for her. I thought it would be pretty awesome working for my cousin. You know, easy street. I had no idea she was so megalomaniacal. It's been a drag. I asked to quit after you stole my keycard . . . that was you, wasn't it?" Mitch readily answered.

I nodded.

"Anyway, she said I could quit after this big event and then she stuck me in here," Mitch explained.

"Say, Mitch, why are the corridors so . . . empty?" I asked.

"Oh, that's due to the battle. Most of the soldiers are in the hangers waiting to be deployed. The rest of us are in these gunnery stations waiting for a chance to blow one of the heroes out of the sky," Mitch explained.

"Really?" I asked.

Mitch shrugged. "What? Most heroes are jerks. They care more about their endorsement deals and looking good on the news than actually saving people . . . you know, being heroes."

"And killing them makes that go away?" I asked.

Mitch shrugged again. "Heroes, villains, they're all the same to me. They both want power, some have it, some don't."

"And the civilians that are being killed by the fortress as we speak? Their lives don't matter?" I asked, starting to feel anger toward this boy's laissez-faire attitude.

"Okay, so, I'm not really cool with that part. But I'm also not the boss, you know what I mean. Besides, it's just New Haven, this little Podunk city is barely a blip on the world radar. Londinium and Wu Shan won't even lift a finger to help, so clearly the heroes don't care that much," Mitch explained.

"Why wouldn't Wu Shan or Londinium come help?" I asked.

Mitch snorted a laugh, then said, "Oh, they hate New Haven. All the other fortress cities do. It's all because of the first Major Miracle and the formation of the first Fortress City. She was a real piece of work, only let certain people in, usually just those with an ability that she found useful. That may be in the past, but a lot of cities can hold a grudge. It doesn't help that New Haven always holds it over all the other fortress cities heads that it was the first, even though those cities are significantly larger and have much higher cultivators. Even my big bad cousin is a little fish in a city like those two."

I was confused. I had only heard of Wu Shan as part of the story Para gave me, but I didn't really get any information from him about it. There was still so much about this world I didn't know or understand, "Your cousin, Terminus . . . erm, Terry, is 88th Milestone. Are you saying that's . . . weak?" I took a second to finally check Mitch's Milestone, a 19 flashed briefly over his head.

"For New Haven, no, that's actually pretty strong for a Tier 1," Mitch said with a shake of his head. Then as if he just realized he was answering my questions like I was an idiot, he asked, "Shouldn't you already know this stuff?"

"My head got messed up a while back," I said. "Lost a lot of information."

"Oh, right, I think I heard about that," Mitch said. "Anyway, anything else you want to know, or can I open the door now?"

I had so many questions. So much about this world that I just didn't know. Still, this was neither the time nor the place. "You're right, we should get this moving along. Go ahead and open the door."

"Right," Mitch said, putting his keycard to the pad next to the door. The door slid aside revealing a very nervous looking Sam.

"What took you so long?" Sam demanded, rushing inside.

"Sorry, Mitch and I were having a serious philosophical discussion regarding the meaning of life, the universe, and everything in it," I said, knowing she wouldn't get the reference, and neither would Mitch for that matter.

"Well, you can do that later, right now, we need to crash this fortress," Sam said.

"Woah," Mitch said in response. "Terry is really not going to like that."

"No, I don't imagine she will," I said. "For now, it's nap time Mitch."

"Okay, just let me lie down first. I heard about this one henchman that fell and hit his head so hard he woke up thinking he was a sidekick," Mitch said, moving into one of the corners and sitting down. "Okay, go ahead."

What an odd henchman! Anyway, I popped a Void Burst and sent him into dreamland.

"Right, so I need you to start with blowing out some of the rear thrusters," Sam said, looking out the monitors. "We need to slow her down but not stop her. Once she begins to backslide, the thrusters are the only thing that will reduce impact."

"Okay, tell me where to start," I said, mentally preparing myself to start imploding some engines.

32

On the bridge of the flying fortress, Terminus glared angrily at the woman in charge of keeping the fortress flying. There was another shudder as something distantly exploded, "What the hell is going on, Captain!"

The Captain, an older woman, much older than Terminus, stuttered out an answer, "We . . . we don't know ma'am. Several engines have been destroyed stalling our forward progress."

"I can see that," Terminus snapped angrily. "I want to know how. How is this happening? None of the heroes can even get close, not with my negation field in effect. So please, enlighten me?"

"It . . . it seems to be . . . sabotage," the Captain stuttered out another answer.

"Where are my security forces? Why haven't they put a stop to this?" Terminus asked angrily.

"They are still in the hangars, waiting to deploy into the city," the Captain answered, only realizing too late that was not what Terminus wanted to hear.

Terminus snarled. She couldn't blame the captain this time. It was her plan that put her security forces . . . her soldiers there. "Fine, then get me Kidnap, right now," she snapped.

The Captain turned swiftly to the communications office, "You heard her, open a transmission with Kidnap."

"Yes, Captain," a young man replied.

Kidnap's voice came through the speaker on the console a moment later. With an angry hiss, he asked, "What?"

"Kidnap," Terminus said, her voice icy. "Where are you?"

"On the ground," Kidnap answered.

"Why are you on the ground?" Terminus asked, suddenly confused.

"Because that freak Dr. Portal blew open the hangar doors and vented us into the atmosphere," Kidnap answered, angrily.

"How the hell did he do that?" Terminus demanded.

"He can still use his Abilities," Kidnap replied. "I don't know how or why, but he can."

Terminus snarled. That didn't make sense. The only way he would have been able to use his abilities was if he was more powerful than she was. And the only way he could be more powerful than she was, was if . . . he still had the power amplifier. Then she urgently asked, "Did he fall out with you?"

"No, he teleported inside the van, it kept him from being sucked out. Ransom fell somewhere nearby, but And managed to grab ahold of the fortress. If he isn't already inside, he will be soon," Kidnap replied.

Terminus turned swiftly to the captain, "Find And, find him now!"

"Yes, ma'am," the Captain said, snapping off a salute.

Then something else occurred to Terminus. "Did you say, he teleported?"

"Yeah, he can teleport, and create some kind of explosions. Suddenly, the freak has all kinds of abilities he never had before," Kidnap said just as another explosion shook the fortress.

"He's sabotaging my fortress!" Terminus screamed. "Kidnap, you and Ransom need to get back up here immediately! Captain, get those soldiers out of the hangars and find that bastard and kill him! Now!"

"Yes, ma'am," the Captain said.

Terminus crossed her arms, her jaw clenched tightly shut. All her plans were falling apart all over again. And once again, Dr. Portal was at the heart of it. "When he's dead, I'm going to mount his head over my office door."

33

Encircling the fortress's two bottom levels were staggered engines designed to keep the fortress moving but also giving it the ability to turn and rotate as needed. It was slow to move as these engines were not the most powerful engines . . . then again, the fortress was considerably larger than a commercial airliner back on my world, so my sense of scale was probably off.

Around the rear third of the fortress, the goal was to take out twelve engines, six from each of the two levels. I needed to take out two engines at a time, as near to simultaneous as I could get. Unfortunately, it was at this point I learned that I could not open more than one portal at a time. As such, that meant traveling through the air ducts once again. The idea being that once I was in one location, I could open a portal to drop a Void Burst at another location while I dropped a Void Burst at my current location. According to Sam, it needed to be done this way to prevent the fortress from rotating.

Once those were out of commission, I needed to do the same to the underside of the fortress. Thankfully, Sam seemed to know exactly where to target.

"Okay, four more and we're done," Sam said just after I appeared back in the gunnery room.

"Great, I just need a minute to catch my breath," I said, leaning back against the wall.

"Hurry up about it," Sam said. "If we don't take out those engines in the next twenty minutes, they might be able to compensate with the remaining engines."

I groaned. It would take almost fifteen minutes to fully recover my energy levels. I was literally getting tired of this. It was a lot of teleporting with very little time in between to recover.

The loudspeaker suddenly came to life, the mechanical voice shouting, **"Warning! Intruder Alert! Intruder Alert! Warning! Intruder Alert! Intruder Alert!"** The loudspeaker kept repeating itself then added a nice loud siren and red flashing lights to go with it.

To top it off, the speaker on the gunnery console crackled to life as well. "All stations report in immediately with appropriate id numbers and locations."

"Okay, rest time is over," Sam said.

I was about to Teleport when I felt an explosion shudder through the fortress, this one not caused by me.

"What was that?" I asked.

"It felt like it came from the front of the fortress. Did someone destroy an engine up there?" Sam asked.

Rather than guess, I opened a series of keyhole portals searching through the front of the ship.

"What if someone did?" I asked, seeing but not quite believing what I had just seen.

"It will throw off my calculations. It could put us into a spin or crash us into the city instead of the wilds," Sam answered.

That didn't sound good.

"Okay, um, I don't know how to say this, but And is back and he looks . . . angry," I said. Angry might have been an understatement. Apoplectic with an all-consuming rage might have been more accurate. From what I could see, it looked like he ripped one of the forward engines out of the fortress from the outside, basically making himself a door. And now he was destroying everything in his path. Whether by accident or on purpose, I didn't know.

"You need to stop him," Sam said urgently as another shudder ran through the fortress.

Sure, good idea. I agreed completely with her. I just had no idea how to stop the rubber man. "I'll happily do so if you can tell me how to stop him."

"I don't know," Sam snapped. "Push him back out the hole he came in through."

Right, I supposed that could work. "Okay, wish me luck," I said, teleporting up into the ventilation shaft to begin worming myself across the fortress. As I got closer to the engine room And was destroying, I started to feel the pull of the depressurization. I had a feeling that with the engines I'd already destroyed and now And's rampage, it wouldn't be long before the entire fortress depressurized. And with our current altitude above the city, that could do bad things to a person's body.

When I finally got to the vent opening just above the engine room, I took a minute to make sure I was good with the oxygen levels, I personally wanted to avoid hypoxia. But my breathing was easy enough if slightly labored, we must have dropped low enough now that the air was more breathable.

Then I got another view of And. He didn't look right. He was blue around the nose and eyes while the rest of his skin looked cherry red. That was the hypoxia I was worried about. Though it seemed like he had suffered much worse. His rampage now was probably a result of the associated confusion.

I felt bad about pushing him back outside, but he would more than likely survive the fall, he was made of rubber after all. I opened the first Void Burst between him and the hole in the hull. It popped and he slid across the floor a few feet. When he stopped, And began looking around wildly for the source, which couldn't be good for me. I quickly created a series of Void Bursts, sucking him rapidly back toward the hole, his hands scrambling to grab onto something, anything. Just as I was about to eject the more advanced henchman, he surprised me.

And started sucking in air and not stopping. He inflated like a balloon until he was large enough to block my planned exit for him.

"I see you," And said, breathing out slowly and deflating for a moment before he sucked in more air to re-inflate himself.

I didn't have much time to teleport out of the ventilation system and into the hanger when his two inflated fists slammed into the airduct I had just been using. I appeared back in front of And and he grinned, letting the air out.

"I know you . . . I don't like you," And said, his words slurring, the hypoxia still in effect.

"No, what are you talking about? You and I are buddies," I said, using my calming doctor voice. The one I generally used to try to get tweakers in the ER to calm down long enough for me to sedate them properly.

"No," And insisted as he continued to deflate. "You hurt brothers," he said, then looked around in confusion. "Where? Where did they go?"

"They are waiting for you upstairs. They sent me to get you. They know you're sick," I said.

"No, you lie!" And shouted, his elastic fists flying at me rather suddenly. I teleported away.

"I see you. You can't trick me," And said, redirecting his fists.

I teleported again up onto a catwalk that ran between the engine rooms and the fists followed a moment later, though it was far enough away now, I could shift out of the way. Then he surprised me again, he grabbed ahold of the catwalk railing and slingshot himself up and tackled me. We both fell. Worse, he kept his grip on me so I couldn't use Teleport to escape the fall.

I landed hard on my shoulder and thankfully he let go. I wish I could say I took that moment to Teleport to safety, but when I felt my shoulder crack and pop, I knew with just a glance that it was dislocated and my health bar dipped a little bit lower as the damage began to accumulate. I looked for And, but he was gone. Or I thought he was right up until he hit the floor a few feet away from me and bounced like a misshapen basketball.

And bounced a few more times before he bounced to a slow stop. His complaint of "Owee," was mostly ignored as I was in too much discomfort to care that much, Hippocratic Oath be damned.

I was just glad to find out the henchman could feel pain. Hopefully, that would keep him down for a minute. And speaking of pain, I needed to get up and move and then I needed a wall. I was a bit slow to get up, but once I was on my feet, I ran. Straight to the closest wall. It took a couple of really painful hits to force my shoulder back into the joint. And let me just say, this is another thing Hollywood got wrong. Does it work, sure, but there are better ways, which are a bit slower but much less painful.

"You hurt me," And said, finally climbing back to his feet.

"You hurt yourself . . . and me," I said, holding my arm immobile. I could use it if I really needed to, but it was going to hurt.

And shook his head in denial. It didn't last long before he was back on the attack. I teleported again, but my aim was off. I was in too much pain. I appeared in the air a foot off the ground and facing the wrong way. I hit the ground and rolled forward, right over my recently dislocated shoulder, stunning me with pain for a moment. It provided more than enough time for And. One of his rubbery legs extended and kicked me, hitting my already bruised ribs and lifting me bodily from the ground. I was sent tumbling across the metal flooring, rolling over my already injured shoulder several times in addition to having the wind knocked out of me. I would have bet I had several cracked or broken ribs now as well, but I wasn't in a position to check beyond a glance at my health bar, which had depleted quite a bit further.

I barely had my breathing back to an almost normal state when I heard And chuckle. It confused me. He sounded almost gleeful, which worried me more. I was hurt, but after hearing that sinister chuckle, I focused in on the rubberized man. "You push me out, I push you out," And said, already running at me.

Only then did I realize where I was standing. I was right in front of And's makeshift door.

"I got you now!" And shouted, his hands splayed out as he was reaching forward to push me as he ran headlong at me.

I didn't have time to think, he was about to push me out and I couldn't be sure I would be able to safely Teleport back or open a Portal or find a way to land safely. So, I blindly used Teleport, aiming for somewhere nearby. I could barely focus but I didn't need to move far. Just a few feet to my left or right. I was suddenly no longer looking at And running at me.

I look left then right before I saw the villain. I watched as And's head turned to look at me, even as he continued running forward. He ran right out of the fortress. He cried out in shock before his voice was swallowed up by the wind and he was gone. Just like that.

I dropped to the deck. I was in so much pain. I was so tired. And I still wasn't done.

I didn't know how long it had been, but I needed to get back to Sam and then deal with the last of the engines.

Once my energy bars were both back up over half, I took a few deep breaths trying to refocus. I couldn't afford to mess up a Teleport now. I teleported into the torn open vent in the ceiling and began a very painful trek across the fortress. Until I dropped boneless into the gunnery room . . . an empty gunnery room. Sam was gone. Mitch was gone.

"Well crap," I said with a groan.

The speaker crackled to life behind me. Terminus's voice greeted me, "Hello again, Dr. Portal."

I closed my eyes and groaned. This was just not my day.

Terminus then stated, "I have something that belongs to you. And you have something at belongs to me. So, here's my offer. I give you the woman engineer. You give me my working device."

Double crap!

34

I took a peek outside the gunnery room with one of my keyhole portals. There were at least a dozen guards, all with their rifles aimed at the door. After seeing that, I knew I wouldn't be able to run through the fortress unobstructed anymore, or at least not going that way.

"Come to my throne room with the device, we'll do the exchange there. You have thirty minutes, or the woman dies," Terminus's voice echoed in my head as I thought back on what the mad woman demanded.

Obviously, this was a trap. One in which the possibility of me dying was fairly high. If I went to her she would just kill me, then Sam, or Sam and then me. She would probably torture me first for information on the device I didn't have. Honestly, I wasn't sure what made her think I had the device in the first place.

I stifled a groan as I teleported again through the airducts. I couldn't afford to be heard now and get caught. I needed a way to even the odds. And without Sam to help me, I had no idea which engines to destroy to finally crash the fortress. Thankfully, I had a backup engineer . . . sort of.

Finally, I teleported into the storage closet where Nick was still resting peacefully. I gave him a quick check over again and he was still out. I knew it was dangerous to even contemplate waking him, but I needed his help if I was going to save Sam.

I tried shaking him gently at first, then not so gently, but all I got was a groan of pain and gasp of even more pain before his eyes fluttered for a moment then closed again.

I cursed under my breath. I needed to wake Nick up. In order to wake Nick up, I needed to heal his injury, something I wasn't able to do. But then I reflected on something I had been thinking about when I got impaled by the warp hunter. What if healing him wasn't what I needed to do at all? What if . . . I could simply reverse the damage? Could I manipulate the cells and move them back in time, to a time before they were damaged?

"You're insane, Dr. Malory," I mumbled to myself as I sat down and started reaching for my Nanos.

I felt for the all too familiar rhythm of fast and slow, sending them my mental request. Trying to convey what I needed. To take something back to the state it was in at a previous point in time. It felt just like when I first tried to use Portals. I could tell almost immediately that I didn't have enough power to do it. Not nearly enough.

I wanted to rail in anger at how helpless I felt. In my desperation, I mentally pleaded with my Nanos to show me a way, any possible way to heal Nick. This time, I felt something different from them. It was still a manipulation of Time, but I wasn't reversing time. I was . . . accelerating time. I was accelerating healing, more specifically, I was accelerating the body's natural healing ability. It was able to relate what I knew about the body's ability to naturally heal with my ability to manipulate time. It was powerful and fast. Just like that, I understood how to target my time manipulation to accelerate the healing in a specific area of the body. It was exactly what I needed.

I checked my Status. I needed to see what it said.

Davis Malory
Aliases: Dr. Portal, The Physician
Occupation: N/A
Alignment: Neutral
Milestone: 31st

Nano: 7,501,135/7,875,000
Body
Athleticism: 25
- Strength: Average (3/10)
- Agility: Above Average
- Accuracy: Above Average
- Speed: Below Good
- Stamina: Average (1/10)
Resistance: 3
- Physical Resistance: Average (2/10)
- Energy Resistance: Above Average
- Mental Resistance: Above Average
Recovery: 6
- Physical Injury: Average
- Nano Energy: Average (5/10)
Ability
Power: 64
- Time: Average
o Time Compression: 65%
o Accelerate Healing: 3-Injury Scale Reductions
- Space: Below Good (13/25)
o Void Burst: 5.8-Uses at Maximum Size
o Spatial Awareness: Passive senses may be enhanced for up to 5-Seconds
o Portal: up to 5.8-Foot Diameter
o Teleport: 5.8-Uses
Control: 64
- Time: Average
o Time Compression: 20-Seconds Uncompressed Time
o Accelerate Healing: up to 2-Inch Diameter
- Space: Below Good (13/25)

o	Void Burst: up to a 68-Foot Range and up to a 5.8-Inch Diameter
o	Spatial Awareness: up to 68-Foot Range
o	Portal: Travel 0.48-Mile Range
o	Teleport: 68-Foot Range

I grinned. '3-Injury Scale Reductions'. I could work with that. Assuming the Nanos worked off my medical knowledge and the scale it was applying was the same as the scale I used back home. On Earth, we used a scale to determine the severity of an injury. Minor was the lowest level. These were things like cuts, scrapes, and bruises to the body and extremities. Moderate was the next level. This was for things like fractured or broken bones. Serious was for things like open fractures and head wounds. Severe came next. These were injuries that could kill if not treated with some urgency, deep lacerations and the like. Critical injuries were things like gunshot wounds to the chest and abdomen, higher chance of death and more urgently in need of care. And last were maximal injuries, basically this meant you were going to die no matter what treatment was provided. Although, with superpowers, that may no longer be the case.

Anyway, it was just what I needed to reduce Nick's injury. My gold energy bar was still low, but I should at least be able to take him out of danger. Waking him up . . . that was still questionable. I know I should have used it on my shoulder and ribs first, but I needed Nick more and my power was already running low. I placed a hand over the dark purple contusion near the man's temple and closed my eyes. I could feel my Nanos enter Nick without any resistance, the small orb of them telling Nick's Nanos they were there to help. With a thought, my Accelerate Healing went to work. The purple discoloration faded rapidly. The effect was more than I hoped for. Nick's eyes began to flutter and open without my prompting.

"Wha . . . what happened?" Nick asked groggily.

"You hit your head pretty hard," I said, sitting back and feeling even more tired.

"Where are we?" Nick asked, blinking as he tried to take in the surroundings.

"Terminus's fortress," I answered.

"Oh," Nick said, not quite registering what I said. Then he sprung upright about to shout before he blinked dizzily and laid right back down again. Then he asked softly, "How? Why? Huh?"

"Terminus attacked the city. We tried to escape in the van," I explained.

"I . . . I remember," Nick said, looking around from where he was laying. "Wait, where's Samantha?"

"Terminus got her," I said. "Look, a lot has happened, and I don't have a lot of time to explain. I need your help if I'm even going to have a chance at saving her."

Nick groaned as he leveraged himself into a sitting position against the wall and asked, "What do you need?"

"Sam and I were working on crashing the fortress. We've taken out several engines and the fortress has lost some altitude and has begun sinking toward the wilds. We didn't get to finish so I can't be sure we took out enough engines to finish the job. She said we had four left," I explained.

"And you need me to tell you which engines to take out next?" Nick asked. "Does that mean you're abandoning Samantha?"

"I'm not abandoning her. But I do need to finish what we started, but with a few changes to the plan," I said.

"What changes?" Nick asked.

"I need the crash to be . . . less gentle but still survivable," I said. "To do that, I need to know which engines to take out. Which means I need you to tell me which engines I need to take out to make that happen."

"First, I need to know what you've done already," Nick started.

I gave him a quick rundown and general locations of the engines we took out so far.

"Okay, if they are already compensating then you'll need to take out at least eight more engines, two directional engines and six levitation engines, as close to the rear of the fortress as you can," Nick said.

"I can do that," I said. I assumed the directional engines where the ones on the sides of the fortress and the levitation engines were those under the fortress. "Now, I need one more thing from you. And I need you to trust me."

"You've gotten us through this so far," Nick said. "I suppose I can trust you a little further."

A few minutes later, Nick was helping me limp my way into the throne room with more than a few soldiers escorting us, most of them looked like they were just waiting for the chance to pull the trigger.

"Dr. Portal," Terminus hissed when we finally entered her throne room, something she herself called it. "We meet again."

"Indeed, we do meet again," I said, mocking her. I smirked as I felt her waves of negation being disturbed. I was already getting under her skin.

"Do not mock me," Terminus snapped.

The throne room hadn't been repaired after I basically blew it up a few days ago. There was still plenty of rubble and the throne was still broken into several large slabs of stone. It was on one of these stones, a bound and gagged Sam sat.

"When you say things like 'we meet again', how can I not mock you?" I asked. It was so unbelievably cliché. I mean, I knew that heroes and villains had a way of speaking in this world, but that was too much.

Terminus snarled. For a moment, I thought she was going to rush me. She took a calming breath and smirked. "And yet, here you stand. Surrendering like a good little hero, all to save the damsel in distress."

"Not exactly a hero," I said, the smirk never leaving my face. A quick Time Compression, a keyhole sized portal, and a Void Burst, and an explosion shook the fortress again, jolting me forward slightly as I felt the deceleration.

Terminus's eyes widened and I felt her negation waves speed up, making the gaps smaller than before. "Such power," she said. "Is the device amplifying your ability so much you were able to change your ability?"

"Wouldn't you like to know?" I taunted her.

Terminus snapped. "Give it to me. Give me the device now!"

"I'm afraid I can't do that just yet," I said. I was stalling. I knew it. She probably knew it. But she probably also knew I wanted something from her.

"If you want to leave this place alive, you'll give me the device now," Terminus demanded, raising a sleek white pistol and aiming it at Sam.

"I understand you want the device. I really do," I said, trying to calm her down. I needed more time to recover my ability. Every second gave me more uses of my ability. "But first, you're going to let my friends here leave."

"And why would I do that?" Terminus asked, sounding amused.

I smirked. Another Time Compression, Portal, and Void Burst sent another engine into terminal failure. The fortress shook again, and I felt the room tilt. Sam almost tipped off the stone fragment she was sitting on. That explosion was accompanied by more alarms, these sounded much more urgent.

"What have you done?" Terminus demanded, wobbling on her feet slightly.

"What?" I asked, feigning ignorance. "You mean this?" I asked, doing it again and taking out another engine. Except this time, it felt different. The explosion was longer. In fact, it sounded like multiple explosions were being set off. The fortress tilted even further.

"Stop that, stop it immediately or your friends die," Terminus demanded, trying to aim at Sam but with the wobbling of the floor beneath her, her aim was all over the place.

"No, I don't think I will," I said. This time it was all bluff. I was fairly certain that last detonation did significantly more damage than I intended. "You're going to let Sam go with Nick. As soon as they are safely away from this place. I'll give you what you want. Or . . . I continue to break your fortress, one engine at a time."

Terminus snarled. "Fine," she said, then pointing to Nick, she said, "Take her and leave."

Nick looked at me hesitantly.

"Go ahead," I said. I knew well enough that they wouldn't get past the door. Not with all the guards out there. I also knew this was part of my plan.

Nick rushed forward and pulled the gag from Sam's mouth first. "Nick, you're alright," she said, sounding relieved.

"I am, are you okay?" Nick asked, working to untie her feet.

"I'm fine," Sam replied. "Just ready to get out of here."

"You and me both," Nick said, helping Sam back to her feet now that she was free. He slowly guided her toward me and the exit behind me, being careful of her broken arm.

"Now, the device," Terminus insisted as Nick and Sam stepped past me.

"Here's the thing," I said, mentally preparing myself for the crazy I was about to pull. "I destroyed the device."

"Liar!" Terminus yelled.

I rolled up my sleeves and lifted my shirt, showing her, I didn't have anything on me. "I'm afraid it's true."

"Then how? How are you doing this?" Terminus asked, as another shudder ran through the fortress as a secondary explosion went off. "How are you able to get past my negation field?"

"How much do you know about your Ability?" I asked, trying to buy more time again. "Never mind, I'll assume you know everything, or at least you think you do. You see, when you use your negation field, it's actually more of a negation wave. I just act within the gaps in those waves. It lets me do things like this," I finished, destroying another engine. I was about to take out one more when I felt the fortress shudder again, only this time it tilted several degrees at once, throwing Terminus off her feet and creating a large gap in her field from the shock and surprise.

This was my chance. I teleported across the room and opened a portal, pushing Sam and Nick through and stepping in after them before the negation wave knocked it out.

"Now what?" Nick asked as he climbed back to his feet and looked around.

We were in another hangar and inside another van.

"Strap in, we're in for a very bumpy ride," I said, pointing to a couple of empty seats. I was barely able to keep on my feet as the last dregs of my energy left me. I could feel the nano-fatigue setting in rapidly.

Nick moved fast, securing Sam first then himself.

I sunk into the seat next to him and fumbled as I tried to strap in. The fortress shook again followed by a rumbling. I didn't notice when

Nick started trying to help me strap in, but I was glad he did. In the next moment, the fortress's shaking became violent. Then the van started sliding across the hangar, knocking into another van and bouncing around it as it slid toward one of the doors where it slammed hard, cracking the windows.

Unfortunately, I didn't see much after that as the Nano-fatigue really set in and blackness engulfed me. The good news was, if I died during the crash, I wouldn't be conscious to feel it.

35

With a groan of pain, the world came back into focus. Dim orange light was filtering in from somewhere above me. Or was it below me. My arms were hanging above me which suggested I was upside down.

"Physician, you still with us?" I heard Sam asking from somewhere nearby.

I groaned in response.

"Nick, you alive?" Sam asked next.

"Yeah," Nick said, then groaned similarly to how I did. "Just for the record, Physician. Your plans suck."

I agreed wholeheartedly.

"Shut up, Nick," Sam said. "We're alive, are you really going to complain?"

Nick didn't respond. I could hear the clicking of something metallic next to me followed by a thud. I opened my eyes again and saw Nick was lying on the roof of the van. I blinked away the spots from the blood still rushing and pooling in my head and tried to take in our surroundings. There were glass shards everywhere. Tools and supplies that were stored in the van were also scattered around us.

Nick slowly climbed back to his feet and moved to get Sam free first. He was extra careful with her arm. It looked like the splint came lose but the arm was still set in place.

I breathed out a small sigh of relief as it set in that they were both okay. Traumatized. But alive.

With another groan of pain and discomfort, I moved to undo my own restraints. When the buckle clicked free, I fell in a manner that was very similar to Nick's fall from a minute earlier. I winced and held my breath through the pain in my ribs and shoulder. Once it faded to something manageable, I breathed again, though not so deeply as to disturb my ribs.

And speaking of my ribs. I moved my hand to cover the ribs I broke. With a thought, I used my Accelerate Healing. I winced as I felt the pain of my ribs knitting back together and the bruising fade. More importantly, I saw my health bar jump up. I also learned something knew about my ability as a result. While it healed the injury, it also made me feel all the pain associated with that healing process. At least it was over in almost an instant. With the injury reduced to a minor status, I did the same for my previously dislocated shoulder. I enjoyed the additional bump to my health bar. When it was done, I breathed out a sigh of relief. I was still achy. And my ribs were still tender. But I was functional . . . more or less functional.

"Now what?" Nick asked, yet again.

"We rest and recover," I said. I had no interest in moving. I hoped to whatever deity ruled this world that the heroes were finally on their way. "The damned heroes better be here soon. I've got nothing left." While my health bar looked much . . . healthier, I could not say the same for my gold and black energy bars.

"Are we on the ground? Can we get out and walk back to the city?" Nick asked.

I sighed. So much for rest. First, I mentally tuned into my Spatial Awareness. I could feel the van and its contents. What I couldn't feel was Terminus's waves of negation. Either she was knocked out again or the fortress broke up and we were too far from wherever she landed. Second, I opened a few keyhole portals in an effort to figure out where we were. Outside of the van was a mess. There was no way we were leaving the van or hangar in its current condition. As if that wasn't enough, the hangar door appeared to be underground, buried in the crash. Eventually I found the outside again. We were in the wilds, which was a relief. With my alternate plan, I was worried we would end up crashing inside the city.

Eventually, I stood and opened a portal for us. I just hoped the crash scared off any beasts.

"We lived," Nick cheered suddenly, startling Sam and me both. Then he surprised us both when he pulled Sam close and gave her one hell of a kiss. As soon as he realized what he'd done, he apologized to the blushing woman. Something told me she didn't mind all that much.

A few minutes later, Sam finally asked, "Now what do we do? I can't see the city through the wilds."

"Now we wait for the heroes to finally show up," I said, finding a comfortable looking spot against one of the trees to sit back and rest against.

"Is that safe?" Samantha asked. "I mean, this is the wilds. There are beasts."

I shrugged, then answered, "With my Spatial Awareness, I would sense anything coming." That said, I continued walking toward the tree I picked out. Only to be proved wrong a minute later as a gunshot went off and I felt something impact my shoulder from behind. It felt like I'd been kicked by a horse or something that kicks really hard. My face planted into the dirt.

"Dr. Portal," Terminus gasped out, suddenly fading into view.

It was my turn to ask, "How?"

"My negation ability doesn't just cancel out abilities. I can wrap myself in its effects, negating all senses from detecting me. Not your eyes. Not your ears. Not even that Spatial Awareness you just told the others about," Terminus answered, her footsteps now crunching as she moved closer. Using one of her feet, she rolled me over. "I just wanted to look you in the eyes before I kill you."

Terminus looked like she was on her last leg. Her outfit had multiple tears in it revealing deep gashes and dark purple bruises already forming. Blood trickled from her temple and nose. One side of her head and face appeared to have been burned, removing a few layers of skin and some of her hair. For an 88th Milestone, she sure didn't look it.

Standing over me, she pointed the gun at my forehead. This felt way too familiar at this point. It was just like when that thug pointed a gun at me before I came to this world. But unlike that time, I had the ability to fight back. Time slowed as she began to pull the trigger, my Time Compression barely taking effect before I opened a Portal in the path of the bullet. I opened the other end behind her. Time sped up again as my power ran dry. But it was enough. The bullet slammed into her shoulder, just as it had done to me. She was sent stumbling forward, tripping over my body but not falling.

I aimed for the shoulder that was connected to the arm holding the gun. I hoped the damage would be enough to make her drop the weapon. From my position on the ground, I could see a new tear in the back of her outfit at the shoulder. Unfortunately, I only saw a bruise forming as the bullet fell to the ground, unable to break her skin.

Terminus spun around. She looked frazzled and angrier than before. "Now I'm going to make you hurt," she said, pulling the trigger rapidly. I felt those familiar kicks in my legs, arms, and shoulders until she ran out of bullets, each shot dropping my health bar until it was flashing in warning with barely anything left. She wasn't lying about making me hurt. The injuries weren't maximal, but they were definitely critical. It wouldn't take long for me to bleed out at this point. And unfortunately, I would be in pain for all of it.

"Before you die," Terminus said, leaning down close. She put her hands on my face and turned my head to look at the terrified Sam and Nick. "You can watch your friends die."

I didn't have the strength to look away as she stepped over me and walked toward the pair. I weakly mumbled, "Stop. Don't hurt them." But it was useless. I just didn't have the strength left.

Terminus didn't say anything as she raised the gun and pointed it at the pair.

Sam looked to me, begging for help. For me to do anything to save her . . . to save us all. But I had nothing left.

"Goodbye, maybe the next engineers I hire will be more useful," Terminus said, pulling the trigger.

I expected to hear a cry of pain from Sam or Nick, but the cry came from Terminus. She had dropped the gun and was cradling her hand which was now smoking as if burned. Then Terminus fell back as a flash of light impacted her shoulder, cutting clean through her shoulder, in one side and out the other.

"No," Terminus cried in pain as she fell back. Pushing backwards away from the source of the shot.

It was then I saw the faint blue field formed in front of Sam and Nick. Ward. Ward was here somewhere. He protected them.

Then I heard the sweetest voice I'd ever heard in my life. Light's all too familiar voice stated, cleanly, clearly, and with authority, "Terminus, you are under arrest, surrender now, or face the consequences!"

"No," Terminus hissed. "You can't stop me. I can't lose to some third-rate hero. I won't let you stop me."

As much pain as I was in, I was aware enough to feel the waves of negation start emanating from her body again. I watched as Light came into view then faltered. He felt it.

Terminus scrambled forward and picked up her gun with her free hand and took aim. But I couldn't let her do that. I was tapped and out of energy. I knew that this could be dangerous. Dangerous enough to possibly kill me, but I just couldn't let my friend die like that.

One more time, I thought to myself. I slowed time as I felt a gap in the negation wave. My vision turned blurry immediately and I felt a severe pain spike through my head, warning me that this was a bad idea. I pushed through anyway. I activated a Void Burst next to Terminus's hand.

I vaguely saw the gun warp and twist around her hand then explode in a haze of red. Terminus's scream followed immediately but it sounded far away as the dark embraced me once more.

EPILOGUE

I honestly didn't know if I would wake up again. After using the last dregs of my Nanos to stop Terminus, I was prepared to die. I knew the risks and I did it anyway. As consciousness slowly returned and I stared up at the white hospital room ceiling, for a brief moment, I considered that it was all a dream. That I was shot back in that alley and the last couple months had been one long hallucination.

When I turned my head to the side and saw Light dozing in the chair next to my bed, that thought ended and another began. Though it was more questions. Mostly, I just wanted to know what had happened.

"Light," I croaked. My throat felt raw and dried out. I licked my lips and swallowed, trying to restore some moisture. I tried again, this time my voice came out a little bit clearer, "Light."

Light stirred slightly but didn't rouse.

I was saved from any further attempts to wake my friend when another familiar friend entered.

"Ah, Davis, you're awake," Ward said.

"Yeah, was I out long?" I asked.

"About a day," Ward replied. "We healed your wounds easily enough, but you really drained your Nanos. All things considered. A day really isn't bad. I've seen it take weeks to recover from Nano-exhaustion."

I nodded weakly. It was good to hear that my injuries had been healed. It explained why I wasn't in any pain, other than a hunger pang from my stomach reminding me that it had been more than a day since I last ate or drank anything. "Water?" I requested. My throat was still dry and scratchy.

Ward smiled softly and crossed the room toward the sink. The sound of running water followed, though only briefly. Ward moved from the sink to my bedside, now with a glass of water in hand.

I thirstily drank the entire glass.

"Better?" Ward asked, taking back the empty glass.

"Much," I replied. "What happened? I mean, did you guys catch Terminus?"

"We did," Ward said, grinning broadly. "After you blew up her hand, she wasn't in any mood to fight us . . . or anyone for that matter."

I cringed as I remembered that moment, hazy though it was.

"So . . . it's over?" I asked.

"It is for her," Ward said. "But I need to ask, are you the reason her flying fortress crashed?"

I nodded. "Well, Sam, Nick and me. They told me which engines to destroy. And that was after we took out a number of the weapons stations to open a path for the heroes to attack. Speaking of, where the hell were you guys?"

Ward flinched at my question. "Please, try to stay calm. I don't want you to strain your Nanos and end up back asleep, or worse, dead."

I frowned but nodded, forcing my shoulders to relax and ease the tension they were suddenly feeling.

Ward sighed before he spoke. "Things in New Haven are . . . not good right now. The Hero Association is in a bad way after the attack. Especially since Major Miracle . . . disappeared."

"Disappeared? What do you mean, 'disappeared'?" I asked.

"As in he's gone. It looks like he ran away," Ward answered.

"But isn't he some kind of super overpowered hero? Why would he run away?" I asked.

"Mental Star thinks he ran because he was afraid of facing another Terminus. Major Miracle almost died the first time he faced Terminus, so his fear is somewhat understandable. Still, that doesn't alleviate him from any of the responsibility he bears," Ward stated, not condoning Major Miracle but still understanding him.

"I certainly don't approve," I said with a frown.

"I understand," Ward said.

"So, what happens now? What will happen to Terminus?" I asked.

"Terminus will likely be sent to the moon," Ward answered.

It looked like Ward was going to continue, but I interrupted. I needed to ask, "The moon?"

"Yeah, we have a penal colony there," Ward replied. "It's a funny story. It was once a villain's base, but I can tell you that story another time."

"So, what happens to me?" I asked.

"We will set you up with an apartment and a small stipend until you find work. I know it isn't much for all that you've done for us, but it's the best we can do," Ward said.

I suppose that made sense. I wasn't actually a hero. Though I must say, it felt damned good to be one for a while there.

"For now, rest, recover. We'll chat again soon," Ward promised.

Ward left not much later, and I laid back and closed my eyes. Eventually I settled into a comfortable sleep and not a forced unconsciousness.

A few more days passed with me sitting around and doing nothing. Sam and Nick paid me a visit before they were whisked away. They were relocated by the Hero Association to different fortress cities with new identities and told to avoid working on such projects ever again. It was sad to see two of the only friends I'd made in this world get relocated but I sort of understood. If a villain was to ever find out about the device Terminus commissioned and then learned who made it, their lives would be in danger once again. Unfortunately, that meant they couldn't rebuild and perfect the device for me to use to go home. I hoped my sister would understand the delay . . . I hoped she was okay.

Light hardly left my side, claiming something along the lines of him owing me a life debt for saving him from Terminus and almost losing mine in the process. I asked Ward if there was such a thing and he just laughed. Still, it seemed that Light took it seriously enough because the man had become my shadow.

As if Light shadowing me wasn't enough, I was also forbidden from cultivating more Nanos. According to Ward, if I tried to cultivate and absorb more Nanos, I risked exhausting my Nanos again, which would probably kill me after already suffering exhaustion so recently. Which was a real shame, after the Nano-exhaustion and all the fighting, I lost two Milestones.

Davis Malory	
Aliases: Dr. Portal, The Physician	
Occupation: N/A	
Alignment: Neutral	
Milestone: 29th	
Nano: 6,155,271/7,875,000	
Body	
	Athleticism: 25
-	Strength: Average (3/10)
-	Agility: Above Average
-	Accuracy: Above Average
-	Speed: Below Good
-	Stamina: Average (1/10)
	Resistance: 3

-	Physical Resistance: Average (2/10)
-	Energy Resistance: Above Average
-	Mental Resistance: Above Average
	Recovery: 6
-	Physical Injury: Average
-	Nano Energy: Average (5/10)
Ability	
	Power: 67
-	Time: Average (2/10)
	o Time Compression: 67%
	o Accelerate Healing: 3.2-Injury Scale Reductions
-	Space: Below Good (14/25)
	o Void Burst: 5.9-Uses at Maximum Size
	o Spatial Awareness: Passive senses may be enhanced for up to 5-Seconds
	o Portal: up to 5.9-Foot Diameter
	o Teleport: 5.9-Uses
	Control: 67
-	Time: Average (2/10)
	o Time Compression: 22-Seconds Uncompressed Time
	o Accelerate Healing: up to 2.2-Inch Diameter
-	Space: Below Good (14/25)
	o Void Burst: up to a 69-Foot Range and up to a 5.8-Inch Diameter
	o Spatial Awareness: up to 69-Foot Range
	o Portal: Travel 0.49-Mile Range
	o Teleport: 69-Foot Range

But it was odd. My Milestone dropped to the 29th. But it still required the Nanos for the 32nd Milestone just to get back to the 30th Milestone. Even stranger, my Space Power and Control both increased by one enhancement point and my Time Power and Control increased by two enhancement points. How did I lose Milestones but still get stronger? I tried asking both Ward and Light and they were both as puzzled as I was. Still, more than a million Nanos were just gone.

When it was time to leave the Hero Association and try to make my way in this world, Light and Ward were there to see me off, though I was pretty sure Light was going to follow me.

"Where do you think you're going?" Hammer asked, blocking the exit.

"It seems my hero days are done," I said. "Thank you for all your help. I don't think I would have survived if it wasn't for the training you gave me."

Hammer didn't budge or even twitch. Then he repeated the question, "Where do you think you're going?"

"To my new apartment," I answered.

"Wrong," Hammer said.

"Wrong?" I questioned, looking to both Ward and Light who looked equally confused. "If not there, then where?"

Hammer grinned and produced a letter from one of the pouches connected to his belt.

I quirked an eyebrow and studied the envelope for a minute, trying to decide if it was a trap of some kind before I took it. It was nice cardstock. On the front it was addressed to David Malory, a.k.a. The Physician. On the back was an official looking wax seal with an 'H.A.' stamped.

I pealed the wax away and opened the letter. I barely got past the 'Dear Mr. Malory' when Hammer Jack spoke, sounding excited, "You're going to Hero Certification as my Sidekick candidate. If you can take out a villain of the 88th Milestone, I'd like to see what you can do with some real hero training. It starts tomorrow, transport has all been arranged. Don't let me down, sidekick."

I tried to protest but Hammer was already walking away, whistling a tune I didn't recognize.

I turned to Light and Ward, "Did you two know about this?"

"First I've heard of it," Ward answered.

"Same here," Light said, though he sounded much more excited than Ward. He then quickly asked, "So, are you going to do it? Are you going to try to become a hero? With your Milestone, you should easily be able to make sidekick."

"Light, calm down," Ward said with a chuckle, putting a hand on the excited hero's shoulder. "It's a big decision. It's also dangerous as he's already learned. This kind of work, it isn't for everyone."

"But he's so good at it," Light protested.

Ward chuckled again as I felt my face redden in embarrassment. "That he is. But he also nearly died several times in the last week. If he chooses to become a real hero, he'll be exposed to that kind of danger on a regular basis. I'll say it again, this life isn't for everyone."

He wasn't wrong. I did nearly die several times in the last week. But I also saved countless lives when I stopped Terminus. I probably accomplished more good in my weeks as a hero than I ever did as an M.D. It was also kind of exciting and terrifying. And my life as a doctor was meaningless now. In a world with superpowered healers, what good was a doctor. I didn't really know how to do anything else but be a doctor. And this world was so different from my own. How long would it take to learn enough to find a new career? On the other hand, being a hero was something I could do now . . . sort of. I would need to go to the Hero Certification and then be Hammer Jack's sidekick for who knows how long. It was kind of like doing my residency all over again. I was surprised by how much I was starting to like the idea. I would still be able to help people. Wasn't that why I became a doctor in the first place?

With my mind made up, I looked to Ward and asked, "Ward, what are the benefits like? Salary, health insurance, that kind of thing? And what about the retirement plan?"

Ward smiled broadly but it was nothing compared to Light's, his teeth were literally shining.

"Light, do you have an ability to make your teeth shine?" I asked.

Light suddenly covered his mouth with his hand.

Ward and I both laughed heartily.

"It's a reflex," Light said dejectedly.

"So, when you're happy, your teeth glow?" I asked through my laughter.

"Pretty much," Light said with an embarrassed shrug of his shoulders, getting more laughter from both Ward and me.

When the laughing finally ended, Ward clapped me on the shoulder and began telling me about the benefits of being a hero. "Let me tell you all about the life of a hero . . ."

AUTHOR'S NOTE

Thank you all very much and I hope you have enjoyed this adventure. If you enjoyed the story, please leave a review as it helps us authors tremendously.

The Physician will return soon so keep an eye out for updates.

For news, please visit my website at <u>M.A. Carlson</u> or <u>Patreon - M.A. Carlson</u>

Please also follow me on Facebook at <u>M.A. Carlson</u>

To find similar stories and connect with authors, check out:
<u>GameLit Society</u>
<u>Spoiled Rotten Readers</u>
<u>LitRPG Books</u>
<u>LitRPG Rebels</u>

www.ingramcontent.com/pod-product-compliance
Lightning Source LLC
Chambersburg PA
CBHW070859180626
46817CB00003B/826